Hamelin
STOOP

Hamelin STOOP

The Eagle, the Cave, and the Footbridge

ROBERT B. SLOAN

HAMELIN STOOP—THE EAGLE, THE CAVE, AND THE FOOTBRIDGE.
Copyright © 2016 by Robert B. Sloan.

All rights reserved, including the right of reproduction in whole or in part in any form.

Printed in the United States of America. For more information, contact Twelve Gates Publishing at www.twelvegatespublishing.com.

www.12GatesPublishing.com

ISBN 978-1-4956-1972-4 (hardcover)
ISBN 978-1-4956-1973-1 (paperback)
ISBN 978-1-4956-1974-8 (e-book)

For purchase or information, contact www.HamelinStoop.com or visit www.12GatesPublishing.com.

November 2016

To Sue
and
to our Children and their Spouses—
all 14 of them!

Chapter 1

Trackers from Another World

THE CAMPFIRE WAS ALMOST OUT, BUT IT DIDN'T MATTER that they were letting it burn down to its last smoky smell. The trackers were coming, but for just a moment longer, Simon wanted to look at her lying in the crook of his arm and at the infant asleep between them.

Funny what you think about when you should be panicked. Would their baby boy have his momma's blond hair? She was still, but Simon knew she wasn't asleep, so it didn't surprise him to see the tear slowly run from the corner of her eye down onto the baby's head. She opened her eyes.

"Okay, we both know what we've got to do," she said.

"Are you sure, Johnnie?" Simon asked. "There's got to be another way."

"No," she said in a loud whisper and sat up, cradling the baby in both arms. "I will *not* let him be taken by those monsters! They almost got us last night, and they won't miss again. There's nothing else to do."

For a brief moment, Simon wished he had stolen the two-year-old '49 Chrysler he had seen the day before. But there was no time now for regrets. They were stuck with fleeing the trackers on foot. Still, he tried to argue. "But . . ."

"I had the dream again. They won't miss the next time."

"Johnnie, look, not *all* your dreams happen. Sometimes they're just—"

"If I'm wrong, we can still come back and get him, but I won't let them take him back there!"

Simon didn't know where "there" was, but he knew that Johnnie, his wife of more than a year, was determined that, if they were caught, their baby boy would not be taken along with them—no matter what.

"Okay," he agreed. "We both know what we've got to do."

"I left the bag of sand by our mesquite tree," Johnnie said. "You know the one."

Simon smiled at the memory but then turned his thoughts to their plan. "They'll be closing in on us again tonight. I'll make sure there is enough of a fire for them to find us." He stood up and looked at the fire. He stirred the embers with his foot and asked, "Is . . . is that blood on one of the baby blankets?"

"Yes."

"Where'd it come from?"

"Don't worry, Simon. It's mine."

He looked down.

She touched his arm. "It's okay. Just be sure they see you've got him when you leave. The tree first, then run like crazy toward the Little Cliffs. And be sure they're behind you when you—"

"I know the plan. They won't get him. I promise."

Simon looked again at the fire, added a few more dried mesquite branches to it, and quickly felt the sharper smoke in his nose and eyes. He pulled their light blanket around them all again. It was about three o'clock in the morning. He lay there without sleeping. If things went as they did last night, it wouldn't be long before Ren'dal's men tracked them down again. He would move out first, and then Johnnie. He waited and closed his eyes.

----◦----

What was that? He had dozed off, but he thought he heard something. In an instant, they both were wide awake, their hearts pounding. The baby squeaked, and they could sense the soft movement in the brush. Simon slowly rose to a crouching position and took the baby, who cried softly as he was pulled from his mother's chest. Simon wrapped him in a blue blanket and tiptoed away. Johnnie never moved, but her eyes and ears strained to follow Simon's every movement. He was quickly gone, and she could hear Ren'dal's trackers as they followed.

----◦----

The trackers wanted the mother and the father too, but they had been given very clear—and threatening—orders to make sure they got the baby. They followed as Simon moved off into the brush with the bundle in his arms. They tracked him quietly at first, keeping space between themselves and the figure with the bundle. Now that the father and baby were separated from the mother, they would make sure their noises didn't awaken her so they could come back to get her. But first, above all, the baby.

About fifty yards away from the campsite, their prey began acting strangely. And his pace quickened.

"What the devil is he doing?" hissed Thurel.

"Don't know," said Procker, the other tracker, followed quickly by, "Hey, where'd he go?"

"We better not have—"

But there he was again just ahead, though now, with the bundle still in his arms, he was running.

"Pick it up," said Thurel. "He must know he's being followed!"

The man and the baby were heading east from the campsite. Why was he running? There was no escaping now. There was nothing east of them but more empty ground, with no cities or small towns for miles in the direction he was headed—no one to help. They might as well run too and get it over with—get the baby and then head back to grab the woman. But Thurel was starting to look wildly around. They hadn't scouted this side of the campsite before approaching—how could they have been so *stupid*? His nostrils flared with a new smell: water! It wasn't rain; it was flowing water, and now the tracker could hear it—it was nearby!

"Procker, you hear that water?" he yelled.

"Yeah, so?"

"So? So don't let him get to it, stupid! Get him!"

"Who cares? What's he gonna do? Swim carrying the kid?"

But now, though still about forty yards behind Simon, they were close enough to see what lay before them. Thurel took it all in and groaned.

The father, with his bundle, was running pell-mell toward what locals called the "Little Cliffs." From the top of the Little Cliffs was a sheer drop of a hundred feet right into a collecting pool of the Middle Concho, which from there flowed mostly eastward toward San Angelo, Texas, where it joined other waters to form the Concho River.

"No!" roared Thurel, screaming and running furiously toward his prey. The sharp eyes of both trackers had enough light from the breaking dawn in front of them to capture Simon's silhouette. They saw the young father race to the edge of the cliffs and—after looking back toward them and hesitating momentarily—throw the blue blanket and its contents over the cliff with a furious two-handed cast.

It had been an extremely wet spring, extending all the way through June in that part of West Texas, and the waters of the Middle Concho a hundred feet below were already flowing strong, well fed from the surrounding watershed. Only seconds later, when the trackers made it to the edge of the Little Cliffs, Simon was on his knees with his head buried in his hands. They grabbed him immediately and loudly demanded to know—though they had seen his violent heave—where the baby was. All he could do was look down toward the river below. By the time they ran around the top of the sheer drop and scrambled down the hillside next to the cliffs, all they could find was the muddy, blood-stained blanket caught on a riverside branch. They searched the banks and the shallows and then the rocks, scrubs, and tall grasses on the near riverbank slightly downstream. But the baby was gone.

While the trackers furiously looked for the baby, Simon got to his feet and began to run. But Thurel saw him. "Procker! Go get that fool!" Procker easily ran him down and tackled him from behind. Simon was young, athletic, and wiry, but these were hardened men, clearly heavier, stronger, and trained to fight—he was no match for them. And they were in no mood to be gentle. Thurel yelled, "Hold him, Procker!" And when Simon tried to wrestle free, Thurel arrived in time to slam him hard in the stomach with his knee, which doubled him over with a gasp of pain. Procker then added a two-fisted hammer blow to the back of Simon's head that made his eyes bulge and stunned his neck and upper back. He went to his knees, and the brief fight was over.

They pushed Simon back toward the campsite. "You fool!" Thurel screamed in his ears. "You have no idea what you've done! Ren'dal will go crazy!"

Procker was so mad, he suddenly began to pummel Simon with his fists.

"That's enough, Procker!" warned Thurel. "You know what we were told. Ren'dal wants *him* too. So we gotta have him healthy enough to make the trip back. Right now, you better be thinking about catching that woman—and then figuring out how we're gonna explain letting that baby get killed by his own father."

Chapter 2

The Mother's Loss: Leaving the Baby

THERE HE WAS, RIGHT WHERE SIMON HAD HIDDEN HIM just minutes earlier. Hard to believe he was still asleep. Simon had done his part, so now it was up to her. Johnnie headed south at a brisk pace toward a place she knew well. It was a forty-minute walk to get to the children's home where she was raised. Though there was an easier way to approach the main house—especially in the semidarkness of the early morning, still a short time before sunup—she stuck to the wooded path she had known as a child. The two-week-old, tightly swaddled boy she carried in her arms wasn't heavy, but he was starting to squirm.

She could hardly think about what she was soon to do. She knew what it was like to be separated—in her case, stolen—from her mother. But what else could she do? She had escaped from Ren'dal as a child of twelve, but it was too late to go back to her mother and father. Besides, Ren'dal's spies had probably been watching her all these years. She knew she was a lot older, but she looked to be only about nineteen, and that's what Simon thought too. Simon—her husband for so short a time, and now he too might soon be caught and taken back with her to Ren'dal's world. But first, the baby. Not much farther to the house. There was no time to cry, and she had no choice anyway, since the trackers, if they didn't have Simon by now, soon would.

Johnnie approached the Upton County Children's Home from the north and paused at the edge of the woods, just short of the clearing that marked out the houses and grounds of the home. There she could see the north side of the main house. That was where the screened porch was just outside the kitchen. It got a lot of traffic, being the main spot where deliveries, especially food and milk, were made. He would be quickly found there, so that's where she would leave her baby boy.

She could feel it pounding on her from the inside—every motherly instinct she possessed was rebelling. But she knew what she had to do. And there was no more time for second-guessing. She crouched at the edge of the woods on her knees with the little boy in her arms and nursed him one last time. It felt so good to hold him. She closed her eyes . . .

———◦———

She could still remember the simple wedding ceremony. It had been done by the justice of the peace in Whitney, Texas. Simon had managed to convince someone in the county clerk's office to help with the marriage license, even though neither of them was twenty-one. The last thirteen months had been the happiest days she could remember, going back longer than anyone would believe.

She had been officially placed at the children's home some seven years ago after she showed up in tattered clothes, tired and hungry. All anyone ever knew about Johnnie was what a man driving by on the road had said later: "I seen the girl walking down the road from the north and was going to stop and get her. She looked lost, but then she up and disappeared into the woods!"

Shortly after that, she had appeared in the front yard of the children's home. She didn't speak at all at first, except once or twice in answer to their questions. She had initially mumbled what sounded like "ge-hon" but then got quiet. After some time, she began to talk more fully, though she was always cautious and withdrawn. She had a way of lowering her gaze and watching her surroundings, as if she didn't want anyone to recognize her. So with no other clues about who she was or where she came from, they named her Johnnie, which was as close as they could come to matching her first mumbling sounds with a familiar name. And, of course, they gave her the last name Smith, everyone's favorite name for unknown people.

The staff at the children's home treated her well—they gave her clothes and food and sent her to the local school. And she always knew—though never said—it was certainly better than the terrible place she had come from. In her earliest years at the home, different people would occasionally ask her where she came from, but she wouldn't say or would just shrug as if she couldn't remember, and they soon grew tired of asking. They had sent pictures of her all around to various children's agencies and police departments, hoping that her parents or other family members would recognize her and come forward, but no one ever did. So Johnnie had grown up at the home, keeping to herself, learning the ways of life just outside the little town of Middleton, and suspecting that she was being watched.

Everything changed for her when Simon showed up. She was seventeen, according to school records, and Simon was twenty when, one cold January, he was hired as a general handyman and helper at the home. He had wavy light-brown hair, was about six feet one, and kept a slender but muscular build—all the girls noticed him immediately. He was assigned to work with Mr. Edwin Moore, the chief handyman, who had more work at the home than he could do by himself. Simon was told to stay outside—especially away from the girls—to work on the van, the old truck, and the tractor, which all usually needed some repair. He also was assigned to do the various kinds of maintenance that Mr. Moore needed to get done.

But it hadn't taken long for him to notice the quiet—but very attractive—girl named Johnnie. They quickly fell in love. Simon and Johnnie started to talk secretly almost every night, with Johnnie whispering from the bathroom window of the girls' house. She knew the other girls saw them stealing glances at each other, but her housemates never said anything to those in charge at the home. And Mrs. Frendle, the cook, had certainly noticed that whenever young Simon had a Saturday off, Johnnie would ask to "take a walk" in the woods north of the home. But Mrs. Frendle had only given her a raised-eyebrow warning and had evidently kept their secret. Simon always promised to take her away from there, and as soon as she graduated from high school the following May, they ran away to get married. Four months later, she was pregnant . . .

———◦———

The baby burped, which woke her from her light slumber. How long had she dozed? She quickly patted his back. No time for a fresh diaper.

She covered his face again with the edges of the blanket, hurried out of the woods, and crossed the last twenty yards to the small porch at the side of the house. She slowly opened the screen door—the hinges squeaked as always—and tiptoed inside. She took in that familiar stale smell of the porch, a mixture of old spills, empty bottles, and its concrete floor. But no time for memories now. She placed the infant in an empty wooden box, where, according to the label, there had once been cans of tomatoes. She then scooted the box with its squirming contents closer to the concrete steps. It was a good spot to be noticed, just outside the solid wooden door that led from the porch into the kitchen. Next to the box stood empty milk bottles, which would soon be picked up when the milkman—probably still Mr. Tomson—came for his early morning delivery.

Johnnie had to hurry. Ren'dal's trackers would soon be back at their campsite, probably to take her back to the place she had hoped she would never see again. Maybe they wouldn't take Simon with her. But she feared that the trackers wanted all three of them—the two of them and the baby. Now Simon would know the truth she had never told him—about her and where she came from. After one last look at the box and her son asleep within it, she turned to go.

Near the steps, she spied a clipboard with order forms and a pencil attached to it by a string. Johnnie remembered it was used by Mrs. Frendle for placing and checking off orders delivered to the side porch. She had earlier considered writing a note for Mrs. Frendle, but she never had the time. And now that she had the means to write something, she wasn't sure what to say. Maybe she should write a note for those who would find her baby, or maybe she could leave a clue that would help her recover her son one day. She started to write quickly.

What was that? Something startled her. Was it just one of the cats roaming outside the porch? A footstep? Someone moving about in the kitchen? Whatever it was, she panicked. Jamming the unfinished, hastily scribbled note halfway under the box, she quickly slipped out the screen door. Head lowered, she hurried across the dirt service road, reentered the woods, and picked her way back north to the place where she and Simon had made camp. The heaviness in her chest from leaving her baby was soon replaced by a knifing sense of dread in her stomach as she feared what now lay ahead. She could hardly breathe. Her lower body ached, but she walked quickly through the woods. She and Simon had been dodging Ren'dal's men for several months, but the tracking had intensified since the baby was born. In the last few days alone, there had been several close calls. She had to get away from the house and back to the camp without leaving any clues as to where the baby was.

Chapter 3

Mrs. Frendle Finds the Baby

NOT LONG AFTER JOHNNIE'S RETREAT INTO THE WOODS, the milk truck arrived at the children's home. The driver pulled up the service road toward the porch where deliveries were made and where now, early in the morning, there would be empty bottles just inside. The milkman, a Mr. Ken Tomson, liked to begin his rounds on the north end of FM 2463 and work back south along the road toward Middleton. The children's home was less than two miles north of the town, and he always started there. Mr. Tomson was a small, slight man with a thin mustache and short, balding hair. He had a good head for numbers and might have made a good bookkeeper, but he dropped out of college because his father thought it cost too much. His father, a retired army major, got him a job from old Mr. Peeper, the local dairyman, and here he was. Mr. Tomson kept careful records of how many empty bottles he took back in, how many deposits he should credit, and how much milk he had sold.

Since the children's home was his biggest customer, he felt like he had done a lot of work by the time he unloaded the several gallons of milk he delivered there each day. This morning, as usual, he parked his truck by the porch, carried the milk crates toward the house—each plastic crate holding four gallons of milk—and carefully placed his dairy products on the floor of the screened porch. He picked up the empties but didn't notice the box—much less its living contents—lying just next to the cold milk bottles.

In fact, the unfinished note that Johnnie had torn from the clipboard and stuck under the tomato box, with half of it showing so it would be noticed, was so close to the crates of milk that it got wet from the condensation dripping down the bottles, leaving only a few partial lines readable. She had intended to sign the short note, but she didn't finish it. The only visible word that looked like a name was the odd word *Hamelin.*

Mr. Tomson never saw it. He checked the clipboard and wondered why Mrs. Frendle had left it on the concrete floor. But his work there was done, so he took his leave of the porch and didn't care when the screen door slammed behind him. The kitchen help would be up and stirring about anyway, so the loud bang wouldn't bother them, and as for the orphans, well, it wouldn't hurt them to be up and moving as well. Hadn't his father always roused him at five thirty every morning?

The noise didn't immediately make the baby cry, but it did wake him up. Several seconds passed between the frightened, arms-jerking, startled look caused by the thwack of the screen door and the piercing cries that erupted from the little but powerful lungs. But by that time, Mr. Tomson was already back in his truck, starting up the motor. He didn't hear a thing. As he pulled out of the dusty driveway and back onto the pavement, he brushed off his uniform trousers with one hand and steered with the other, satisfied that he had a good start to the day. His father, the old major, would be proud, he hoped.

———

Mrs. Frendle was the head cook of the children's home. She was in her late fifties and slightly overweight but never slow in getting things done. She always wore a long white apron and kept her mostly gray hair tightly wrapped in a bun pinned to the crown of her head. She was a good cook, though Mr. Stephenson's tight budget made it hard for her to do all she wanted. She was always busy and kind to the children as a general rule, but she didn't put up with laziness—or foolishness—from anyone. She had two other full-time staff to help her (though, she always said, "It's hard to get good help") as well as a rotation of three or four children every day to help with the kitchen chores. But she was, as always, the first one up that morning and already hard at work.

She had just dropped her first batch of kneaded bread onto the greased pans when she heard Ken Tomson's truck pull into the driveway. She heard him out on the porch making his delivery. *There he goes, rattling around*, she thought. She heard the screen door slam—*he always does that*—and then, moments later, there was what at first sounded like a cat wailing. *Probably caught its tail in the screen door*, she thought. But as the sound of the truck drifted away, the crying got louder. It went on and on, with only short gasps in between, a lot longer than any cat she had ever heard cry. In fact, now it didn't sound like a cat at all. It sounded like a baby. *But it can't be a baby*, she thought.

So off to the porch door she went, her brow knitted and her eyes sharp. She opened the door and stepped down onto the first of the two steps that led to the porch, and at her feet, right there on the stoop, was a baby in a box. It was quite a shock.

Later on, as she told the story, Mrs. Frendle could hardly remember what she had done next, though no one blamed her that she got a little rattled by the whole thing. However it happened, she looked down at the box, and there, wrapped in a blue blanket, was the baby, his face red, his eyes closed, and his arms pushing out in jerks! So she just lifted him right out of the box, cradled him in her arms—Mrs. Frendle had children and grandchildren of her own, after all, though they were all grown now—and took that poor thing right into the kitchen, all the while patting him and cooing to him.

It didn't take long for the news—and the cries—of the baby boy found in a box on the porch of the children's home to spread. There was chatter everywhere as the staff and the children crowded around in the kitchen to see. But Mr. and Mrs. Stephenson, a couple in their late twenties who served as the main "house parents" and managers of the home, saw things differently. They were new there, and it was their first job of that sort. They had been hired because they had good references but also because the Upton County commissioners had a hard time finding couples willing to take on jobs like this. With no children of their own, they were very unsure as to what to do with an abandoned baby. It was one thing to have orphans and other needy children from ages six to eighteen to house, feed, and supervise, but caring for a newborn was an entirely different matter.

Mrs. Frendle managed to quiet the baby down. Though she had no baby bottles, she wet the end of a clean towel with some milk and let him suck on it. The other staff, along with the Stephensons, worked to settle down all the children, who were even more excited than the time the litter of puppies was found under the main house.

But Mr. Stephenson was very upset by the whole turn of events.

"For heaven's sake, where did he *come* from?" he said. He looked around, expecting someone to answer.

"Well," said Mrs. Frendle with a bit of exasperation, "he didn't just walk up here."

"Obviously," said Mr. Stephenson, who nodded while he spoke, as if everyone agreed with him. "We'll have to report this to the county authorities. I'm sure they'll want to get him into the right hands immediately."

As it turned out, the two commissioners of Upton County—a county with one main town, Middleton, only a few paved roads, and a small population—spent a lot of county time at the Dairy Dream, talking with the retired ranchers about next year's hopes for the high school football team. They were just easygoing, storytelling fellows. They were elected mostly because nobody else wanted the jobs. And they didn't have much of an idea either as to what they should do with the baby. They made a few calls to some state officials, and the county sheriff did work fairly hard to solve the mystery of where the baby had come from, but he had a very small staff and an even smaller budget. He did question Mr. Tomson and even checked one lead as far north as Jones County in the little town of Hamlin, Texas, but learned nothing. The note that was left was no help either, because of the water damage.

Mrs. Frendle found him on July 10, 1951, and in those days the federal government left these matters to the states.

Since Texas had already cut back on the number of homes for children (and what few there were, public or private, were crowded), there just wasn't any other place to take the baby. Before long, a state judge ruled that since "the infant was found near Middleton" and since the Upton County commissioners had "a children's home in their county and a child in need of help," then they could "provide for him" as well as anyone else.

Never mind that the Upton County home typically didn't take children younger than six. The home now had its thirty-first boy to go with the twenty-seven girls, making fifty-eight in all. Within a few months, the Stephensons and the sheriff gave up their efforts to find the baby's parents and accepted the fact that, like it or not, the baby boy was theirs to take care of.

Chapter 4

Johnnie and Simon: Captured

A S JOHNNIE APPROACHED THE PLACE WHERE SHE AND Simon had camped, she could see that Simon had indeed already been captured and was being held at the site. One of Ren'dal's men stood next to him. So far, the plan seemed to have worked, but her stomach turned over when she got a closer look at Simon. He looked defiant but also beat up—there must have been a struggle. Had he talked? She'd have to assume he hadn't. He was seated on the ground with his hands tied behind his back, his shirt torn, and his face red and swollen on one side.

Johnnie could see only the one tracker. She took a deep breath and, making no effort to be quiet, stumbled into the small clearing. She glanced around wildly, but before she could rush toward Simon, as she had intended, the other tracker jumped out from hiding and grabbed her by the wrists, twisting them behind her back.

She struggled fiercely to get free, her body, head, and eyes turning and twisting in every direction. "Where's my baby?" she screamed, looking at Simon, whose head was down. "Where's my baby?" she screamed even louder.

"You tell us," said Thurel, the tracker who had grabbed her.

"Where's my baby?" Johnnie bellowed.

"Your fool husband threw him off the cliff and into the river!" yelled back Procker. He kicked Simon fiercely.

Johnnie roared, "No!" and then fell limp to the ground on her face, as Thurel bent over her now but still held her down by the arms. She wailed as only a mother who has lost her baby can. "Why did you do it? You were supposed to hide him!"

"They'll never get him now," spat back Simon through a bloody lip.

"I *told* you she didn't have the baby!" yelled Procker.

Thurel yelled back in a language neither Johnnie nor Simon could understand, but it sounded like a curse.

Johnnie and Simon were marched westward through the woods. She was pretty sure where they were going. Not far from there was the cave she had walked away from some seven years ago, shortly before she was first seen wandering along the road near the children's home. Anticipating what would happen next made old, chilling memories flood back.

———◆———

She had escaped Ventradees once, but would it be different now? Most of the children from her village were made to work as laborers, though she—along with a few others—had been raised apart from the main group and treated somewhat better. There had been twelve girls and twelve boys—all about eleven or twelve years old—who had been raised separately. They were well fed but seldom allowed time to themselves. They worked to maintain the order of Ren'dal's mansion. Everything there was built around a constant regimen of service and attention to meticulous detail. No casual conversation among the children was permitted—though occasionally they chanced it. Obedience was everything, and almost no one ever dared an escape. One boy who tried, Jacob, was quickly caught, and she never forgot what happened. She and the other children heard the lashing sound of his punishment and then his muffled groans and crying the following days, before he returned to work, weak and pale. No one ever asked him—nor did he describe—what happened. But stories were whispered around by Ren'dal's guards and those who supervised the children. Soon everyone, even the children, knew. It was worse than a normal whipping, and he had nearly died in agony.

But things were not just cruel; they were also strange there, even beyond the constant fear and boredom of their regulated lives. At first no one noticed the oddest effect Ventradees had on them, but after six months it was becoming apparent, and then later, by the end of their first year of captivity, it was clear to all: the children were not aging or growing. Ren'dal was furious when he was told, as it apparently ruined some plans he had for the children. Johnnie could still remember the story that had spread: how, in his fury, he had disclosed some secrets.

"Why is this happening?" Ren'dal had demanded to know from his chief holy man.

"We don't know why, my lord. They just don't age."

"Is some fool giving them the special water from Osmethan?"

"No, my lord. We've checked everything—their food, their water."

"So what is the matter?" he bellowed.

"We don't know, my lord. Except that something is different with these children, the ones you specially brought here from—" Neither Ren'dal nor the holy man ever said where the children came from, but the children remembered their hometown, even though they were forbidden ever to speak of it. Ren'dal's tirade had continued.

"Then *kill* them!" he raged on.

"But we also need them to run the house, sir. Especially to serve you," the holy man added. "At least they won't have to be replaced. And surely some use can eventually be found for them. Besides, the way you got them here was a stroke of genius, the tale of which is already legendary and told the world over."

Slowly, Ren'dal's temper cooled as he listened to his flattering servant.

"My lord, I'm sure *you'll* think of some way to overcome this. They aren't old enough now, but give yourself time to come up with another plan. Who knows, they may start growing eventually."

And time is exactly what Ren'dal had and what the children—cursed to be forever the same age and never to return to their families—endured. Year after year and century upon century.

Escaping had always been at the back of Johnnie's mind, but once she committed to it, her opportunity came along soon. There was a strong, blistering windstorm one night, and Ventradees was strewn with trash and tree limbs. The next morning, she was assigned to a work detail under the authority of a tall, silver-haired old woman whose mouth seemed forcibly pulled into a scowl. Her head craned and her blue eyes twitched back and forth as if she were always counting the children. They were led outside Ren'dal's main house and ordered to clean the grounds between the house and the walls of the city. They gathered up trash, stacked the fallen branches, repaired a blown-over wooden fence, and at the end of that long day, picked up rocks near a low spot in a collapsed portion of the outer city wall.

Johnnie's chance came late in the day as she worked near the low spot on the wall. The woman looked directly at her, longer than usual, and then glanced at the low spot. She turned away, making nothing of it, and yelled to one of the boys, "Hey, you! Bring that wagon over here and start loading up these rocks!" As everyone's attention was on the boy, Johnnie quickly stepped over the low spot, ran a few steps, ducked behind a higher portion of the wall, picked up a big rock, and waited. If the woman noticed she was gone and started yelling, Johnnie would just walk back inside, holding the rock as if she were cleaning up. But there was no sound. No commotion. Johnnie stood there. She could hear the woman barking instructions on the other side of the wall. She could even hear the sounds of the children picking up the debris and loading rocks and fallen branches into the wagons. But there was no sound of alarm. Apparently she wasn't yet missed.

She waited. She remembered how loud her own breathing sounded to her, but she waited. The rock grew heavy in her arms. Then the work crew and the stern woman seemed to be moving away from the low portion of the wall. Slowly, Johnnie put down the rock and waited some more. The last thing she remembered hearing was the woman yelling, "Okay, people, let's get this trash out of here and leave the carts with the rocks over there. The builders will know where to find them when they fix the wall. Let's head back."

Johnnie kept waiting. It started getting darker, and still no one had noted her absence. No guards running, no dogs barking. It just grew darker and quieter, except for the sound of her own breathing and heartbeat. Not knowing where to go, she started running, though she knew she should run away from the wall and not alongside it. She could make her way out somewhat in the growing darkness. She was in the woods just outside the city walls, and she ran under branches, through bushes, around anything that she could see.

Eventually, she had to stop to catch her breath. She waited, breathing heavily, hands on her knees, listening for anyone who may have been following her. She heard no sounds, no yelling from a search party. And then she thought of what had happened to Jacob, and she started running again. And she ran and ran until, exhausted, she tripped over something in the woods and fell. She wasn't hurt, but she was paralyzed with fear. *What have I done?* she thought to herself. *They'll find me, just like they find everyone who tries to escape.*

Exhausted and afraid, she fell asleep. And that's when the really strange things started happening. At first she wasn't sure whether she was awake or dreaming, and even now, when she thought back upon it, she still didn't know what had happened—it was like her memories and her dreams merged. She remembered falling asleep in the woods, but when she woke, she was just outside the mouth of a small cave. That was also the start of her strange dreams of an eagle and a mysterious, beautiful woman, mixed in with dreams of flying. The dreams occasionally came back, but they made no sense to her, so she never told anyone about them, not even Simon. From the hilly area where the little cave was, she had stumbled down onto a road and found her way to the children's home. And so began her seven years on this side of the cave.

It turned out she was right. She and Simon were pushed along to a spot out near the base of a short hill. She continued to yell at Simon about the baby, putting on a show for the trackers. But Procker finally slapped her hard and told her to be quiet. Once inside the mouth of the cave, Ren'dal's trackers lit torches and pressed along the walls to the left of the first inner chamber until a hidden door, known to them, opened. Johnnie and Simon were left tied up outside the door, while Procker and Thurel went on through it. The trackers, judging from the voices, met up with two other men a short distance inside the doorway.

There was loud yelling among the four. Johnnie and Simon couldn't hear all of it, but some of it was clearly a nasty argument over pay, the loss of the baby, and how angry Ren'dal was going to be about their failure. At one point, Johnnie kept hearing Simon's name come up in the argument, and she was afraid they were going to kill him right there. Suddenly Thurel and Procker returned and looked at Simon.

"You! Stupid husband! You are free to go!"

"What?" Simon responded. "We're free?"

"No, fool! Don't you listen? Not your pretty wife. Only you! You may go."

"I'm not leaving my wife."

"You killed my baby," said Johnnie suddenly. "Go ahead and *go!*"

"I will not!" Simon yelled back at her.

"So do you choose to go to Ren'dal's kingdom? Even though you are free to leave?" Thurel asked pointedly.

"I told you," Simon answered angrily, "I'm *not* leaving Johnnie. If that means I have to follow you to hell, then I'm coming."

The other two men emerged from the darkness, and the four men looked at each other and nodded.

"You heard it yourself," said Thurel to the two strangers.

"So get up," said Procker after he untied their ropes. He gave Simon a kick with the side of his foot. "You're going with them now," he said as he pointed to the two men. Then Procker and Thurel left the cave.

Johnnie was relieved they didn't kill Simon, though she tried to look like she didn't care. The new handlers pushed them along one of the tunnels of the cave, and the underground journey back to Ren'dal's territory began. The handlers were short and stooped, with big feet and large heads. Their chests were small, but their arms looked powerful. They had torches, bags of equipment with small hammers, other tools of some sort, lots of thin rope, and provisions— mostly bread, water, and dried meat. They clearly knew their way through the underground tunnels.

They moved along at a steady, almost relentless pace. At first Johnnie was afraid their new guards wouldn't care whether Simon made it back, but it was soon evident they meant to deliver both of them to Ren'dal.

The day had started with the couple being chased by the trackers and abandoning their son. It was about to get worse.

Chapter 5

The Journey to Ventradees: The Cave

THE TWO TRACKERS JABBED AND KICKED JOHNNIE AND Simon down the path. Their new guides usually spoke only to each other, except when barking commands like "Move!" "Keep up!" or "Over there!" Their names, as Simon and Johnnie learned along the way, were Carnell and Brackley, with Carnell apparently the leader. The path was broad enough for walking, but since the two guards used torches—one guard in front of them, usually Carnell, and one behind—Simon and Johnnie could see only as far in any direction as the torchlights allowed. The smells were musty, like those in an underground cellar or a damp basement. Their surroundings were at times almost a forest of glistening formations. The walls, ceiling, stalagmites, and stalactites sometimes shone brightly but at other times were more like dancing shadows, depending on their size and how close the torches came.

At one point, Simon could tell that they came to an intersection, where they crossed what looked like another—though narrower—footpath passing to their left and right, but they didn't turn. Their steep downward trek eventually flattened out. "Now we can make better time," said Carnell.

Johnnie moaned and doubled over slightly at the waist.

"Keep going, you!" growled Brackley from the rear.

"Shut up!" yelled Simon. "She's just had a baby!" Without a second's hesitation, Brackley slapped Simon's face with an open right hand and then grabbed him by the lapels of his shirt, pulling him closer, face to face.

"She'll do as I tell her!" he snapped coldly.

Simon stared back at him, but before he could respond, Carnell yelled, "That's enough! We're supposed to bring them both. Let her rest, and—by Chimera's breath—don't hurt him. I don't want to have to carry him."

Brackley released Simon with a push. They rested there a short time before starting again.

The ground stayed level for a while, but within another hour of walking, it started another steep descent. It was slowgoing. Simon tried to help Johnnie whenever she stumbled or winced in pain, but she pushed away his efforts. The path flattened out again, twisted some left then back right, but from there stayed mostly straight. They came to another intersection, this one more of a fork, and the guards led them sharply to their right. The path then inclined steadily downward. Simon and Johnnie found themselves in a narrower shaft but still able to walk upright.

Almost immediately, they noticed the change in the air along the new path they took. A hot breeze hit them, and the smell of burning rubber assaulted their nostrils. It reminded Simon of the time he threw an old tractor tire onto the garbage fire back at the children's home.

At that point, they had been walking for several hours. Finally, Simon spoke again. "Please. I won't cause any more trouble, I promise, but *please* just give my wife a break. I'm tired, and I know she is too." Johnnie said nothing, but she did look up at Simon, as if agreeing, and then looked at the lead guard.

"Okay," Carnell finally said. "We'll probably need it before we get to the tough part. But only a moment's rest."

It was obvious Johnnie was getting weaker, but the time needed for her to eat, drink, and rest was more than the two guards were willing to give. Before long, they started up again.

The smell and the heat got worse with almost every step. The area where they were walking grew slightly larger, judging from the light and shadows that bounced off the surrounding walls. Occasionally, Simon thought he could hear the faint hum of a few voices in the distance. Johnnie's head was down, and she held one hand to her abdomen—she didn't seem to hear whatever it was he was hearing.

The smell weakened slightly, and with no visual warning, the walls on each side disappeared and the ceiling above vanished into blackness. Simon realized they must have emerged from a corridor into what looked like the floor of a valley. He could see by the far-off twinkle of the torchlight, as reflected against the minerals and rocks in the walls, that the new space extended in all directions.

Walking across the floor of the black valley brought them to the source of the scorched, rubbery smell. This was not a dry valley bed. Some kind of river of hot, oily sludge flowed slowly past them. Simon paused to look at the bubbling liquid, and a jab in the back from the rear guard reminded him that—as nightmarish as this was—it was no dream.

The guards pushed them onto a small raft. Johnnie sat on it, head in hands, taking slow, short breaths. Simon kneeled next to her. The raft was slowly poled across the dark river, and now he thought he could hear the voices again. Johnnie lifted her head in a sign of recognition. The sounds were coming from somewhere around them, echoing off the walls—or perhaps even up from the hot, murky river. They were constant, low, weeping sounds, from voices that had grown weak from age or crying, or both.

The smell burned in Simon's nostrils. Johnnie's head sank lower between her knees. Simon tried to breathe through his mouth to stem the stench, but that made his throat burn, and he could almost taste the oily rubber.

Finally, they reached the other side, and even Johnnie moved quickly to get away from the river. They walked straight toward the almost sheer wall of the valley. Then the guards drove them to an opening in the wall. It was perfectly straight and rectangular, which meant it had been shaped by someone.

"Okay, now we go back up. Keep moving, you two," said the trailing guard. "Keep close to the person in front of you. I don't want you stopping or falling back on me." The guards extinguished their torches, and Simon and Johnnie soon realized what he meant. Once all four of them were inside the opening, they began a cramped, stomach-wrenching climb in pitch blackness—on a stairway that resembled an angled ladder up a jagged, narrow tunnel. They were climbing in what seemed to be a single-person shaft, and the steps were shallow in depth and very steep. The only place to grab for support was the next step above at about chest level. Carnell led. Johnnie was second, holding onto Carnell's belt, and Simon was just behind to support her. Brackley, the rear guard, occasionally pushed Simon, but mostly to make sure he didn't stumble and slip back.

The guards grunted and cursed as the group moved slowly, trying to push their prisoners faster, though it was obvious that Johnnie's strength was failing. At one point, the steep pitch of the steps lessened slightly, and they all paused, standing up and leaning forward on the stairs to rest.

Finally, the torturous ascent ended. Carnell pushed open a round, hinged door like a manhole cover. Then they climbed through the opening onto level ground. The torches were relit, and they all sat a while. Johnnie drank a few sips of water and lay on her back, panting and occasionally groaning. In the light of the torches, Simon could see that they had climbed out onto a level space at the top of the river valley and they were resting not far from the edge of the valley wall. Just slightly ahead, he could see one end of a rope bridge strung across the black chasm to his left. He couldn't make out where the other end stopped—it just disappeared into darkness. He was dreading the thought of crossing that bridge; it had only thin ropes for support and wooden planks to walk on, and it swayed high above the canyon of blackness, with its updrafts of heat and its river of hot, noxious sludge below. Simon lay down next to Johnnie and closed his eyes.

He had almost passed out from exhaustion when a high-pitched woman's voice wailed, "Here! I'm here! Come get me . . . fly away . . . fly away!" He reached for Johnnie, but she no longer lay next to him. The captors ran toward the voice. Simon looked beyond the bouncing lights from their torches, and there, standing at the side of the rope bridge, leaning toward the chasm, with her elbows lifted and her arms bent like wings, was Johnnie, crying, "Here I am . . . here I am . . . over here!"

Chapter 6

The Journey to Ventradees: The Final Leg

T HOUGH THE GUARDS WERE WELL AHEAD OF SIMON AS
they all raced toward Johnnie, Simon's voice got to her
first. "Wait, honey. Wait for me!" Johnnie looked at him,
and for a moment, she leaned away from the yawning abyss
in front of her. Her arms slowly began to drop.

But the guard closest to her yelled fiercely, "Get back
here, woman!" at the same time as the other bellowed, "Are
you *crazy*?"

Simon could see the panic on her face as the guards
approached. "No!" she yelled, and she leaned out and raised
her elbows and arms again. "Hurry!" she wailed, and then
she let herself drop.

"Johnnie!" Simon screamed.

The first guard—Simon could now tell it was Carnell—
caught her by one ankle and held on, but her dead weight
pulled him onto his stomach and dragged him toward the edge.

"Hold her!" shouted the other handler, who was only a
step behind. The second guard grabbed his partner by the

belt and wrapped his right leg around an upright post that supported the bridge. The guard who had Johnnie pulled her up enough to get a second hand on the same leg.

"Now what?" yelled Carnell. Just then, Simon grabbed the top rope of the bridge with his right hand and, leaning over Brackley, grabbed Carnell. Together Simon and Brackley pulled Johnnie and Carnell slowly back to safety.

All on the ground, they panted and huffed. Finally, as he leaned over Johnnie, Simon said to the guards, "I wish I had it in me to thank you, but we wouldn't even be here if it weren't for you and your despicable bosses."

"Yeah, well, ya better be glad I caught her," snarled Carnell, "'cause if she'd dropped, we'd have just thrown you after her."

"Yeah," said Brackley, "then you, her, and your precious baby could all have fallen to your deaths on the *same day*." He snorted with what might have been a laugh, but Simon wasn't listening anymore. Johnnie was unconscious.

But the guards weren't paying him any attention either. They had already recovered their torches, wrapped them again, and relit them. "Time to go," one of them said.

"What?" said Simon. "Look at her. She can't move. We've got to stop for a while and take care of her." He put his hand over her face. "She's burning with fever."

"Can't," said Carnell. "No time."

"But—"

"Enough!" Carnell hesitated but then said, "There might be something ahead to help her. Now grab her. We'll have to carry her."

They moved out again, with the two guards taking turns carrying Johnnie over their shoulders. In addition to the faint hope that she might get some help, Simon was immediately surprised and relieved that, instead of crossing the unstable rope bridge, they turned right and entered a tunnel that was a little easier going than their previous paths. Carrying Johnnie slowed them down some, but they still walked hard.

The path descended slightly as they went. The torches gave off enough light that Simon could see the walls, and after about an hour and a half, they reached the end of the tunnel. They walked through a large room, through another narrower area, turned a corner, and then came into another large space. The air was fresher, as if a door or window were open, and Simon thought he heard the faint sound of running water.

The lead guard walked toward the sounds and laid Johnnie down on her back. In the light of the torch, Simon could now see a small pool next to a glistening cavern wall.

"Give her some of this water," Carnell said.

"You sure about that?" said Brackley. "You know—"

"Shut up," Carnell snapped back. "I know what I'm doing. If the woman dies in our keeping, *we'll* pay, not Thurel or Procker."

"But—"

"Quiet!" Carnell looked at Simon. "Give her some of that water. Might break her fever. But don't stay too long around that pool. Or get too close." Then he turned back to Brackley. "Stay here and watch them. Make sure they don't . . . you know."

"But—"

"Don't make me repeat myself." And he turned his back and walked away with one of the torches. Brackley, left there with Simon and Johnnie, growled under his breath but stayed. Simon was already busy crouching at the pool, cupping his right hand with water and bringing it to Johnnie's lips while he held her head up with his left hand.

Johnnie began to move her lips to take in the water, and within a minute, her eyes fluttered open and looked—though still unfocused—at Simon. The water helped, so he splashed small amounts on her forehead and cheeks to cool her fever. He took a few sips for himself when he could. The water was surprisingly fresh. Johnnie coughed and tried to raise her head and shoulders but fell back. She mouthed something, but Simon couldn't hear what.

"What, honey? What is it?" he asked.

"Hot . . . burning . . ."

"I know," he said. Simon splashed more water on her neck and upper chest. Brackley, who was supposed to be watching them, snorted in disgust, strolled off a few paces, and sat against the cavern wall, his torch wedged within a small cluster of stalagmites. As Simon kept giving Johnnie water, he noticed that Brackley was nodding off. The fresh water was certainly helping, but her fever had to be broken if they ever hoped to escape. He pulled Johnnie's shoes off and, as quietly as he could, slid her—clothes and all—into the pond.

As he held her, her legs slowly sank, so the pond was evidently deep, and he lightly bathed her face.

"So good . . . better . . . feeling better," she whispered. Simon smiled and was amazed to feel strength and movement returning to her back and shoulders. She was supporting her head, even moving her legs, and now looking more clearly at him. He could see the light of the nearby torch flickering in her eyes.

"Hey!" yelled Carnell, who had suddenly returned. "Get her out of there! Fast!"

"But it's helping—" Suddenly Johnnie screamed and disappeared beneath the water. Simon didn't completely lose his grip, but a handful of her long hair was all he held. He pulled her back toward the surface, but whatever had her was stronger, and he was being dragged into the water himself. With his other hand, he grabbed for Johnnie's shoulder, under her armpit, clutching at clothes and flesh. His head was pulled under with her, but she now had enough strength to fight and thrash her legs against the unknown force.

Simon felt the guards holding his legs in support. His right hand slipped momentarily, but before Johnnie disappeared into the depths, he was able to get a better hold and pull them both out enough so she wasn't completely submerged and could breathe. Whatever it was still had her, though it seemed that it was momentarily regripping. Simon hugged her close and pulled with all his might. But before the guards could get them out, he and Johnnie were both pulled back under. The guards pulled them above water again, but the unknown force powerfully churned the water and jerked them back in a cruel tug-of-war match. By the third time, Simon and the guards could see what held her—a long, snakelike tentacle belonging to a living mass, a creature of some sort several feet below. It had wrapped its tentacle at least twice around her, and it tightened its hold.

One guard screamed, "The torch!" and Simon could see the torchlight illuminate the water around him.

"One more big pull!" one of them yelled, and Simon supported their efforts by pulling Johnnie as hard as possible. Then he, Johnnie, the wrapped tentacle, and something resembling a huge, earless cat's head on the other end of the tentacle emerged from the pool. One of the guards jabbed the torch directly at the head, at what might have been an eye, and when the creature's head sputtered, squealed, and returned to the safety of the water, the guard jammed the torch onto the tentacle that remained around Johnnie. She screamed as the fire also burned her leg. The monster then loosened its hold, which was enough for Simon and the guards to pull her free.

Simon and Johnnie tumbled backward, and the creature vanished into the depths of the pool.

All of them lay there breathing heavily until Brackley said sharply, "I *told* you! She shouldn't have been given that water!"

"Shut up!" roared Carnell. He grabbed an iron tool that resembled a bar and hook from his bag.

"No, you shut up," Brackley yelled back. "What if Chimera hears of this? That was probably one of his—"

Carnell aimed the iron tool at Brackley's face. "No one will know, will they? Not if we keep our mouths shut. I know I will. Will *you*?"

The other one, clearly at a disadvantage sprawled on the ground, looked at the weapon and nodded.

"'Cause if word ever got back, then I'd *know* who talked, wouldn't I?"

Carnell kept the iron weapon at Brackley's head.

"I'll be quiet, okay?"

Simon and Johnnie witnessed it all but said nothing.

"Good," said Carnell. "Then there's no problem. Gather our stuff and let's go."

"Go?" said Simon. "But we've been up for hours. It's got to be night. We need rest. Can't we just stop now and wait 'til morning?"

"You fool. We rushed all this time to be right here at night. We came for the darkness of this place."

Brackley snorted in agreement. Simon and Johnnie realized there was something else here, besides the creature in the pond, that their guards didn't want to see, especially in the light, so there was no point in arguing. Johnnie was still weak but also clearly better. The burn on her leg was almost healed, though a scar remained. Simon sensed there was something strange—good and bad—about that water, but there was no time to get more.

Carnell and Brackley rummaged in their packs and pulled out ropes, small hooks, rock hammers, and other special tools.

"Now we climb," said Carnell.

"Please don't let them pull me up with those ropes," Johnnie pleaded. "I had a dream. They intend to kill us."

"Honey, I don't think we have a choice. But I'm sure they don't want to *kill* us."

"Please," she whispered. "The—" But she stopped and closed her eyes.

Simon held Johnnie as she lay on the cave floor. Both of them stared up as Carnell climbed the steep sides of the cavern. He threaded the rope through the hooks as a way to pull himself up. The torches were held by Brackley, still on the ground with Simon and Johnnie; Carnell needed very little light to make his way up. He seemed to be moving in an upward circle, bouncing on and off what must have been a spiral ledge to support his feet and using the ropes and hooks to keep his weight pulled toward the wall. The sweeping turns seemed to get smaller and smaller until the climber disappeared somewhere near the center of the ceiling. He obviously had found an opening out of the cavern.

"Okay, I made it!" Carnell yelled back down. "Now send the woman!"

Johnnie groaned. "Please, Simon, no . . ." But Brackley was already moving, and Simon knew he couldn't fight it. With a few quick twists of a rope around Johnnie's upper body, passing it under her shoulders and armpits, Brackley had her in a crude harness. He hooked it to another rope dangling from above, and through a series of hooks, pulleys, and other supports, pulled Johnnie up. She moaned softly as she was lifted, twenty feet, thirty, and then more than halfway up.

But suddenly there was a massive crack of lightning, followed immediately by a loud clap of thunder. The hole at the top of the cavern—Simon now realized—led outside the cave. Even more startling was the length and power of the lightning. Though the hole was relatively small, the lightning hit so close to it that the cavern seemed to shake, and simultaneously—for at least three to four long seconds—the whole inner space was filled with light. In fact, strangely enough, somehow the glow in the room lasted longer than the lightning that struck above and just outside it. The entire room vibrated with radiance, as if the lightning from above shot between and around them, bouncing off the walls at every angle with rays of shimmering brilliance.

Several things happened at once. Carnell, who was managing the simple pulley system from above, groaned as if he'd been struck by the lightning. Simon's hair stood on end, but he nonetheless had a clear vision of the inner formations of the cavern. He was sure that Johnnie saw the same thing, judging from her piercing scream when the light went out. Brackley, who was pulling Johnnie up, lost his balance in all the confusion, and though he continued to hold the rope, he fell and dropped some of his tools. The pull of the rope slid him toward Simon, and Johnnie quickly dropped about fifteen feet.

The guard fortunately collided with Simon, who instinctively grabbed the rope with one hand to keep Johnnie from falling farther and—for the same reason—grabbed Brackley by the shoulders with the other. Johnnie's fall was short but violent, and she dangled in midair, twisting and shrieking, "Simon, help me!"

Brackley and Simon stabilized their balance, and the guard slowly got to his feet, still holding the rope. He yelled to his partner above but got no answer. Johnnie twisted and turned halfway up. "You've got to let her down!" yelled Simon. The guard hesitated. In one swift move, Simon grabbed a metal bar of some sort hanging loosely from the guard's bag and held it up as if to strike. "I said let her down!"

"Go ahead, fool. Hit me with that, and I'll let this rope go, and she'll be flat as a bug on this rock floor." Simon looked at the guard and back up at Johnnie. Then a voice, weak but clear, sounded from above.

"Pull her on up. I'm okay." It was Carnell.

After a long pause, Brackley sneered at Simon and said coldly, "I think you better help. I'm getting pretty tired."

Simon dropped the bar and grabbed the rope. They pulled Johnnie up to the opening, and Carnell pulled her through it. Then Simon was harnessed, and just before Brackley started to pull, he gave him a hard knee to the stomach and said, "You better hope I don't accidentally let this rope slip."

Simon doubled over and coughed in pain. He responded weakly, "You haven't got the guts." He straightened up, gasping from the strike, and then added, "You're too afraid to fail your boss—what's his name? Ren'dal?"

"You'll find out soon enough," Brackley said with a scowl. "And you won't talk so brave then."

The two glared at each other, but Carnell's voice broke the silence. "Get with it down there! I'm pulling him up now!"

So Simon was pulled to the top, and Brackley quickly gathered his scattered gear from the floor and, using another combination of pulleys and hooks, swung himself up the wall and through the opening.

Carnell was weak and still dazed by the strike of lightning, but he was able to lead Johnnie and Simon away from the opening, which seemed to be on a rocky, almost dome-like area. They traveled only a few hundred yards, but now even the guards were ready to make camp. Johnnie and Simon were too exhausted to talk about what they had seen when the lightning filled the cavern, but they both thought about it as they fell asleep. Johnnie dreamed about the mysterious woman, the eagle, and flying. But now these images were mixed with scenes of ropes lifting her, with her arms stretched painfully above her head, and someone she couldn't recognize standing close by.

Chapter 7

Caring for the Baby

"**W**ELL, HE HAS TO HAVE A NAME," SAID THE CLERK AS he widened his already bulging eyes, leaned over the counter, and looked back and forth from Mrs. Frendle to Mr. Stephenson. Mr. Tapley, the county clerk, was thin and short and had noticeably full eyebrows to go with his big, round eyes. He was talkative and usually helpful but stuck to the rules of his office.

"He doesn't, I assure you," shot back Mr. Stephenson.

"Well, of course he has a name," interjected Mrs. Frendle, giving Mr. Stephenson a frown. "It's just that we don't *know* it." She looked back at Mr. Tapley, whose bushy eyebrows raised a notch. "This is the baby that was left at the children's home. I'm sure you read about him in the paper. The sheriff told us to get some kind of birth certificate for him. He'll have to have that for school someday, and besides, he belongs to the children's home now."

Mrs. Frendle nodded at Mr. Stephenson when she reached the end of her comment, as if to remind him that the baby really did belong to the children's home. Mr. Stephenson turned his mouth up at the corners and shot a glance at Mr. Tapley with a slight roll of his eyes.

"Well, again," started in Mr. Tapley, "I'll need a name if I'm going to make him a birth certificate. So let's see," he continued, closing his right eye and putting the tip of his pen near his tongue, to help him think a little bit before he wrote. "You're giving July tenth as his birthday . . . right?"

"That's right," answered Mrs. Frendle. Mr. Stephenson just shrugged.

"But," said Mr. Tapley, with a note of persistence in his voice, "I *will* need a name." Then, after another pause, and this time in a more helpful tone, "What do you all *call* him?"

By this time, Mr. Stephenson was also leaning on the counter, and he pointed to Mrs. Frendle with his thumb and said, "Well, *she* calls him 'the baby I found out on the stoop.' Or sometimes just 'my stoop baby.'"

"That's much too long," said Mr. Tapley. "Any *other* names for him?"

"Well," started Mrs. Frendle, "there was the note that was left by his mother—well, I say it was his mother, but really, it's just because the note looked like it was written by a woman. Anyway, the note did use the word *Hamelin*, or something like that, and that's the only thing that looked like a name."

"Well, not much to go on."

"It can't be helped!" she said. "The note was all wet from the cold milk bottles. If Mr. Tomson hadn't set his blamed bottles down right next to the note, then we'd know more."

"But he *did*," said Mr. Stephenson, exhaling as he spoke. "So, why don't we just use the name Hamelin. How's that?" he asked as he looked at the clerk.

"Fine with me," said Mr. Tapley. "Some kids got worse."

Both men looked at Mrs. Frendle, whose face at first was stock still. Finally, she blinked her eyes slowly, and Mr. Tapley took the cue. "Okay, then," he said, "that's the first name. But what about his *last* name?"

All three of them stood silently. Finally, Mr. Tapley added, "Well, since you've been using it—what about the name Stoop?"

"Oh," began Mr. Stephenson, "I don't know . . . pretty odd thing to name a baby."

Suddenly Mrs. Frendle said, with a sigh of exasperation, "*Fine! I* found him, and I found him out on the *stoop*. Everybody's been calling him 'the stoop baby' anyway. So that'll be *just fine!*"

The way Mrs. Frendle pursed her lips when she said the words "just fine" made the two men look at each other with raised eyebrows, but neither said a word. She reached into her purse, pulled out a small handkerchief, which she crumpled in her right hand, and dotted the corners of her eyes. She put it back in her purse, snapped the purse shut, and glared at the two men.

"Well, okay then," said Mr. Tapley, who quickly bent over his official piece of paper—he wasn't about to ask for a middle name—and wrote very carefully the words *Hamelin Stoop*.

When Mr. Tapley finished entering all the information in his books and giving Mr. Stephenson an official birth certificate, Mrs. Frendle turned and strode toward the door. As she left, Mr. Stephenson muttered, "Well, you can bet that taking care of him won't be as easy as coming up with that name." But only Mr. Tapley could hear it.

Mr. Stephenson and Mrs. Frendle headed back to the children's home in the pickup. She was in no mood to talk, so she pretended to nap on the drive, but she was really puzzling over how to care for Hamelin, her stoop baby. She could see the children's home in her mind, with its white picket fence around the front yard and the half-moon dirt driveway between the fence and the paved road. The biggest problem would be space . . .

The children's home faced the road. The first floor of the main house had her kitchen and a big dining hall, as well as some private quarters for the Stephensons, with a bedroom, living room, and small guest room. The guest room might be of help, but the Stephensons weren't likely to offer it. There was the sitting room the staff used for breaks and the little living room near the front door, which was for visitors. Well, certainly *her* areas were available.

Mr. Stephenson stopped to gas up the truck before leaving Middleton. Mrs. Frendle opened her eyes as he was outside, but she kept picturing the home. The upstairs wouldn't help. It was just one long hallway with the boys' bunkroom on one end of it and the sinks, showers, and toilets on the other. With thirty boys already, you sure wouldn't put a baby up *there*.

Mr. Stephenson got back in the truck and slammed the old door, but Mrs. Frendle, her eyes closed again, hardly stirred. Ideas were forming.

Behind the main house were two other, smaller houses, each designed for twelve girls, though now there were three extras. But even with the other children ranging in age from six to eighteen, they could make do with a baby, whether the Stephensons liked it or not.

By the time they got back to the home, Mrs. Frendle had determined to take charge. Even before the state judge decreed that the children's home would have to keep Hamelin, she had already done most of the work caring for him. But now that it was more permanent—at least until he was adopted, if that ever happened—she would *have* to have some help.

When she and Mr. Stephenson walked into the dining area, several of the staff were looking after Hamelin. Mrs. Stephenson had heard the truck pull up and was already walking into the area.

"His name is Hamelin Stoop," announced Mrs. Frendle immediately, while also moving her eyes rapidly from person to person, daring anyone to object or look amused at it. No one said a word or glanced away. "I'll keep Hamelin during the day, mostly, but I'll need some help."

"We can *all* help," said Mrs. Regehr, one of the housemothers for the girls, as she glanced at the other women of the staff. They nodded, though Mrs. Stephenson looked away.

"Good," said Mrs. Frendle. "But I'll especially need someone to take Hamelin at night. I'm in the kitchen early, and I just don't think I can do that and manage a baby at the same time." Everyone was quiet. Mrs. Frendle waited, looking at each woman until her eyes lit on Mrs. Stephenson. This time, even though Mrs. Stephenson wasn't looking back at her, Mrs. Frendle just stared and waited. Finally, Mr. Stephenson broke the silence.

"Look—" But his wife interrupted him.

"No!" And she looked at Mrs. Frendle. "We can't." But she couldn't hold off Mrs. Frendle's stare. She looked down again and this time pushed her lips down and sniffed. Then with her voice slightly higher than usual, she said, "We are hoping to have a child of our *own.*"

Mrs. Frendle put her hands on her hips, held her stare for a moment longer, and loudly exhaled before picking up Hamelin and walking to the kitchen.

Mrs. Regehr followed behind her. All anyone could hear Mrs. Regehr say, before the door closed behind her, was "Jessie . . ." It was unusual for anyone to call Mrs. Frendle by her first name, but the two women were about the same age, and both were widows. No one heard the conversation, but after that, they shared Hamelin.

At night, Hamelin stayed in the girls' house where Mrs. Regehr was the housemother. She took care of him from evening until early the next morning. She herself had raised two children, a boy and a girl, and now also had three grandchildren living in Canada. But after the death of her husband, Norm, she had not wanted to move in with either of her children, so she had accepted a job at the children's home.

When Hamelin woke up during the night, she fed him, changed his diapers, held him, and talked to him as long as she could. But early each morning during the school year, when she had to get the girls up and ready to catch the bus, she handed Hamelin off to Mrs. Frendle, and he would spend his mornings in the kitchen, though away from the stoves and the doorway.

For the most part, though he was moved around a lot, Hamelin Stoop was a normal baby, spending his day in a playpen and sleeping in a crib. The kids and staff at the home did notice one unusual thing about him physically—a mark on the top of his right foot. At first some thought it was just a birthmark, but it wasn't the right color. It was more black or blue than red or brown. And apart from the color, it just didn't look like a birthmark—it was more like a tattoo, though of course no one could figure out how a baby could have a tattoo. It was two straight lines that leaned toward each other at one end but didn't touch. At the narrow end of the lines was a circle. And there might have been a mark between the two lines. There were different ideas on what the mark resembled, but the most frequent opinion was a clown's hat.

In spite of being passed around a lot, Hamelin was well taken care of. After Mrs. Frendle prepared breakfast and the children came down to eat, she placed him in the dining hall, where he always drew a lot of attention—whether he was in his crib or later in his high chair. The kids would walk by and make faces at him or pat him on the head. Some of the boys would pinch him playfully, and the girls would talk to him or hold him. But still, Hamelin, especially as a toddler, often sought attention from the kitchen staff or some of the older children—holding out his arms to be picked up. However, he never approached Mr. or Mrs. Stephenson.

After lunch, Mrs. Frendle put him in his bed for a nap. She usually placed his crib where the dining hall opened to the reception area near the front door, which was also where the stairs led to the boys' room. In that spot, just about anybody in the house could hear him if he cried.

When the children came home from school, starting with the elementary children around three thirty, Hamelin was usually up from his nap about then. Some of them would talk to him or play with him until they tired of him and moved on to other activities. At six o'clock, there would be supper in the main dining hall, again with all the children around, and then it was back to Mrs. Regehr for bed.

With this pattern, Hamelin was always around lots of people. They watched over him, and Mrs. Regehr and Mrs. Frendle grew very fond of him. He belonged to everyone, though in some ways to no one fully. Even as a toddler, he could feel that.

Chapter 8

Back to Ventradees

THE NEXT MORNING, THE MARCH TO REN'DAL'S TERRITORY continued. Johnnie was still weak but definitely stronger. The burn on her leg was almost completely healed. They now traveled outdoors, and the fresh air helped them all. That evening, as they made camp, she and Simon freely whispered to each other, not caring if the guards noticed.

"After all we've been through, there's no point acting like we're still mad at each other," said Simon. "Besides, it's obvious they've been told to keep us alive."

"But the question is *why*," said Johnnie. "Ren'dal needs us, or he would have killed us already. But his reasons won't be good." She grew quiet, her head down and her eyes closed.

"Honey, I know you've got some bad memories, things I don't know about. But please, talk to me. I've got to know what we're up against if I'm going to get us back."

Johnnie took a deep breath and looked at Simon. She smiled faintly and shook her head. "You have no idea how bad it is . . ."

But he pressed on. "What do you think Ren'dal wants with us?" And then, in an even quieter whisper, he said, "The baby is safe and—"

"Shh!" Johnnie shot a look at the guard and then back to Simon. "Never, *ever* mention our son again, as if he's still— just *never*! Ren'dal hears everything."

He nodded. He waited but soon asked again, "What does he want with us?"

"I don't know. But if he was only angry that I escaped or worried about what I would reveal about his world, I'd probably have been dead a long time ago."

"What do you mean?"

"I mean, I'm pretty sure he's been watching me for years."

"You really think so?" replied Simon.

"Yes. Growing up in Middleton, I used to notice odd-looking men—like those trackers Thurel and Procker— looking at me but acting like they weren't."

"Why would Ren'dal keep track of you?"

"I don't know. But it's clear now that he wants me *and* you, Simon. All that talk when the trackers handed us off to these cave guides—there was something odd about it."

"Honey, the whole thing's odd. But what did you notice?"

"I mean, it was like you had to *agree* to come—like they wouldn't just take you without you *letting* them."

"Well, I wasn't going to leave without you."

"I know—but so did they. Yet they still wanted you to *agree*."

"Honey, it was hardly a decision. I love you—how could I have done anything else?"

Johnnie smiled slightly, but her expression changed quickly as she added, "You're missing my point. Another thing—the trackers, and these guys too, seem pretty worried about the baby being dead and not bringing him back—and that's what bothers me the most."

"Well, they've got us, but not . . ." He paused and stopped himself from saying, "our son." Then he continued, "At least we're together. Besides, I'm not giving up on getting back home. I know I'm not putting up a fight right now, but I can promise you that I marked in my mind the exit in that cave and memorized every path and turn we took so I'll know how to get us home."

"Wherever home is."

"I'm *glad* they want both of us," Simon continued, "because then I can watch out for you. I love you, Johnnie, and I'll never let them harm you."

Johnnie smiled and, with a soft shake of her head, thought about saying, "Thanks, my dearest, but you still don't understand," but she didn't. Instead, "I love you too," was all she said. And before they fell asleep, they looked for a long time into each other's eyes. Johnnie saw hope in Simon's eyes and tried to show some in hers.

That night, as often happened, she woke up abruptly. She thought about things she didn't have the heart or the will to tell Simon. Her mind filled with images of her baby. She could almost feel him in her arms. Was he okay? Was Mrs. Frendle taking care of him? And she now especially worried about Simon. He was brave enough to put up a good fight. But he couldn't begin to imagine what they were up against. He had no idea how many soldiers Ren'dal had, how cruel Ren'dal could be, and how almost impossible it would be to escape once they entered the walls of Ventradees, the place of subtle lights and twilights, like nowhere on earth. And what would Ren'dal do to Simon when it was reported to him that Simon had killed the baby?

Her mind filled with memories of the cruelties she had seen in Ren'dal's territory. She had lived there for hundreds of years, and though she, like the other children, never aged, she had often wished to die.

She remembered again what had happened to those few workers outside Ren'dal's quarters who had tried to escape, especially the young boys. They were punished cruelly. Those who never returned were killed, the children figured from the conversation of the soldiers who hunted them.

But the punishment for those brought back was worse than dying. Ren'dal had what he called the "Scorpions' Whip." Just one lash from that whip would cause the whole body to convulse with pain, and the agony would continue for days after, as if a potent venom had entered the victim's body. Johnnie knew of only one person to receive more than two lashes: Jacob. She could still remember his cries at night, calling for his mother and father, begging for death.

Finally, she fell asleep.

———◈———

The next day started off early, but Carnell didn't push as hard.

"Why so slow?" growled Brackley at one point, only to be answered with a dazed glare.

They stopped earlier than usual for their midday break, and while eating, Simon and Johnnie heard the two guards argue. Brackley was still complaining about the slow pace, but Carnell was in no mood to be pushed. Finally, Brackley approached them and announced, "We're stopping for the day. Carnell's still weak from the lightning. We'll start off early tomorrow."

Simon was glad to hear it, since Johnnie was still tired. That afternoon, when things were quiet and Carnell slept, he finally had the chance to ask her about the cavern and the lightning.

"Honey, what happened when you were hoisted up? You begged me not to let them lift you with that rope; you were going on about a dream."

At first Johnnie hesitated, but she realized how much she wanted to talk about her dream, as if it would make it go away. "It's one of the worst dreams I've had. In it, I am being strung up by my hands and arms. I'm hanging in midair. There are people all around . . . monsters, wild animals on thrones, even children. And they are all watching me and yelling—especially one hideous creature. All the other monsters seem to be afraid of that hideous one. Then there is a terrible, vicious struggle between the hideous monster and a young boy . . . he looks like a teenager . . . and then I . . . anyway, I'm lashed . . . lashed in front of them all. By a terrible whip. It hurts like nothing you've ever felt . . . one lash . . . two lashes . . . three—"

"Honey, stop. It's just a dream."

"But my dreams happen."

"Not all of them. This one didn't happen."

"But," Johnnie whispered almost in a monotone, her eyes staring blankly ahead, "it was the room. I started remembering the dream when I saw the rope from above, and then the lightning . . . and I saw it . . . it was the *room*! The *same one* in my dream. It had a pond, and the walls were shining . . ."

"But there were no monsters—except for the one in the pond. And there wasn't anyone or anything else—no wild animals, no children, no teenage boy—"

"I'm telling you it's the *same room* . . ." And Johnnie began sobbing uncontrollably, hands on her face and elbows in her lap.

"Honey, honey, it's okay," Simon said as he held her in his arms and rested his head on hers. "It was just a dream. It didn't happen. It *won't* happen." He held her for a long time, running his hands through her hair and kissing her shoulders. He hoped he was right, because what he didn't tell her was that, when the cave was illuminated by the lightning, his immediate impression was that he was standing in the midst of four giant thrones.

———

It was dark when they arrived at the city walls. They had traveled for days, though Johnnie and Simon lost count of how many. Johnnie immediately recognized the stones that formed the giant walls, even though she had hardly ever seen them from the outside. She and Simon were handed off to uniformed soldiers, who hustled them along the side streets of the city. They were led through a small opening in an inner wall and then found themselves at the edges of a large courtyard. Then they were taken through an unmarked door, down a long hall, and into a large room, where they were thrown at the feet of an imposing figure. The soldiers slavishly bowed and addressed him as "Lord Ren'dal."

The room was not as gaudy as Simon had imagined for the "son of Chimera," as Johnnie had called him. It was big but felt closed in, having no windows. There was a smoldering fire behind what could have been something like a raised throne. A few tapestries hung here and there, but this was evidently Ren'dal's private quarters.

In addition to the soldiers who delivered Johnnie and Simon, there were other armed men a short distance from Ren'dal. In a shadowy corner of the room to their left stood another man—a large, lonely figure who was overweight, bald, and dressed in black pants and a shirt of brown animal skin. The shirt was sleeveless with a deep neckline that showed his thick, hairy chest. He had the arms of a blacksmith and the scowl and humped shoulders of an abused man. He held something in his hand, but Simon couldn't make out what in the shifting shadows of the room. Johnnie, however, knew what he held.

"So 'home again, home again, jiggety-jog,' eh, Magda?" said Ren'dal as he smiled slowly and blew air out his nose, his head bobbing back slightly.

Johnnie shuddered at the sound of her real name, one she had not heard in years. Simon looked at her quizzically and then remembered hearing that Johnnie was the name given to her when she was found.

"I suppose you're proud of yourself, getting away from us for so long. I must admit, it was surprising that a mere child could have possibly escaped this city. But you don't look so clever now, Magda," he said, looking her over fully. "But my, how you've grown—yes, quite a young woman you are now," he added as he licked and then pursed his lips.

Ren'dal was tall, lean, and dressed in strange clothes. His clothing covered his entire body from the neck down. His shoes were almost like ballet slippers except for the furry ball on the toe of each foot. Johnnie had always seen him in a strange hat, which he wasn't wearing now, but there was still no mistaking the long, strawy brown hair and the large, beaklike nose. He was clearly the same sneering figure she had seen in passing so many times as a child.

"Speak up!" he yelled. "What's the matter with you?" He paused, leaned in, and continued sarcastically, "Oh, excuse me. I forgot to address you by your new name, *Johnnie*— what a silly name for a girl. I suppose you couldn't bear to tell them your true name, Magda. Well, let me remind you of some of the things you left behind." And with that, he turned to the corner where the hulking, apelike man stood. "Snardolf, come here and remind Magda of life in Ventradees."

And now Simon too could see clearly what the large, round, lumbering man carried in his hand. It had all the appearance of a whip, but its component pieces were unlike the parts of any whip Simon had ever seen. From the cord-wrapped rod that proceeded from the handle, there were tightly braided strips of leather. The individual strips each splayed out again into multiple strands of smaller, writhing tentacles shaped like a rat's tail. Moving and slithering as if alive, each taillike strand looked to be of a hard thread of fine metal. And at the end of each thread was a broad, upraised tail that moved constantly and resembled a scorpion's stinger. Each stinger moved randomly, it seemed, but never in all their movements did they tangle or knot up.

"You recall the Scorpions' Whip, do you not, Magda?" asked Ren'dal. He had a way of speaking that was bouncy in tone, even when—or maybe especially when—the words were cruel. His mouth was usually stuck in a sly, almost whispering kind of smile, and his eyes betrayed an amused, quizzical look. Always the showman, Johnnie remembered. Always prepared to dance with every word, his arms and hands moving smoothly to express outrage, ridicule, and, above all, a mocking sarcasm.

Johnnie's heart sank, and her eyes showed it. She knew what was coming.

"I'll take that as a yes," mocked Ren'dal. "I was *sure* you wouldn't forget it. It's been waiting for you all these years.

You've seen its work. You've seen its . . . power." And then he spoke to Simon, wrinkling his brow in a look of feigned concern. "*You*, of course, have not, but you will . . . when it's used on your wife. Maybe that will give you an appreciation for the way things are done here in Ventradees!"

Johnnie was still on her knees, but now her whole back and body crumpled before him, exposed. The dread of the whip had doubled her up in fear. Her worst nightmare was now only seconds away; the stories and the screams of tortured children she remembered from years ago were all now about to explode across her back. Trembling and groaning lowly, she waited on the floor in front of Ren'dal for the first lash.

Simon realized with horror what was about to happen, and for a split second, remembering Johnnie's dream, he even glanced up to see if there were ropes above set to hoist her up—there weren't any, though that didn't mean his wife was safe. He dived forward to cover her back with his own, but the guards anticipated his movement and quickly pulled him several paces away from Johnnie.

"No!" he screamed. "Are you going to hit a woman, you *coward*?"

"*Coward*?" said Ren'dal as he jerked his attention from Johnnie's back to stare at Simon, his eyes bulging. "Me? A coward? Oh, no, my brave, young lad. A coward is what she has been for running away, for hiding out in another world. A coward is what you are now, as you stand by helplessly, too *weak* to help your wife. And a coward is what both of you will be day after day when you do *nothing* but our bidding." Ren'dal leaned close to Simon, speaking in a teeth-clenched whisper. "And a *coward* is what a man is who *kills his own son* instead of protecting him."

With that, Ren'dal looked at Snardolf and nodded, and the Torturer raised the whip.

But Snardolf had been trained by long years of painful practice. Raising the whip was one thing, but he knew never to give the stroke without a final sign from Ren'dal. So with the whip raised and the living ends of it writhing and whirling above his head, Snardolf waited, and Ren'dal paused. A soft groan came from Johnnie. A slow smile touched Ren'dal's lips as his eyes closed.

After a long pause, he drew in a deep breath and said, "There, there, young Johnnie. Did you really think that I would welcome you back here with Snardolf's whip? Why, we're so glad to see you. We wouldn't *think* of harming you. Don't you see? We have *missed* you. We *need* you back here. In fact, I am so"—and he stopped briefly with his eyes turned upward, as if searching for the right words—"*happy* that you have come back, especially with your husband." He looked at Simon with a freezing look, but the soft, almost musical flow of his voice continued. "Yes, we're glad to have you *both*. And what a wonderful young family you appear to be: Johnnie, a child belonging to this world, and you—Simon, isn't it?—by your own consent now a son of Ventradees."

Johnnie and Simon stole a quick look at each other.

"No, no," he continued, his words dripping rapidly from his rounded lips. "We wouldn't harm you in the least, would we? We want you both healthy and strong. You, young wife—perhaps one day soon a young mother again—we want you *especially* healthy and strong. And you, young husband, you're joining us to take care of our dear Magda, just as a young husband should. We have great plans for the both of you."

The guards, at a glance from Ren'dal, helped Johnnie to her feet. She rushed to Simon's side, and the two of them stood trembling.

"There, there, I'm so sorry we appear to have frightened you," Ren'dal said with his best toothy smile. "All is well. Take them away."

The guards led the two to the exit, but then he flicked his hand, and one of them pulled Simon back while the other pushed Johnnie away. "Simon . . . young husband," Ren'dal continued, and the smile vanished and his voice lowered. "I know your intentions. You want to protect your wife, take care of her, and at the first opportunity, you will try to escape. I don't advise it. You came here voluntarily, but now you are ours. To attempt escape would be—how shall I put it?—a very *painful* mistake."

And then, without warning, he stood back, and the soldiers who held Simon instinctively stepped back. Johnnie, who was still in the room but a few paces away, turned at precisely the moment when Ren'dal gave Snardolf the signal. Snardolf, who still had the whip raised, cracked it forward with a lightning speed that caught everyone but Ren'dal by surprise. Even the guards flinched as the lash of the seven scorpions tore across Simon's back and left side. He screamed in pain and shock as his body convulsed and he fell to his knees. Ren'dal leaned down and fiercely whispered in his ear, loud enough for Johnnie to hear, "*That* is for killing your son. But can you imagine what a *second* stroke would feel like? Maybe I should show you *now!*"

He paused as if his throat was stuck. His face puffed and his eyes watered. His nose and cheeks turned red as he breathed in rapid gasps. "The baby—the *baby boy,*" he stammered as he stretched out his arms with his fingers flexed as if to grasp Simon's neck. But slowly he caught his breath and regathered himself. He let his arms fall.

"This time I'll let you *imagine* what another stroke would do to you," he said, again in his hissing whisper. "All the ancient stories say that the sixth stroke kills. To tell you the truth, I've seen *two* strokes cause people to wail and beg like slaves, *three* to leave them shivering in agony for weeks, and a fourth . . . well, you don't want to know."

All the while Ren'dal breathed these threats, Simon shuddered with convulsive groans that made the soldiers nearest him swallow hard and perspire. Johnnie had screamed simultaneously with the lash, but her captors held her back.

The guards picked up Simon at Ren'dal's signal and all but dragged him from the room, since he was nearly faint with pain and barely able to add support with his legs. Ren'dal's words chased them all out of the room. "So, husband of Magda, remember this the first time you think about escaping."

And then he laughed. He could be heard to laugh by all, especially Johnnie, as she was pulled away reaching for Simon and as Ren'dal danced for himself and apparently no one else in particular. He clasped his hands in front of him and performed a piper's jig on his toes. "The tune has come round again! The girl thought she had escaped us!"

He twirled and spun before the fire, and Snardolf slowly returned to his corner of the room. Then in two voices, both monotone but one high and one not, Ren'dal answered himself line by line in alternating voices and chants.

It is all according to the plan,
She comes back, new wife with man.

Both from there and now from here,
The hour is near for the one to appear.

Once the tremors have begun,
The sun is risen, the time is come.

With birth pangs, sword, and lash to fear,
The hour is near for the one to appear.

Chapter 9

Hamelin's Friends

HAMELIN GREW INTO A CURIOUS THREE-YEAR-OLD, always on an adventure or running around. Always, it seemed to others, in search of something—or someone. He loved exploring Mrs. Frendle's kitchen cabinets and drawers. "Hamelin, get out of there!" or "Put that back!" she often barked out, loud enough for everyone to hear. Once she lost him for more than twenty minutes when he crawled inside a series of lower cabinets that were connected side by side. "What—are—you—*doing* in there!" was not really a question so much as an explosive warning when she finally found him. "Come *out* of there!" She thought about giving him a big swat—"I'm going to bust your bottom!" she had promised when she spied him in the cabinets—but she was so relieved to find him she just gave him a big hug and kiss and decided the swat could wait. "Now stay out of *trouble*," she yelled after him as he raced off to his next adventure.

Besides enjoying the many spaces and the constant activity of the house, Hamelin liked exploring outdoors too—at least as much as the staff would let him. The main house was on what was once farmland, before the county bought it. The home faced west and had one paved road running in front of it. To the north, it was bordered by some brushy woods, which Hamelin was especially drawn to. To the east, behind the main house and not far from the girls' houses, he found other fun places to play: there was a work shed where an old tractor and rusty pieces of equipment were stored and a barn with plows and some other old farm implements. Then farther east—about the distance of a football field away—there was a small pond, usually called a "tank" by people in those parts, and then the woods picked up again just beyond it. Hamelin liked to go there when someone would take him—to play, to skip rocks, or to just stare into the water at reflections of the sky and the clouds on sunny days.

Hamelin sometimes spent time with Mr. Moore, the handyman who had worked at the children's home for several years. Mr. Moore usually covered his bald head with a straw hat, and his face was ruddy and weather-beaten. He moved steadily but not quickly, always working and usually smiling, unless some repair wasn't going well and had him sweating and muttering—although the worst that he ever said was "Dat-burn it!" Mr. Moore tried to teach Hamelin how to fish at the pond, but Hamelin didn't like handling the live bait, or even the small fish they caught, so he wasn't much interested. Still, he liked Mr. Moore a lot and often followed him around, trying to help.

At other times, some of the children, especially the girls who liked school, would use him as their student. "Come play school with us, Hamelin!" was often heard on summer afternoons. Sometimes his attention span was too short to play their games, but other times he stayed long enough to learn something new, like letters, words, and numbers.

Growing up in the children's home wasn't at all like growing up with parents and siblings, but it wasn't bad. Sometimes there were children at the home who were mean or just ignored him. Or if the adults weren't around, a few of the kids might give him a swat or a thump on the head. But most were nice to him, and Mr. Moore—and especially Mrs. Frendle—wouldn't allow anyone to pick on him for very long.

Though he didn't know the exact moment when it happened, Hamelin's world changed when a brother and sister at the home—Bryan and Layla Collier—started showing him a lot of attention. They had been at the home for several years, and Bryan was one of the boys the other children looked up to. He usually sported a blue jean jacket with the collar turned up and, on special occasions, a straw-colored cowboy hat. He was lean, athletic, and quick to smile and always seemed to know what was going on around him. One of Hamelin's earliest memories of Bryan was when he sneaked around a corner and up to where Hamelin was sitting one afternoon. With his back hunched and his fingers curled, he took exaggerated steps and snickered like a cartoon villain. "I'm . . . gonna . . . *get you*, Hamelin!" he said in a low, crackly voice as he grabbed him and tossed him into the air. Hamelin squealed in pure joy, and Layla, usually never far from her brother, said, "Bryan! Don't scare him!" Even when Bryan was in a hurry or busy with a task, he still always gave Hamelin a wink and a pat on the head.

Layla, who was about fifteen months younger than Bryan, also showed Hamelin a lot of attention, helping Mrs. Regehr and Mrs. Frendle take care of him whenever she could. Layla had dark-brown hair that tumbled off her head in big curls right down to her shoulders, and Hamelin loved to grab big handfuls of it. "Hey, go easy on the hair, Hamelin," she always said as she released his grip. But she would stick her head right back into his face so he could grab again.

Layla often read books to him. They loved to read stories of strange, exotic places and adventures, and they would spend hours and hours immersed in them.

By the time he was almost four, Hamelin would wait on the front porch of the children's home every afternoon for Bryan and Layla to return on the school bus.

He never expected what would happen when Bryan graduated from high school. They tried to explain it to him, but it was a painful shock when Bryan moved out of the children's home. Of course, all the high school graduates left, but Hamelin was too young to know why that should happen. He just knew that he missed Bryan terribly. For weeks, he could feel his chest rolling over on the inside whenever he thought about his friend.

Hamelin wasn't the only one who missed Bryan. One day he found Layla sitting just outside the old shed. He could see that she was crying.

"What's wrong, Layla?" he asked.

"Oh, Hamelin, I didn't see you." She stood up quickly and wiped the tears from her eyes with the palms of her hands. She was wearing her hair in big pigtails that day, and it made her look more like a little girl.

"Why are you crying, Layla?" he asked.

He looked into her red, teary eyes. "Well, Hamelin, I . . . I guess I just miss Bryan, that's all."

"Oh," he replied. "Are you going to leave too?"

"Oh, no," she said, but then stopped herself. "Well, I mean, I'm not leaving *soon*, Hamelin. I'm going to be here with you for at least another year." She knew a year was a long time for a little boy, so she thought that was a good thing to say.

"Is Bryan going to come back?" Hamelin asked.

"Well, sure he's going to come back. But it's just hard for him to visit us right now. He lives more than two hundred miles away in a big city called Abilene. He has a job there, and he hopes to save up enough money to go to college."

"What's college?"

"Oh, it's like a big school you can go to after high school, if you want to."

"Do *you* want to?"

Layla paused for a second but finally said, "I do, Hamelin. You know, I'm going to graduate from high school too. Then I'll probably go to Abilene. Bryan and I plan to live together there, and I'm hoping to get a scholarship—some money—to go to college."

Hamelin just looked at her.

"You understand, don't you?" she asked.

He shrugged and looked down, his hands in his pockets. "I miss Bryan, and I don't want you to go away too."

Layla couldn't help it; she started crying again. And she could tell that Hamelin was about to cry too. He kept looking down, but his nose got wrinkled up.

"Hey," she said. "It's way too hot out here, don't you think? Let's go in the house and read some *Robinson Crusoe*. You want to?"

"Sure," he said. And the two of them went off into the house. They read from *Robinson Crusoe* for a while, and Hamelin listened to it with no interruptions.

He sat there quietly after she finished a chapter, and he seemed to be thinking.

"What'cha thinking about, Hamelin?" Layla asked.

"What books does Bryan like to read?"

"*The Count of Monte Cristo*," she said. "He *loves* it."

"Could we read that one?"

"Sure."

And so, even though Hamelin was a little young for it, they started reading Bryan's favorite book.

———

Hamelin had just turned four when Layla started her senior year of high school. They spent a lot of time together throughout the year. One day during December, as he played outside, a figure approached from the distance. He could almost make out who it was, but his hair was a little different and his clothes more rumpled: it was Bryan! He had taken a bus and was walking from the bus stop. He was visiting for two weeks to celebrate the holidays with Layla and Hamelin and all his other friends. Hamelin was overjoyed.

Everyone was delighted to see him. After a long day of activities, Hamelin and Bryan rested by the pond.

"Thanks for taking care of Layla for me, little guy," Bryan told him.

Hamelin looked a little somber. "You've been gone a long time. I missed you."

"Yeah, buddy. I missed you too. I wish I could visit more often, but I just don't have a car yet. Eventually, when I save up enough money, I can buy a car. Then I can come by more often."

"You promise?"

"Cross my heart," said Bryan.

The Christmas holidays passed quickly that year, and so did the rest of the school year. Which meant the day that Hamelin dreaded was coming up: high school graduation. Soon Layla would have to leave.

One afternoon, shortly after graduation, he and Layla read *Gulliver's Travels* together. After finishing a chapter, she lowered the book.

"Hamelin, you know I love you, right? I don't want to leave you," she said, "but I got a partial scholarship to Hardin-Simmons University. I'm moving to Abilene with Bryan."

Hamelin didn't say anything.

"But we're both going to work hard, so maybe Bryan can get that car before long, and then we'll come back to see you as often as we can."

When Layla finally left in early June, it was the hardest day of Hamelin's life. The final moments of her leaving all happened in slow motion. She hugged him good-bye as he stood on the front porch. She climbed into Mr. Moore's pickup. Mrs. Frendle went to Layla's side of the truck, said something, and handed her an envelope. Layla nodded. Mr. Moore started up the engine and slowly pulled out of the driveway. All the other kids stood around waving good-bye. Hamelin held back the tears that were forming—he didn't want any of the older boys to make fun of him. But as the truck turned left, Layla looked out the back window at the group. When her eyes met Hamelin's, she put her hand on the window and started crying. He couldn't help himself; he felt tears coming. The slow motion stopped. He covered his face and ran into the house as the truck headed toward the bus stop.

Why did Layla have to leave? And why didn't *he* have any family? At least Layla had Bryan, and now he had nobody. Well . . . he still had Mrs. Regehr and Mrs. Frendle and some of his friends. But why didn't he have a mother and father? Well, Layla and Bryan didn't have their mother and father either. But *why*? And why did his mother and father leave him in a tomato box, like Mrs. Frendle told him, by the kitchen steps of the side porch? And why did he have the stupid name *Stoop*?

The summer dragged after Layla left. Even with the other kids from the home around during the summer, it just wasn't the same. Hamelin was going to be starting kindergarten the next year, but he really wasn't looking forward to it. If only Layla could be there to take him to school the first day . . .

One day in late July, with a hot sun and no clouds, Hamelin was sitting on the porch doing nothing when he heard Mrs. Regehr. "Hamelin! Hamelin! Where are you?" She came out of the front door with a wide smile and an envelope in her hand. "Hamelin, you got a letter today. It's from Layla!"

Hamelin's eyes widened as she handed him the letter. "Really?" he said. He tore the envelope apart, removed the letter, and stared at it. Smiling, he pushed it back in her hands. "You read it, please." Then he sat cross-legged on the front porch and looked up into her face, the same way he often listened to Layla read the books they shared.

The letter read,

```
Dear Hamelin,


I miss you so much. I can't believe you're
now five years old and will soon be starting
school! I wish I could be the one to walk you
```

to your room on your first day. You are going
to do so well in school, especially since you
already know your ABCs and numbers!

Bryan told me to tell you hi and that he
misses you too. We'll come see you as soon as
we have the chance.

Hamelin, always remember that, even though
we're not there, we love you. You are a very
wonderful boy. We believe there is something
very special that will happen in your life.
Keep waiting and keep hoping.

Love,
Layla (and Bryan)

After Mrs. Regehr finished the letter, Hamelin sat very still for a moment. He said nothing, and the silence caused her to say, "Hamelin, are you okay, honey?"

Then, with Mrs. Regehr still holding the letter, he got up and ran. He kept running until he came to the pond. He stared at his reflection at the water's edge. "Keep waiting and keep hoping," she'd said. He knew how to wait, but he had no idea how to hope. His chest hurt more than ever, and it hurt so bad the pain came up into his eyes, and soon his tears were dropping and making little rings in the pond, disturbing his watery reflection.

———

There was one other big change that summer. The Stephensons and Mrs. Frendle decided that Hamelin was old enough to move out of the girls' house where Mrs. Regehr stayed and into the main house. He didn't want to, but

Mrs. Regehr assured him it would be all right, and a couple of the older boys were told to make sure that none of the others picked on him. But sometimes he cried at night, though he tried not to let the other boys hear him. One night, one of them yelled, "Shut up, Hamelin, you big baby!" One of the seniors yelled back, "Shut *yourself* up! Leave Hamelin alone."

And alone was just what he felt. He wanted Layla and Bryan to come back.

Chapter 10

The Summons

"DOESN'T THE FOOL HUSBAND KNOW WHAT IT TAKES TO make a baby?" roared Ren'dal. He was not a patient creature, and after four years, Johnnie and Simon still hadn't conceived a child.

"But, Master," Katris began, "you can't expect—"

"Don't tell me what I can't expect!" he screamed. He stared at her with drawn-in eyes and a pointed face.

Katris was a middle-aged woman who had been captured on one of Ren'dal's excursions. She had soft brown hair, which would have fallen into the middle of her back if she had not kept it pinned up on top of her head and covered with a scarf. She was in her midthirties when she was captured and brought to Ventradees. Within just a few years, after difficult work around the city streets, she had been brought to Ren'dal's quarters and in rather short order became the head of his household.

She had managed to get word back to her family in Parthogen that she was alive, but both she and they knew that, even though Ren'dal did not have a right to her, it was better for everyone that they not attempt to rescue her. She certainly would have left if she had ever had the chance, but no one left Ventradees without Ren'dal's permission, and everyone knew the punishment for even trying.

Katris knew how to keep Ren'dal's household functioning and usually knew how to handle his moods; she was practiced at subtly calming his rages before he got out of control. Thanks to her, the household ran smoothly and the servants stayed safe—she usually knew how to stop Ren'dal from abusing them.

"Certainly you are right, Master," she began. "You have every right to expect exactly what you want." The redness in his face drained slightly. "My suggestion—and it's only a suggestion—is that your plan, perhaps your finest ever, has a better chance of success if you can wait just a bit longer."

"Are you saying I have not already been patient with those two?"

"Of course you have. But the ways of women can often be mysterious." She looked up and offered him a faint smile.

"Yes . . . ?" He waited for her to continue.

"The woman, Johnnie, has certainly had plenty of time after these several years to recover from her other pregnancy, but her son's murder is another matter altogether. That wound might require a little more . . . healing, especially since it was by her husband's hand. Also, if I may be so bold . . ." Katris looked away. She finally said sheepishly, "Being watched all the time will probably not help her chances for conception, my lord."

Ren'dal breathed out heavily, almost with a snort. But he begrudgingly agreed he would have to wait.

Waiting, however, was not the real cause of Ren'dal's anxieties. He feared a summons from Chimera. The plan was really not his plan; it was Chimera's, and the order was for it to be completed as soon as possible—and Chimera would not tolerate failure.

And fulfilling this plan wasn't exactly easy! Arranging to have a child born of two worlds was not the kind of thing his idiot brothers, Landon and Tumultor, could do. It was hard enough to communicate with those on the other side of the Atrium, much less find a child who had parents from both sides. If only that group of captured children had continued to age! Chimera's plan to usurp the Figure's high throne— Ren'dal looked around nervously, almost as if someone could have heard his thoughts—was an audacious plan, to say the least. Not that Chimera wasn't wise and bold enough for such plans, of course. Ren'dal glanced around again, but this time, he looked up as well. He was trying as hard as he could. If the fool woman and her husband would just get on with it!

Though he tried to deny it, he could feel Chimera's approach. And when he came, it was usually at night.

———

Ren'dal lay in his bed and stared upward. The shades of night had long since closed over Ventradees, and now he lay awake. He felt himself slowly sinking into a greater darkness, and at first he thought it was the beginning of sleep. As he sank lower, however, he could smell the wispy odor of a failing fire. Had Katris allowed the fire in his bedroom to go out? The smell remained, and now he found himself sinking into a pool of shadows. Wave after wave of darkness came over him, and in those fleeting moments, he knew that Chimera was coming. Whether he was still in his bed or floating elsewhere and off into the night, he couldn't tell. He began to hear the crashing of a waterfall just before he felt the final, dry waves of darkness cover him. Now he felt himself traveling facedown while still going down, down into the depths of an ocean of blackness. Then, at the last second his body spun, and now standing but still sinking, he looked back into the darkness and saw a pinpoint of light coming toward him. The pinpoint of light grew larger and larger but somehow didn't seem to grow brighter.

The place where he was felt like a globe, and the pin-prick of light, coming ever closer, began to illumine the outer edges of the massive sphere that held him. The bottom of the globe began to fill, and Ren'dal could smell and feel, as well as see, the creatures that were filling it. At his feet were muddy tadpoles and frogs, and above the frogs, coming near his waist, were swarms of gnats. The light continued to come closer—or maybe the globe that held him was being pulled toward it.

The light was now close enough so that the form of Chimera's face was taking shape. The darkness around the encroaching face was not scattered but rushed toward Ren'dal and buried him even deeper into the spherical pit of blackness. But he could see the darkness, and he could also feel it. The upper half of the globe was now filled with Chimera's face, which expanded downward and seemed to grow body parts—wings like an eagle, legs like a goat, and a lashing tail like a snake. These three animal parts flowed from a face that bore little resemblance to anything human, though his eyes, a very faint nose, and a narrow, wide mouth could be seen.

Being summoned before Chimera in the past had always, at this point, produced a scream from Ren'dal, but except for those few instances when these visions had been nightmares, the screams had done no good. And Ren'dal knew, without screaming, that this nightmare was not a nightmare. Though it was nightmarish, this was a summons, and now he stood before Chimera. The mouth barely moved, and the eyes opened only in snakelike squints, but Chimera's voice could be felt in every part of Ren'dal's body.

"I am not pleased," he said. "The plan has been very clear, has it not?" Ren'dal knew not to speak. He briefly looked into Chimera's eyes and nodded before turning his head away.

"There must be no failure," the voice continued. "As much as you fear looking at me, I remind you that I too have seen a vision, one that all—but myself—refused to gaze upon, but one that can be defeated.

"When the Figure came to our realm to gloat, all others, even though chained, fell back. But I rushed toward him, and as he left, I grasped the flaming tail of his light. My chains were broken as I ascended with him out of the Abyss. As I climbed, I seized a piece of rock from Nefas, the Pits of Darkness, and it grew into Ventradees, part of the Land of Gloaming, where, with my permission, you now rule. Do not make me regret that decision."

Now Ren'dal knew that he must speak, though he dared not look again into Chimera's eyes. His body trembled from the echoes of the voice within him, but still Ren'dal breathed as deeply as he could and said, "I will not, Father."

"Then understand that I do not fear the Figure. Indeed, I will conquer him yet, when a child, a son of two worlds, bridges the gulf and thereby raises Nefas over the upper regions. I will ascend and raise my throne over the stars of the Ancient One. So this child must be produced! Unlike you, I can and will be patient. Even centuries have been and can be endured, as long as I have success. But the fullness of our opportunity is now, and so I will not wait much longer. The child must be born from this woman and this man, because the time is near. Do you understand?"

And before Ren'dal could answer and while he was still uncertain as to whether he should, the voice spoke again. "Do not fail!"

The face and its three parts began to withdraw in sections, but Ren'dal felt agony even in its withdrawal, as the pain of Chimera's crushing presence reversed itself. In Chimera's wake, the floating creatures chased after him, scurrying to serve him. The muddy, moldy stench they carried lingered even as they left, overwhelming Ren'dal's senses. Rancid, burning smells of rotten apples and damp mud mixed with urine. Chimera's departure sucked at Randal's inner flesh as if a thousand flames were being pulled through his skin to chase Chimera's vanishing light. Hot trailing winds lashed at his back like stems of pampas grass. The absence of Chimera signaled Ren'dal's survival as his son, for now, but the lifting of that abysmal weight of darkness nonetheless left him gasping for air in the suffocating vacuum.

And now Ren'dal did scream. The sphere was stripped away, and then, with a speed that pulled and then turned his stomach, he was thrown backward and felt himself rushing away. And he kept screaming. His screams were the only things he could hear as he hurtled back through the darkness.

Finally, he was awakened by a voice.

"Master! Are you okay?"

Ren'dal opened his eyes; Katris stood over him. Others from the household entered the room, alerted by his wails. He grabbed Katris by her hair and pulled her close to him.

"*Whatever* it takes," he croaked hoarsely. "Do you understand? Make the two of them—that woman with that man—conceive a baby. And don't forget, *I still know where your family lives.*"

She winced in pain and whispered hoarsely, "Yes, Master."

He continued to hold her hair in his fist, but she dared not pull away or say another word. Finally, she slowly touched his hand, and he loosened his grip. She hurried away to do his bidding.

Chapter 11

A Baby in Ventradees

SIMON WASN'T THERE WHEN KATRIS TOLD JOHNNIE WHAT she had to do.

"But *why* does he want me to have a baby?" Johnnie asked.

Katris looked her in the eyes briefly but had to look away.

"I'm not sure," she said slowly, "but I know you must." Katris looked again at Johnnie.

"I won't do it."

"But you must. You and Simon *must* have a baby."

"If he wants a baby around here, then *you* have it for him!" Johnnie yelled. But as soon as she said it, she regretted it. Johnnie knew that Katris had come from Parthogen and that she still had, at least as far as Johnnie knew, a husband and children back there.

"I'm . . . I'm sorry," she said.

"It's okay," said Katris. "If I thought it would help you *or* me, I would do it. But I'm too old, and besides, babies aren't born here in Ventradees." Johnnie had never thought why that was so, but she had known from long ago—and shortly after arriving, Simon had also noticed—that there were no babies about.

"So, why does he suddenly want a baby?" She started to say that he could go steal one just like he did before with children, but she thought better of it.

"I *told* you," responded Katris, this time with a bit more snap in her voice, "I don't know, but—"

"And why *us*? Besides, maybe we can't have children either, here in Ventradees."

"I'm not sure of that either, but I know Ren'dal and the source of this demand well enough to know that this is not negotiable. He wants a baby in Ventradees, and he thinks you and Simon, for whatever reason, *can* have children, so he expects you two to produce a baby."

Johnnie felt the panic rising in her chest at the memory of the son she had abandoned to keep Ren'dal from getting him.

"Well, then," she blustered, "I'll just make sure we don't have any more children."

"You can try every method you want not to have children, which I suspect is what you and Simon have done over the last four years"—and here it was Johnnie's turn to look down—"but the reason why won't matter to Ren'dal. He just expects it, and if he doesn't get what he wants voluntarily, then . . . well . . ."

The thought of Ren'dal forcing them, by whatever methods he might use, finally made Johnnie and Simon give in to the pressure—at least to try again to have children. They wanted children, but the pain of abandoning their son and being brought to Ventradees made them reluctant to have more. It was very plain to them that Ren'dal had wanted their son especially, and now they were expected to produce another child. They talked and argued at length, but in the end, their fears, and partly too their natural desire for children, won out. And Katris, without telling them she was going to, made some household decisions that made it easier for Simon and Johnnie to have more time together and for both of them to be healthier. Katris assigned a younger woman to be with Johnnie constantly, to make sure she had the kinds of foods she needed to be healthy, and Simon's workload changed dramatically. Everyone in Ventradees, Ren'dal's domain, was required to work. But Simon's duties became noticeably lighter than those of others. He was allowed to sleep in a little later and to go home earlier to make sure that he and Johnnie had time alone as husband and wife.

"Of course I want a baby," he said bluntly one night. "But I don't want to produce a baby just because *Ren'dal* wants us to."

"Well, I don't either," responded Johnnie, "and you can be sure that it suits some plan he has."

"And whatever his plan is, it won't do us or anybody else any good," Simon said bitterly.

"I know," said Johnnie, "but maybe another baby here with us can make things a little better. Besides, Katris said that Ren'dal had to have a baby from *both* of us, so surely he isn't going to harm the baby. I mean, he *needs* it for something." And, though they never spoke of their other child, they both also secretly hoped that another child would help them forget the pain of abandoning their first.

———

Soon after, Johnnie and Simon were expecting. The months of pregnancy dragged by, filled with fears, but finally the day came that Johnnie gave birth to a healthy baby girl.

"A *girl*? *Get rid of it!*" bellowed Ren'dal. Katris was as shocked as Simon and Johnnie to hear his command, but there was no arguing. Katris tried every argument and trick of manipulation she knew, but there was no changing Ren'dal's mind. So she came and, with the help of Ren'dal's guards, forcibly took the nursing baby girl from her mother's arms.

Simon struggled with the guards but was wrestled to the floor with a dagger held against his throat. Another guard slapped Johnnie down when she rushed at him. They left the couple on the floor, grieving in each other's arms.

For three days, Johnnie refused anything to eat or drink. She wanted to die. Late on the third night, she stopped crying. Simon never left her side during those days, and he could see something different in her face.

"We've got to escape," she said finally.

"What?" Simon said.

"We've got to leave."

"We *can't* leave, Johnnie. You know there's nothing I want more, but I've studied every conceivable way and thought of every option. If it were possible to escape from here, I'd do it."

"We've got to try."

"Honey, it's . . . it's impossible. We're watched constantly, and even if we weren't, the system of walls and guard stations in this Godforsaken city makes it hopeless to try."

Johnnie looked him straight in the eyes. Her face was red and swollen, but her words were clear. "Simon, I'm going to try whether you come with me or not. If they catch me, I'll try again. If they bring out the Scorpions' Whip, I don't care. The worst thing that can happen is that I'll die trying. I want you to come with me, but if you don't, I'm going to do it myself. I escaped from here once before—"

"But you've often said yourself that you only remember the first part of how you got out of here."

"I don't remember much, but I do know I *tried*, and when I did, somehow the way opened up. I can't just sit here any longer. I'd rather die."

Simon knew she meant it. As much as it hurt to know that she was willing to die trying without him, he also knew that Ren'dal's cruelty had affected her. He tried one more time: "Johnnie, please—"

"*No.*" Her face had no emotion left in it. "This place has cost me two children, and I'm not going to take it anymore without fighting back. And if you're the man and husband I think you are, you'll come with me. If they kill us, at least we'll die together, with neither of us left to mourn the other."

Simon agreed. He would come with her. But he wanted to have something of a plan, and what he left unsaid was that he hoped he could delay long enough that she would change her mind. "Look," he said, "I'll come with you, but we can't go with you in this kind of condition. You just had a baby three days ago, and you haven't eaten anything since then. Promise me this"—and now she looked up again and a glimmer of life came into her eyes—"promise me that you'll eat and get your strength back and that you'll give me at least a month. And I promise you that in a month's time, I'll figure out the best plan I can, and we'll make a run for it. Together."

Johnnie nodded in agreement.

Chapter 12

Johnnie and Simon Meet a Strange Woman

THE MONTH PASSED QUICKLY, AT LEAST FOR SIMON. Johnnie wouldn't change her mind, and there really wasn't much to figure out, because he had no way of knowing exactly what would happen if they ever even made it out beyond the immediate grounds of Ren'dal's quarters. Outside the grounds that surrounded the house was a stone wall that not only was guarded but had no obvious point of entry or exit. The only way in and out of Ren'dal's palace was through the main doors, as far as Simon knew. But he had promised Johnnie, and he at least thought he knew how to get to the main doors late at night. He knew that probably there were other doorways and no doubt private passageways in Ren'dal's palace, like the ones he and Johnnie were pushed through when they first entered Ventradees, but neither he nor Johnnie had ever used them since their arrival, so there was no point in hoping to find an unknown exit during an escape that was already poorly planned.

When he knew he could delay no longer, one night, as they went to bed, Simon whispered, "Tonight's the night. Take whatever you can carry that we'll need, but nothing more than what you can put in a small bag."

They lay in silence, waiting for hours until the rest of the palace retired to their quarters, and in the middle of the night, Simon nudged Johnnie. He whispered, "Do you still want to do this?"

"Yes," came the whispered reply, and the two of them quietly slipped out of bed and left the room. They had no lights, but there was a bright moon outside, and what few windows there were in Ren'dal's mansion allowed enough light for them to make their way out. From their room, they went through a short hallway to the back of the kitchen. They crossed the kitchen, which had coals still glowing in the fireplace, toward a small dining area that also adjoined an even larger banquet hall. Simon kept Johnnie just in front of him and guided her with one hand on her elbow and the other in the small of her back. The plan was for them to go through the small dining area, cross the larger banquet room into the massive foyer, and then tiptoe from there to the front doors, being careful to move quietly along the walls and not in the middle of any area. Simon knew that next to the front doors was a guard station, and behind it was a smaller door that led outside. Their first hurdle would be to get past the guard stationed there.

As they moved along a wall of the smaller dining area, Simon made sure Johnnie stayed close to the draperies that hung against the wall. But just before they were to cross the threshold of that room, he saw movement in a corner next to the banquet hall entrance. Suddenly there was a rapid movement from behind one of the curtains, and he felt a stinging blow at the base of his neck.

The blow was hard and heavy, and Simon was stunned as if hit by an electric shock. He was dazed but sensed some rapid movement next to him, followed by a stifled scream from Johnnie. Then a scuffle, followed by the sound of heavy footsteps along with what must have been Johnnie struggling and banging against the floor. Moments later, Simon, who had for a few seconds been close to blacking out, heard a door shut somewhere behind him. Once again he heard a stifled voice. Regaining his feet, though still woozy, he made his way back toward the kitchen area, this time with less caution.

He felt his way along the back wall of the kitchen and was certain now, as his mind continued to clear, that he had heard a door shut. There was just enough light from a small window high up on the kitchen wall that he could make his way without stumbling. He felt a door. He didn't recall ever seeing a door there, but there it was. A wooden door, and he could now feel the metal handle of it at waist level. He pulled, and the door opened. But in front of him, there was nothing but pitch blackness.

Simon turned and, using his memory of the kitchen's layout, walked to a cabinet where the cooks kept something like matches. These "firesticks," as the cooks called them, were crude compared to the ones back home. They were bigger, about three inches long, and made of bulkier wood, and they flared up by contact with fire, not by striking and friction. He grabbed several and hurried over to the fireplace.

He stuck one of these matches into a live coal, and it burst into flames. He went back to the door, opened it, and held out his old-fashioned match like a small torch. It was a good thing he hadn't tried to follow immediately because what was before him was a long, steep flight of stairs heading down.

Simon took a deep breath, steadied his still wobbly legs, and started down the stairs. He went as far as he could while the match still burned and then lit another one by touching it to the first one just before it went out. He was still in a long narrow stairwell, but now he could see a landing just below him. When he reached the landing, he found that it was only a turn in the stairwell and that the stairs continued downward but now to his left. There must have been forty steps in the first stretch before the landing and at least that many all the way down the next flight. His firestick was nearly out by the time he reached the bottom. He lit another and looked down a long corridor. He could hear footsteps echoing and muffled voices ahead, this time a woman's—it sounded like Johnnie—and a man's, though it was odd and hoarse.

"Johnnie!" Simon yelled. He heard what might have been Johnnie answering, but the shout back was quickly stopped. He ran down that corridor as far as he could until the flaming stick was barely flickering. He felt like he was getting closer, and though he didn't want to run out of matches, he had to see what he was chasing. He touched another match to the hot end of the one he held, and the corridor lit up again.

At the edge of the light's range, he could see movement. He ran toward it and continued as far as he dared in the darkness before lighting another match, but now the sounds were gone. He waited, holding his firestick above his head until—there! Just a short distance in front of him, no more than fifty feet, he could see Johnnie sitting on the floor of the long corridor and a large hulking figure standing over her.

"Johnnie!" he yelled.

"Simon!" she yelled back.

Then in a deep, reedy voice that sounded like air forced from a constricted throat, Simon heard, "Go *back*, you fool!"

But the chase was still on. Just before the match went out, Simon saw the hulking figure grab Johnnie by her shoulders and force her along. Simon quickly lit another firestick, but it slowed him down while the character in front of him obviously knew where he was going and needed no light.

Then just as he thought he was drawing closer, judging from the sounds, the noise from their footsteps seemed to change. Simon pulled another match, lit it, and saw another long corridor open up, this time back to the right. He made his way into it, and though he could hardly see anything in front of him, he noticed an immediate change in his surroundings. He was still in an enclosed area, but it looked more like an underground tunnel, with the walls glistening and what sounded like water ahead. Sure enough, as the corridor descended, water, maybe six inches deep, sloshed around his feet. He tried to lift his feet higher as he moved, but within a few steps, he made a splash high enough to douse his match.

But Simon had seen enough to know that it was quite a distance before the tunnel would turn, so he plunged ahead. He tried to stay in range of the sounds, but he didn't seem to be making up any ground. The creature in front of him was evidently strong enough to carry Johnnie and still move at least as fast as Simon.

Simon's legs were heavy, and his lungs were tearing at him. His head and neck throbbed. He paused.

Then he felt a strong draft of air. It wasn't cold, but since he was drenched in sweat and water, it felt cool. He struggled onward, and a few paces away, there was enough light to see movement ahead. The hulk was dragging Johnnie through an opening next to a huge rock. They were outside now and—no!—the thing was trying to close the rock back on him. The opening was nearly gone!

Simon staggered ahead, reached the rock while there was hardly room for him to squeeze through, and managed, turning sideways, to push himself through just as the creature inched the rock forward some more into the opening. He fell to the ground and looked up to see the creature he had been chasing. There, facing him—with Johnnie lying on the ground on the other side of the massive man—stood *Snardolf.*

Simon pulled himself to his feet and rushed the huge man in a low shoulder tackle, hitting him right at his waist. Snardolf grabbed Simon just below the shoulders with two hands and started pulling him away, as if trying to delicately pull away a cat that had latched onto his trousers, claws and all. Johnnie jumped up and rushed in to fight as well, but Snardolf held her off with one hand and gave Simon a hard blow on the back of his neck with the other. He went down once again, nearly faint.

"Simon—" Johnnie yelled, but her words were muffled as Snardolf clamped his hand around her mouth.

"Come on," he rasped. "We've got to leave him. The *woman* waits!"

Snardolf began to drag Johnnie away, but she kicked and bit his hand with a ferocity that surprised even him. He let her go, but this time his voice changed. "*Please!*" he said. "No more yelling. We can't let any guards find us."

That reference to guards caught Johnnie's attention. She looked around and saw that they were outside the city walls but obviously still close enough to alert Ren'dal's guards.

"Then I'm *sure* not going to leave him here," she answered in a loud whisper. "If Ren'dal or his men find him, they'll kill him."

Snardolf growled. But then he approached Simon, who was still lying on the ground, dazed from the attack. He grabbed Simon by the shirt and tossed him over his shoulder.

Johnnie wasn't sure what Snardolf intended, but she knew she probably shouldn't fight him, so she did her best to help balance Simon.

The unlikely threesome moved farther away from the city walls, across a small creek, and into some woods.

Simon's head throbbed, but it was clear enough for him to be aware of what was happening. He made no effort to get down though, since he couldn't have walked anyway. After what seemed like several minutes, Snardolf stopped. He lowered Simon onto his feet and did so with surprising gentleness. Johnnie supported Simon, putting his arm around her shoulder.

Suddenly there was a rustling movement and the sounds of hastily spoken words in an area of the woods just in front of them. They heard what sounded like wings beating the air and then saw a large dark object shoot almost straight up and disappear into the sky. Snardolf slowly led them farther in that direction, and they came to a small clearing.

The moon lit the area, and on the far side of the clearing was a woman draped with a large shawl covering her upper body and a scarf over her head so that only her face could be seen. Snardolf pushed Simon and Johnnie toward her. She lifted her head and looked for several seconds, first at Johnnie and then at Simon.

"Welcome," she said. "I was expecting only *her*." The woman looked at Snardolf, who shrugged. "Well," she continued, almost with a cheery tone in her voice, "we'll just have to carry on, even with this little surprise."

"Who are you?" asked Johnnie.

"Oh, my dear, I'm very sorry, but I can't say. I know it's rude not to introduce yourself, but really, it's not important. But I *am* a friend."

Simon, who was now gathering his wits, rubbed the back of his head and asked slowly, "A friend?" He pointed at Snardolf. "What about *him*?"

The woman, with a smile and a nod, said, "Oh, he's a friend too."

"The guy who lashed me? The guy who slugged me in the head twice tonight?"

"I'm sorry, my dear, but you must let that go," she said. "He had no better choice."

Simon grimaced. "Pretty hard to let it go when my head's still throbbing." And he moved his hand from his head to his side. "And when I still have the scars from—"

"There's no time for that," the woman interrupted. "As I said, he didn't have any other options. Now, we must be quick."

"I agree," said Johnnie. "Where to from here? Let's get going."

The woman paused. "Going?"

"Yes," Johnnie responded. "Where are you taking us?" She looked from the woman to Snardolf.

"I'm afraid, my dear, that you're not going to like my answer."

"What do you mean?" asked Johnnie.

"Well, you'll need to go back."

"Go back?" Simon yelled.

"We *can't* go back," said Johnnie.

"I'm sorry, my dear, but you *must* go back. If you attempt to leave now, nothing good will come of it."

"Unless we escape!" she said.

"But that will never happen."

"I did it once before. I can do it—"

"Yes, you did escape once before, but, I must tell you, you had a fair amount of help then. This time, you will be caught."

Johnnie was stunned. The woman looked at Simon and continued, "And your husband, *when* you are caught, will be severely treated. I think you know what I mean."

"So why are we here?" demanded Johnnie.

"First of all," the woman began, "I'm here to *stop* you. Snardolf sent us word weeks ago that you and your husband were planning an escape. We had to stop you."

"It's a funny way to stop us," said Simon sarcastically. "Beat me over the head and drag us out to God-knows-where just so you can tell us to go back?"

"I understand your frustration."

"Our *frustration*?" Simon shot back.

"Stop. I said I understand, and I do. But let me finish," she said with a bit of a smile that quickly morphed into a look of sternness. "I said my first reason was to stop you, but once we knew you were coming, we knew we'd have to talk to Johnnie."

"Talk to *me*?" asked Johnnie.

"Yes, as long as you and Simon were in Ventradees, we had no need to communicate with you until the right time. But now you've forced our hand. We have to tell you some things."

"Like what?" asked Simon.

"Well," the woman began, "I hope you'll understand if I tell you only what you need to know for now." She paused and looked at them. Neither of them nodded.

"For now, you must go back and act like none of this happened. Ren'dal may be cruel, but we don't think he will kill you."

"*That's* comforting," Simon snorted.

"He *needs* you."

"Needs us for another baby?" Simon almost laughed.

"Yes, and you must—"

"So he can kill it, too? Well, we won't do it!"

"I understand your bitterness, young man." She looked at him, and he held her gaze with an anger that refused to blink.

Johnnie shuffled her feet and lifted her head somewhat, inclining it more toward the woman.

The woman sighed. "I suppose I must tell you more than you're ready to know, though I do wish you'd trust me." Then she said in a voice that chided Simon, "You'll have to agree that Snardolf and I are the first ones here who have given you any indication that we're on your side. Perhaps Katris . . . but . . ." She shook her head. "Here's what I'll tell you. But understand. After this, I will tell you no more. Once I have finished what little I will say, you will accept my words and act accordingly, or I'll have to leave you on your own."

Johnnie took a step back and let out a long breath. "Okay," she said, "we'll listen." And she looked at Simon, her eyes telling him to be quiet.

"Chimera, lord of Nefas, has given his son Ren'dal a task. He is to raise up a *male* who is born of parents from both sides, from Ventradees and from across the Pillars." Johnnie narrowed her eyes, as if puzzled, and started to speak slowly.

"From *both* . . . But I'm not from Ven—"

"I know what you're thinking," said the woman, quickly interrupting her, "but it's complicated. You're not, but you are." She and Johnnie looked at each other.

Simon's eyes got larger before he squeezed his eyebrows together, looking at the woman and Johnnie, as if they shared a secret. But before he could ask anything, the woman continued.

"Ren'dal has tried to fulfill his mandate from Chimera by resorting to all kinds of evil foolishness. On one occasion—perhaps you heard of it—he acquired, because of human greed, the right to children from across the Pillars, thinking that once they matured and had children, their children would be both from the *other* side and, since they belonged to him by a contract he made with their parents, also from *here*, from Ventradees. In theory he was right, but it didn't work. For many reasons." The woman's eyes bore into Johnnie's.

Johnnie nodded and seemed to understand. But Simon shook his head as if confused and pressed the point.

"So why doesn't he just get a man or woman from the other side—he captured us—to come here and have a child with one of his people here in Ventradees?"

The woman's eyes widened in amazement at the question. "In the first place, I hope you aren't suggesting that you'd be happy for someone *else* to be captured as long as *you* are free!"

Simon looked down.

"But in the second place, it wouldn't work. Those who come to Ventradees, with some unusual exceptions, only do so after they have first died on the other side. Then they descend through other parts of the Land of Gloaming—unless they alter their course—and eventually end up here. By the time they have become residents of Ventradees, they can no longer have children."

"But—" started Simon again.

"I don't have time to explain to you all the regions of this side and how their citizens live, if you can call it living. Again, unless a person's mind is changed, everyone eventually comes to Ventradees, the outskirts of the depths of Nefas, but the laws of entry, living, and dying—and having children—are different in each region of Gloaming."

"So *we*," said Simon, "are the only ones Ren'dal can use to—"

"I'm sorry to interrupt," the woman said, "but in this case it is necessary. Speculation is useless. Who knows what other strategies evil can devise to do its work, especially since it is not limited to the truth? But, yes, at least for now, you two are the only ones he can use. That, unfortunately, is the only answer I can give to your question. Chimera's hopes depend upon you both, because, as you now know from Katris, except for *you*"—she looked at Johnnie—"women in Ventradees do not have children. And, I might add," and now she looked at them both, "the men in Ventradees are equally powerless."

Simon shifted uneasily and glanced at Johnnie. He was, like Johnnie, beginning to see bits of the puzzle.

Johnnie hesitated at first, then spoke in a rush before the woman could stop her, "I know I said we'd listen, but I can't help asking. I think I see why he wants *both* of us, but *why me*? How did this fall on *me*?"

The old woman smiled faintly and sighed softly before speaking. "These are actually two different questions. The first one—'why me?'—no one can ever truly answer. But I think the answer to your second question should now be pretty obvious. You came to Ventradees in an unusual way, *not* by death. But, in addition to that, you also *escaped*, Johnnie. And even though you had some help," and here she paused and smiled softly, "you desperately *wanted* to escape, and you did. Your escape has for now helped Ren'dal, but the Ancient One was willing to take the risk. Your courage matters to our cause."

"How have I helped Ren'dal?"

"Well, you weren't lost from Ren'dal's sight for long. He has an informant on the other side who reported to him about a little girl who was found near Middleton. For reasons we need not discuss now, Ren'dal suspected that it was you, the child who escaped from Ventradees."

Simon looked at Johnnie. He knew some of this story, but it was so strange hearing it told now by another person.

"Ren'dal sent some of his men there, and they kept track of you all those years. You grew, which surprised them. Then you married; the real shock came when they learned you were pregnant. Thanks also, of course, to your loving husband." She winked at Simon.

But then she looked back at Johnnie, and the smile quickly vanished. "Ren'dal saw in your pregnancy the opportunity he has looked for. But he would have to get your baby. So, as you know, his trackers started watching you and Simon, following you everywhere you went, particularly during the last months of your pregnancy. They didn't get your son"—Johnnie and Simon looked at each other, wondering how much the old woman really knew—"but even though they failed to get him, they were told to bring you, Johnnie, on back.

"As for you, Simon, they were told that if you could be persuaded to come *voluntarily*, you should come as well. Of course, they desperately needed you as her husband and an adult man to come so you and Johnnie could have another son. But they needed your *agreement*; otherwise, they would have had no right to bring you to Ventradees."

Simon looked at Johnnie. "Those children that Ren'dal 'acquired' . . ." He held Johnnie's hand. "You're one of them, aren't you?"

Johnnie looked down.

"She is," said the woman softly. "And so she is of Ventradees. And by your own agreement, though the conditions differ, so are you. And now it's clear to Ren'dal that you can have children, even here."

"All the more reason for us to run," muttered Simon, but even as he said it, he could feel himself losing the will to run.

"No, I would advise against that, at least for now."

Johnnie and Simon looked at the woman, at each other, and even toward Snardolf, who no longer looked down but held their gaze as well.

"So what do we do now?" asked Johnnie.

"You must go back and go on with your lives in Ventradees."

"Until when?" asked Simon softly.

"And what if I become pregnant?" asked Johnnie. Her eyes narrowed.

"And what if we *refuse*?" said Simon.

"Well," the woman said, though she spoke slowly, "then I suppose the Ancient One, our great and wise ruler, will no doubt have another plan . . . *without* you."

"Another plan? But what is his plan *with us*?" asked Johnnie. "We know *Ren'dal's* plan."

"And who is this Ancient One, anyway?" asked Simon.

"My dears, those are good questions, but it would be hard to give a simple explanation of our ruler and his ways. And I must admit we really don't know all the details. I wish I could tell you for how long, but for now you've got to go back and buy time until the one comes who can start a rescue, a rescue of you and all those who are being held by Chimera."

"But who is that?" asked Simon.

"Someone who can start the final tremors that will honor the contract, summon the four rulers, build the bridge . . ." The old woman looked off somewhere beyond Simon and Johnnie. "And establish the way that will lead from this gloaming to the Atrium and then to freedom."

They were silent until Snardolf spoke. "Ma'am," he rasped, "it's getting late."

"Yes. It is. Well, my children, that is all I can say. The rest is up to you."

"But—" Simon started.

"No," said Johnnie suddenly. Her shoulders slumped, but her voice was strong.

"No? No *what*?" said Simon.

"No more questions," Johnnie said. She smiled faintly and nodded to the woman. "We must go back."

Simon fell silent. And as they turned to leave, Johnnie looked back and said, "But, ma'am, what if I have another girl? I couldn't bear it if—"

"Shhh," she said, putting her finger to her lips. "My dear, there is more to these things than you know. You must *trust* me. Go now."

———⊙———

Snardolf got them back to Ren'dal's castle just before sunup. He led them back through the same path they took to get there—through the underground tunnel, up the stairs, and past the kitchen. They slipped back into their bedroom unnoticed.

"Simon," Johnnie whispered as they settled into bed face to face, "I don't know how much that old woman knows, but she never mentioned . . ." Simon instantly knew she was talking about their son. "We must remember *never* to speak of . . . that . . . between ourselves again. If Snardolf and Katris knew of our plans to escape, then someone else may be watching and listening."

Simon squeezed her hands and nodded.

Chapter 13

Hamelin Starts School

HAMELIN DREADED HIS FIRST DAY OF ELEMENTARY school. He liked learning his letters and numbers, but he was the only five-year-old from the children's home, and he knew he would have no one to walk with him to class. The first thing he noticed when he got off the bus that day and started walking up the sidewalk toward the school was that all the other kids were accompanied by their mothers or fathers and some by both. Hamelin could feel their eyes as he walked along by himself. One boy pointed at him and said something to his dad, who just shook his head. He so desperately wanted a mother or father with him. Or Layla!

Hamelin walked into the schoolhouse and was overwhelmed with its size. There was a long hallway with gray lockers on each side, big doors, and already dozens of kids coming and going. He was told that the kindergarten classroom was near the main entrance, but he wasn't sure which of these many doors was the one. He just wanted to run away.

Then a sign on one of the doors looked familiar. He knew his teacher's name was Mrs. Blankenship. One of the older girls on the bus had written it down for him so he could recognize the letters. He pulled out the paper, and sure enough, it matched the name on the door—this was his class.

When he walked through the door, all the other children and their parents turned to look at him. He didn't know where to sit, but a middle-aged woman came up to him quickly and said in a friendly voice, "Hello, I'm Mrs. Blankenship. What's your name?"

"Hamelin."

"Ah, Hamelin Stoop! Your place is right over here."

She led Hamelin to his first desk and chair in public school. He sat down, placed his small box of school supplies on top of the desk, put his lunch box under his chair, and waited.

Before long the class started, the parents left, and Mrs. Blankenship took charge. And Hamelin didn't feel quite so alone anymore.

"Okay, children, I want each of you to stand up and say your name," Mrs. Blankenship said.

When it was his turn to say his name, he heard a boy snicker, but Mrs. Blankenship gave a sharp stare to where the laugh came from. It made Hamelin feel a little better.

Then came Beverly, Judy, Bill, Robert, and James. All in all, there were twenty-one children in the class: eleven girls and ten boys.

Hamelin's first day ended up being not too bad, mostly because he knew his ABCs and numbers better than most kids in class. And no one looked at him very much anymore, which was just fine with him.

Since he was the only one in the class from the children's home, he didn't know any of the other kids, who were mostly from the little town of Middleton, though a couple of the children said they lived on farms. Still, he noticed at lunch and recess that some of the other kids already knew each other. Those kids always stuck together.

But Mrs. Blankenship also made them play some games as a class, so before long, Hamelin got to know several of the boys and a few of the girls. They played tag, red rover, and drop the handkerchief. He had fun, especially since he'd never played with so many kids his age before. By the time the first day was over, he forgot how lonely he had felt that morning.

But then the parents returned to pick up their children. Hamelin silently walked past all the children with their mothers and fathers, boarded the bus, and rode it home.

Overall, the first day was okay. Mrs. Blankenship seemed nice, and he'd met a few of his classmates. He wished they had spent more time learning some words, because he really wanted to read. He loved it when Layla read to him, and he wanted to read for himself. He knew she would be proud of him when he could read a book to her.

And so Hamelin's school days began. They were all pretty much the same: get up in the morning, do his chores, have breakfast with the other children, and then take the bus to school. After several weeks, all the children knew one another, and he even had a few buddies he liked to play with, especially James and Billy. Though he saw them only at school, James and Billy were friendly and liked the same games as Hamelin, and he liked to hear them talk about their brothers and sisters.

Afternoons at the children's home were about the same as they'd always been. Being the youngest, Hamelin oftentimes was left to himself. The younger girls still wanted him to play school with them, but now that he was in school himself, he wasn't as interested. He learned how to play baseball and basketball from some of the older boys, and they usually let him play in their front-yard football games, as long as he wouldn't cry if he got hurt. But all the children had afternoon chores, the older ones particularly had homework to do, and before long it was time for supper, more homework or some reading, and then off to bed. The Stephensons wanted things quiet in the evenings.

As it turned out, Hamelin liked living upstairs after all; with all the other boys sleeping up there, he didn't have to go to bed as early. He had his own bed at the end of the room. It was his little corner, and he really liked it. Next to his bed was a small wooden apple crate that Mr. Moore had given him, and there he kept his few possessions: a beat-up baseball glove that one of the older boys had handed down to him, two *Superman* comic books from Bryan, a copy of *Robinson Crusoe* that Layla had given him, and a few toy soldiers he had gotten one Christmas. It wasn't a lot, but they were his.

Hamelin kept his clothes in another small box between his bed and the wall. He didn't have a dresser, but that was okay. He didn't have many clothes anyway. On a small bedside table, he kept his lunch box, his notebook, a tablet, a few pencils, and a small backpack that Mrs. Regehr had given him.

Hamelin's kindergarten year passed quickly, and soon he was in the first grade. His new teacher, Mrs. Adams, was a good teacher, but she wasn't as nice as Mrs. Blankenship.

He figured out how to succeed in Mrs. Adams's class: answer when called on but otherwise don't talk. He liked to read by himself anyway, so that kept him quiet enough for Mrs. Adams. Hamelin had some of the same friends from kindergarten, but about half the class was new, so he made a few other friends.

But he still missed Bryan and Layla. He always felt particularly lonely when the parents of the other children would pick them up from school or when he heard his classmates talk about the things they had done the past summer or during holidays.

One afternoon at the end of his first-grade year, with just a few days left in school, Hamelin was walking down the sidewalk that led from the schoolhouse to the buses. He could see the buses lined up and children boarding them. He would, as usual, be getting on the second bus.

Just then he saw in front of him a curly-haired brunette, about Layla's height, walking toward him.

"Hey," she said, "I've just finished my semester finals at college. I came to pick you up!"

The afternoon sun was behind her, and Hamelin squinted at the young woman walking toward him. He wasn't exactly sure about the voice, and because of the sunlight, he couldn't make her out clearly.

"Did you have a good day at school?" she asked.

Layla? She put out her arms and began jogging in his direction. Hamelin had started his first step toward her when he realized she was looking just beyond him, over his left shoulder. She ran right past him to a little brown-haired girl in a pretty green spring dress several steps behind him. He turned and saw the young woman scoop up the little girl and give her a big hug.

It wasn't Layla.

Hamelin looked around and saw parents and a few big sisters and brothers picking up the other kids. He hurried on, head down, to the line of buses. He got in the second bus and sat in the back alone. He thought about Layla the whole way home. His chest hurt and his eyes stung.

———

Hamelin would celebrate his seventh birthday that summer. No one really knew exactly when his birthday was, but they always celebrated it on July 10, the day Mrs. Frendle had found him. When the day came around, she made him a birthday cake and, as always, retold the story of how she found him: "Why, I can remember it just like it was yesterday! There I was up early in the mornin', fixin' to drop another biscuit into the grease, and I heard this caterwaulin' outside. Well, I tell you, I knew that the milkman . . ." and on she went.

After recounting the whole story again, she smiled at Hamelin and concluded with, "And that's how you came here . . . my stoop baby! And look at you now—seven years old!"

Hamelin's cheeks flushed as some of the girls said, "Aw," and some of the other children cheered and patted him on the back—and he was sure that most of the boys were happy the story was over and they could finally get some cake.

Some of the kids gave him presents, which would usually be hand-me-down clothes or things they had outgrown or didn't have any use for anymore. That's the way most of the kids did it at someone else's birthday, but no one minded.

But one gift especially was the highlight of the day: Layla sent him a birthday card.

The card read,

```
Hamelin,

Happy Birthday! I wish we could be there to
celebrate with you. Once we get a car, we can
visit, but we can't afford one yet.
    We are both working, sharing an apartment,
and going to college part-time. I wish I
could show you some of my literature books
and tell you the great stories I'm reading.
    Keep reading. One day something special
will happen to you, just like in all the
stories with happy endings. Keep hoping.

Love,
Layla
```

One afternoon in the middle of August, Hamelin entered the house, hot and sweaty from playing baseball. Mrs. Regehr was waiting for him near the door.

"Hamelin, would you visit with me for a few minutes?" she asked.

"Okay," he said.

He wondered if he'd done anything to get himself in trouble. She walked into the sitting room near the front of the house, where usually only adults went. She sat down in an upholstered chair and patted the footstool in front of her.

Hamelin shrugged and sat on the soft stool. He looked around at the walls and lamps. Funny, he couldn't remember ever being in the room before.

Mrs. Regehr was still, with her hands folded in her lap. She smiled, leaned forward a little, and said, "Hamelin."

He looked in her eyes and remembered that she had such a quiet face, with smiles and not a lot of words.

"You know," she continued, "I have a daughter who lives in Canada." Hamelin had seen Canada on a map before. It was a big place, far north. "Well, my daughter—that is—I'm going to go there." She reached out both hands and touched his knees. "I'm going to *move* there—to stay."

Hamelin didn't know what to say. For a second, he had a strange memory. He was lying on his back. It was really warm—he was outside in the sun, and he was looking up into the sky, but instead of seeing the sky, he saw Mrs. Regehr's face. Then the memory went away.

"I'm sorry," she said. Hamelin could see that her eyes were starting to shine, but he couldn't see any tears. She stood, rubbed his head, and walked away.

He sat there for a little longer. He thought maybe he should feel something, but he didn't. So he went back outside and walked to the pond.

About a week later, on her last day, Hamelin was quiet while everything happened around him. He had watched her that morning at breakfast and saw that she seemed to glance at him every now and then, but she would look away if he looked at her. That afternoon he and a few of the other boys carried her things downstairs. Mrs. Regehr didn't have much, so it only took a couple of trips with two suitcases and one small case. It all happened so quickly. Otherwise, it seemed like an ordinary day. But then, there was Mrs. Regehr, coming into the foyer. She walked out the front door and headed toward Mr. Moore's truck. He was going to drive her into town to the bus station. Several of the kids had hugged her and were saying their good-byes.

She paused at the door of the truck, turned around, and looked at Hamelin. He looked up again at her and thought about walking over, but suddenly she walked quickly to him. She bent down and hugged him with both arms and began to cry. Hamelin felt a little embarrassed, because she kept her head right next to his and whispered to him, "Hamelin, I love you. I'll miss you, and I'll always remember you." And then she got into the truck, and Mr. Moore started it up and slowly began to pull out of the driveway.

And then it hit Hamelin. She was leaving. He wanted to shout—and inside his head he did—*You can't leave!* But the words didn't come out of his mouth. He just stood there. He noticed that several other kids were still there waving at her and that they would wave at Mrs. Regehr and then look back, and then some of them were looking at him. He was waving too, but he wanted to cry. He didn't want any of the older boys to make fun of him, so he didn't. But he did feel that big turning and swirling in his stomach and chest. Hamelin just stood there waving as Mrs. Regehr rode off in the truck with Mr. Moore.

He stood there for a long time after the truck was out of sight. Finally, all he could see was the dust stirred up by the wheels of the truck. August was always dry. He stared at the dust. Maybe if he just stood there and stared long enough, it would stay there, hanging in the air. But finally the dust settled, and the noise from the truck was gone, and there was nothing left to see but an empty road going south, disappearing over a little rise in the pavement. For a while longer, Hamelin just stood there alone, and then he noticed that he was the only one still there.

He turned to walk back into the house, and standing in the doorframe, looking at him, was Mrs. Frendle. When Hamelin glanced up and saw her, she quickly turned and walked away.

Chapter 14

A Really Bad Year

THE FIGHT DIDN'T LAST LONG, BUT IT DIDN'T STOP UNTIL Mrs. Frendle pulled Marceya Makowski off of Joey Cox. It didn't take Mr. Stephenson long to come running down the steps toward all the commotion and ask his usual, "What's going on here?"

A dozen kids had surrounded the two as they fought, including Hamelin. David Rivers, an older boy, said, "Joey started it. I think he called Marcie a cow or something."

"Did *not*," whined Joey, who was struggling to get to his feet, rubbing a big bruise on his cheek. "She slugged me for *nothing!*"

Mrs. Frendle held Marceya, but the nine-year-old girl, who was tall for her age and would soon start the fourth grade, said nothing. Marceya was a quiet, skinny girl with straight, stringy brown hair that came down to just above her shoulders. Her eyes, now squinting, glared at Joey through her bangs.

"Well, Marcie?" said Mr. Stephenson. "Is that true? Did you hit Joey?"

The answer to that question was getting more and more obvious as Joey's right eye started to close from the bottom. Marceya looked at Mr. Stephenson and then slowly surveyed the rest of the kids. She stuck out her chin and said, "Yes."

"Well, then . . . uh . . . you're going to have to—" Obviously Mr. Stephenson was having a hard time figuring out what to do with a fourth-grade girl who had just roughed up a fifth-grade boy when a voice emerged from the group.

"He made fun of her name," said the voice.

"What?" asked Mr. Stephenson as he turned and looked toward Hamelin. Hamelin repeated himself, "He made fun of her name."

"What do you *mean*?" asked Mr. Stephenson.

"Well, he came through the room here where some of us were just sitting around, and he said real loud, 'Hey, one day I'm going to be a rancher and I'm going to have plenty of cattle and then I'll have My-*kow*-skees.' And that's when Marceya hit him."

"Oh," began Mr. Stephenson, who now looked even more uncertain.

At that point, Mrs. Frendle stepped in and said, "I think I'll just take care of you, Miss Marceya Makowski. I'm sure Mr. Stephenson can take care of Joey." Mr. Stephenson looked at Mrs. Frendle and seemed to agree.

So the whole thing was over as fast as it started. Joey slinked away, and Mrs. Frendle marched Marceya into the kitchen.

Hamelin didn't think it was fair that Marceya was apparently being punished but Mr. Stephenson didn't do anything to Joey, who had started the whole thing. Wanting to defend Marceya, he walked quietly over toward the kitchen and stuck his head in.

Mrs. Frendle, who stood next to Marceya, noticed him. "Now just you get yourself out of here, Mr. Hamelin Stoop!"

Hamelin knew not to fool with Mrs. Frendle when she had that tone of voice, so he backed out quickly. But he did get a quick glimpse, and he was pretty sure he had seen Marcie with a cookie in her hand and maybe even a milk moustache.

At dinnertime that night, Marcie sat where she usually sat, in the area where the girls ate their dinner, but she was more toward the end of one of the tables—with the girls but by herself at the same time. Hamelin walked by with his plate, not sure where to sit. Marcie caught his attention, and when he approached her, she said, "Thanks."

Hamelin paused. He didn't know what to say, so he just sat next to her. He started feeling odd sitting there when Marcie looked at him, a scowl on her face, and said, "You've got a pretty funny name yourself, Hamelin *Stoop*." Then she smiled, just slightly, and that's how their friendship started.

Hamelin learned that Marcie used to live in East Texas. She'd been at the home for only about a month by the time of the fight with Joey Cox, and not many people had really gotten to know her.

"I won't be here long," she insisted. "My parents went to California, and as soon as my dad finds work there, they're coming back to get me." She was two grades ahead of Hamelin and really almost three years older, since her birthday was in October, but still she didn't seem to mind talking to him, and Hamelin was glad to have somebody else to talk to.

But except for his new friendship with Marcie, the school year couldn't have started out worse. There were two second-grade teachers: Mr. Burleson, a nice, middle-aged man whose smile never seemed to leave his face, and Mrs. Kelliman, whom every second grader dreaded getting. Mrs. Kelliman was a graying, middle-aged woman of a rather slight frame, a sharp nose, and glaring eyes, which matched especially well her somewhat pursed lips. She was referred to by the children as Mrs. "Killerman" or "Killer" for short. Mrs. Kelliman was worse than strict: she was mean and uncaring. She piled on needless assignments, her grading was unfair, and the students were a bother to her, unless their parents had money. All the first graders dreaded the thought of having her as a teacher.

For his second-grade teacher, Hamelin got Killer.

After the first day of school, he plopped down in the dining hall at the children's home. A few minutes later, Marcie sat down next to him.

"I heard who you got. Too bad, Hamelin. She's the worst," she said.

"Yeah," said Hamelin. "I don't think she likes me. Already."

"Probably not," said Marcie. "From what I hear, she knows how to be nice to the children of the rich parents. I think that's how she saved her job. They were going to can her years ago, but she started ooing and gooing around the people with money in town. So we're stuck with her."

"Yeah," said Hamelin. "She knew my name, but I could tell she didn't care about me."

"My advice to you is to lay low. Just be quiet any time Killer is around."

"She already told me twice today to sit up straight. I don't think it's going to be a very good year."

"Yeah. Better get used to it," Marcie said.

To make matters worse, Hamelin began to encounter, for the first time in his life, a bully. His name was Patton McBoggerson. Patton was a pretty odd first name, but the rumor was that his father admired a war hero by the name of General George Patton and decided to name his son after him. Hamelin sometimes wondered if Patton was mean because he didn't like his name or because he was so overweight. Whatever the reason, Patton, who was in the fifth grade, especially liked bullying the younger children. He had buzz-cut brownish-blond hair, a loud voice, and a big body that seemed to be everywhere.

Hamelin did his best, whether at lunch or on the playground before or after school, to avoid Patton. But the bully knew how to find him regularly. There was always just a little too much time after the bus dropped them off in the morning or before the bus arrived to pick them up in the afternoon. It was really hard to avoid Patton.

The bullying started early in the school year and got to be a frequent thing. The older boys from the children's home would have helped Hamelin out had they noticed, but since they were always busy with their after-school activities, they hadn't seen the bullying. And Hamelin didn't want to look like a crybaby or a tattletale.

Mrs. Kelliman was supposed to make sure that all the children got picked up safely after her class. But she never paid any attention to Hamelin. She was usually too busy talking to the mothers with expensive cars. One time, when Patton was pushing him around, Hamelin thought for sure Mrs. Kelliman saw it, but if she did, she ignored it, since she did nothing to stop it.

The last day before the Thanksgiving holiday was particularly bad. School was let out a little early that day for everyone, and Hamelin was on his way out of the building when he got shoved hard from behind.

"Oh, excuse me, did I bump you? Hahaha!"

Hamelin turned around—it was Patton. He turned to walk away, his books under his arm.

"Hey, Hambone, where you goin'? Don't you want to stick around and talk? What do ya say, Mr. Stoopid?"

Hamelin just kept walking.

"Hey, aren't you paying attention to me? I'm *talking* to you."

Hamelin kept walking. Patton hurried up behind him and knocked his books out of his arm.

"Whoops, looks like you dropped something."

Hamelin looked at Patton and sighed, knowing that it usually didn't do any good to say anything. He just bent down to pick up his books, and when he did so, Patton pushed him with his foot. Hamelin toppled forward. Patton then kicked a few of his books.

"Oops. Did I accidentally step on your books?"

By this time, a couple of Patton's friends, followers who laughed at everything he did but were really also afraid of him, gathered around.

"Gosh, Hammy, you sure seem clumsy. I hope you didn't tear your nice jeans. 'Cause then Mommy—I mean, your *house* mommy—might have to buy you some new ones!"

That was all Hamelin could take. Even though he was several inches shorter and forty pounds lighter—not to mention about three years younger—he got up and threw himself at Patton. He head-butted Patton's chest, knocking him back a couple of steps, but the bully really wasn't fazed.

"So the little Hambone has a little fight in him after all!" Patton rushed back at Hamelin and gave him a stiff punch to the chest. Hamelin flew back.

He picked himself up—he wasn't going to quit.

"Hey," one of Patton's buddies said, "I think we'd better get out of here."

David Rivers, who was older than all of them, was approaching. Patton and his gang took off. David came up to Hamelin and helped him pick up his books.

"Everything okay here, Hamelin?" he asked.

"Yeah. It's fine."

"Anybody bothering you?" asked David.

"Nope," said Hamelin. "I'm fine."

David walked with him to the bus. "Okay, Hamelin, see you back at the house."

"Yeah, thanks," said Hamelin, and he gave David a quick look.

"Sure," came the answer.

The Thanksgiving meal was especially good that year. Mrs. Frendle and the staff just kept bringing out more and more food. Even the Stephensons were surprised, though Mr. Stephenson at times didn't look all that happy about it. The meal was the best Hamelin or any of the other kids could remember: turkey and dressing, green beans, squash, corn, and cranberry sauce, plus the best desserts ever— pecan pie, cherry pie, and a big carrot cake. Mrs. Frendle and the staff had really outdone themselves.

At the end of the meal, everyone was talking and laughing and ready for an afternoon game of football—a holiday tradition. But then Mrs. Frendle stood and banged her fork against the side of a glass, gathering everyone's attention.

When the room grew silent, one of the boys yelled, "Hey, great meal, Mrs. Frendle!" and all the kids cheered. She smiled, and when the applause stopped, she dropped her head and wiped her eye with a napkin—was Mrs. Frendle crying?

"Children," she said, "I'm not much at speeches, and this is going to be pretty hard to say, so I'll just say it: I'm leaving."

"What?" one of the girls said out loud. And then everyone was silent again. They all looked at the Stephensons, who were looking at each other.

"I haven't told anybody, but I'm just getting too old for this. I love you all, and I'll miss you, but it's time for me to retire. Some of my children need me to help them with their families, and at my age, you just can't go on forever."

Hamelin heard one of the girls sob a little bit and someone else say softly, "No," but everyone else was quiet.

"Please just let me do this and don't make it too hard for me. I'll be here until the end of the year. We'll all enjoy one more Christmas together, and then I really do need to leave. Well, that's about it."

Some of the kids went up to her and hugged her while others stayed in their seats, unsure what to do. Finally, the kids filed out, some to the kitchen to help clean the dishes and others outside to go about their day. The boys went ahead with their football game, but everyone was pretty low key.

Hamelin didn't go with the boys to play football. He waited for the dishes to be done and for Mrs. Frendle to come out of the kitchen that evening. Finally, she did. He was sitting there in the dining hall when she walked out. Their eyes met, and she said, "Hamelin, I . . . I just have to do this."

He ran to her and hugged her, and she hugged him back. But he really didn't know what to say, and Mrs. Frendle didn't either.

Between Thanksgiving and Christmas, Patton's bullying stopped, though he still glared at Hamelin, as if to let him know that he hadn't forgotten him. Hamelin wondered if Patton was just trying to be good before Christmas or maybe didn't want David Rivers to notice.

But even without the bullying, Hamelin felt a pain in his stomach and chest whenever he remembered that Mrs. Frendle was leaving.

Christmas came, and, as always, the children at the home had a big meal together. They read the Christmas story from the Bible, opened presents, and, as they typically did, passed around their favorite used possessions as gifts. But things didn't sound quite as loud and joyful as Hamelin remembered from past years. Then, when December 31 came, it was obvious Mrs. Frendle was packed up and ready to leave, and the home was very quiet.

Again, the boys carried Mrs. Frendle's things to the truck so Mr. Moore could drive her to the bus station. Mrs. Frendle hugged and said good-bye to everyone. When she came to Hamelin, she hugged him especially long, and when he looked up, he noticed the tears in her eyes.

"You'll always be special to me," she whispered. "I'll never forget the morning I found you."

Hamelin's chest felt full and his face was burning, and inside he wanted to explode. *How can she leave?* he thought. *Why does everyone leave?* But he realized that whether staff or children, eventually everybody left—except him.

Unlike when Mrs. Regehr left, Hamelin didn't walk outside to see the truck drive off. He stood just inside the front door listening. He heard the last few good-byes shouted from the children. He heard the two truck doors slam. He heard the truck start and the sound of the motor as it drove off, out of the dirt driveway, onto the paved road. He listened until the sound was gone.

Chapter 15

The Forgotten Birthday

MR. STEPHENSON HAD TO HIRE TWO NEW PEOPLE TO take care of all the work that Mrs. Frendle had done. He brought on Mrs. Daly, a local woman from Middleton, who didn't live at the children's home but was there between eight o'clock and four o'clock every day to order supplies and supervise the kitchen. The other person he hired was Mrs. Carroll, who was from Rankin, a small town about eighteen miles east of Middleton. Mrs. Carroll didn't live at the children's home either, and she didn't talk about her home life, so no one knew much about her or her family, but she worked hard and was a decent cook—though not as good as Mrs. Frendle. And even though she was younger than Mrs. Frendle, she didn't have the same attraction to the children that Mrs. Frendle had. Still, she cooked the meals, and life at the children's home moved on.

The second half of Hamelin's second-grade year picked up almost where it had left off before Thanksgiving, with Patton back to his bullying. Hamelin found a few other ways to avoid him. He stayed in the classroom as long as he could after school, reading or working on his assignments, until Mrs. Kelliman pushed him out the door. He also learned to look for other kids to walk with and did his best not to leave the front door of the building until the bus arrived. Still, he couldn't avoid Patton all the time, so more than once, he found himself being bullied.

The school year finally came to an end, and Hamelin was glad to get some relief from Mrs. Kelliman and Patton. However, when July 10 arrived, something happened that he never expected: everyone forgot his eighth birthday.

Mrs. Frendle had never forgotten, because she loved to talk about how she had found him. But many of the staff were new, and Mrs. Frendle wasn't there to remind everyone. Usually they would celebrate summer birthdays at lunchtime, but when lunch was over and no one yet had even wished him a happy birthday, he was almost certain it had been forgotten. Hamelin quietly got up from the table and walked out.

Marcie saw him leave and followed him. "Hey, Hamelin, what's going on?"

"Nothing."

They walked outside and sat under the shade of one of the big trees in the front yard.

After Hamelin said nothing for a while, Marcie said, "Well, anything happening?"

"Nope."

"Come on, Hamelin. You seem kind of sad. What's going on?"

"I told you—*nothing*," he said sharply.

"Okay," said Marcie. But she didn't leave. She just sat there with him for a while. The afternoon sun was starting to get pretty hot, and the shade they had started out under had moved.

"Hey, let's go over by the old shed and see if we can find better shade there."

There was a little bit of shade on the east side of the shed, so they just sat there in silence, looking up at the clouds. After a short time, they both spotted a black dot high in the sky. They watched as it grew closer.

"What's that?" asked Marcie. "Pretty big bird, it looks like."

"Yeah," said Hamelin. "Could be a vulture, I guess, but it doesn't really have wings like a vulture."

"Yeah, looks like an eagle," she said, "but bigger than any eagle I've ever seen." It was not unusual to see eagles in that part of Texas, but even though the ones around there could be big, this bird seemed unusually large.

"Well," said Hamelin, "it could be an eagle. I've heard the kids who live on ranches say that some eagles are so big, they can lift small sheep."

"Really?" she asked.

"That's what they say." The two of them kept looking at the bird as it soared, climbing above the clouds, dipping shortly, and then going back up. It circled around and then glided down closer until it was just above them, no more than twenty yards overhead. They both stared, holding their breath, until Marcie spoke almost in a whisper.

"Wow," she said. "He's *big*."

And then the huge bird, with a few powerful strokes, took off toward the north and climbed again into the clouds. The two children kept watching it until it was once more only a speck in the sky.

"It must be great to be able to fly," said Hamelin. "You could just go wherever you wanted."

"Yeah," said Marcie. "Whenever you wanted. To fly like that would make you feel really free."

They sat in silence again. After a long stretch, Marcie finally said, "Well, hey, it's getting too hot for me. I'm going in."

"Okay," said Hamelin.

"See ya," she said.

By the end of the afternoon, Hamelin knew for sure that no one was going to remember his birthday. For a while he imagined—or hoped—that everybody was just teasing him and that there would be a big surprise party later that evening. But those hopes faded when supper came and went and there was no cake, no presents, and not even a single person who wished him a happy birthday—not even Marcie. Of course, Marcie was new to the children's home and didn't know Hamelin's birthday. But the others just forgot. The Stephensons. The other children. They all forgot.

After supper, Hamelin sat on the front porch. By about seven forty-five, the sun was down and darkness was taking over. He thought about Mrs. Regehr, Mrs. Frendle, Bryan, and Layla. He thought about the eagle he and Marcie had seen. Then a car drove by, its headlights cutting through the dark and its tires making a rhythmic sound as it headed north on the paved road. He could hear people laughing in the car as it passed. He watched the taillights until they were only red dots in the distance and wished he were going wherever they were going.

That's when he decided to run away. *Nobody cares. And nobody would even miss me if I was gone*, he told himself.

Hamelin put his plan into motion. He ran upstairs and gathered what few things he wanted to take with him: the two *Superman* comic books, his copy of *Robinson Crusoe*, and a sandwich he had sneaked out of the kitchen. Then, with his backpack zipped and hidden under his bed, he waited for everybody to go to sleep to carry out his plan. He'd show them.

Chapter 16

The Cave and the Eagle

I T REALLY WASN'T TOO HARD TO SLIP AWAY FROM THE Upton County Children's Home that night. Hamelin had not undressed fully by the time the lights were out. He took his shoes off and then quickly just slipped under the covers with his daytime clothes still on. Nobody even noticed.

He lay there in bed for what to him seemed like an hour, but he really wasn't sure how long. He then quietly sat up on the side of his bed and slipped on his shoes. He reached under his bed and grabbed his backpack and slowly tiptoed down the long room where the other boys slept. A floorboard creaked. Someone stirred in the bed to his right. He waited. Then he quietly started again.

Hamelin carefully made his way out the door and down the steps. The front door was locked, so he slid the bolt in the door. It stuck halfway, then released all at once with a pop. He cringed for a second and then waited. No sounds from upstairs. He unlatched the screen door and stepped out, closing both doors behind him, making hardly a sound, except for the door clicking in place.

He walked softly down the steps of the front porch, through the gate in the white picket fence that surrounded the front yard, out the half-circle dirt driveway, and onto the paved road. He paused. Which way? The town of Middleton was to the left, and Hamelin didn't want to go that way. To the north was—well, he didn't really know, except that the huge eagle and the car with people laughing had both gone in that direction. So that's the way he chose.

There was almost a full moon, and since it was a Texas summer night, it was still pretty warm, though cooler than the middle of those hot July days. Hamelin swung his backpack onto his back and walked briskly up the road.

He really didn't know where he was going. He figured he would walk as far as he could that night, sleep a little bit in the woods just off the paved road, get up the next morning, and walk to the next paved road that ran east and west off of this one. He would then maybe try to catch a ride into San Angelo, where he had once been taken along with the other children to the Tom Green County Fair. The more he walked, the more he realized he really hadn't thought very much about what he was going to do next; he just knew he was running away.

Hamelin walked what seemed like a long way—though, when he thought about it, he figured it was only about two and a half to three miles. Then just over a slight rise in the road, he saw the headlights of a car zooming toward him. He slipped off the road and ducked into the woods.

He waited for the car to pass and then decided that he might just sit down for a while there and eat his sandwich. Really, he was more thirsty than hungry—why hadn't he brought some water?—and the dry bread and meat just made it worse. But eating gave him something to do while he rested and planned what to do next.

He sat on the ground with his back against a thick mesquite tree. He could look up and see the moon through the branches of the trees, most of which weren't very tall in that part of Texas. He stayed there for a while, thinking of Mrs. Regehr, Mrs. Frendle, Bryan and Layla, and even a few of his friends at school and at the children's home, especially Marcie. Now that he was running away, though, he was glad to be leaving Patton McBoggerson behind. And why couldn't the Stephensons or somebody have remembered his birthday? Before long, he dozed off and dreamed of the county fair, the big bridge over the Concho River that they had crossed in San Angelo, and all the happy children and parents he had seen there.

Though it doesn't happen often in July in southwest Texas, a sudden thunderstorm came up. It wasn't what the farmers would have called a general rain. It was a hard summer shower, and in a short period of time, the wind started to blow, and the first few big raindrops began to fall. In his sleep, Hamelin dreamed that the wind was blowing in his face as he rode the fairgrounds roller coaster high above the people below. But suddenly a thunderclap woke him up, and he remembered that he was out in the woods—not in his bed. Then a big raindrop hit him on his left ear, followed by another on his forehead. By the time he got to his feet and looked around, he could hear the hard rain coming from the other side of the paved road.

The rain intensified and had now reached him, pouring through the branches overhead. Hamelin wondered what he should do. Maybe it would be smart just to stay there, but he had heard the thunder, and he remembered something about not staying under trees when there's lightning, so he decided against it. He grabbed his backpack, got out of the woods and back onto the paved road, and headed north. Out under the open sky, however, he was drenched in seconds. He ran across the road, toward a dark set of shadows to his left. He soon realized that it was a little grove of trees, even more thickly grown together than where he had been sleeping on the other side.

The rainfall grew into a howling, tree-blowing thunderstorm. Hamelin was old enough to know that this was the kind of hard rain that could be over in five minutes or, if it lasted up to thirty minutes, could produce quick-flowing streams in the low places. Not sure what to do, he moved farther westward into the trees and realized the ground was also thick with brush. With his backpack high on his shoulders, he felt his way along through the bushes and trees with both hands, and, with his back slightly bent, he could also feel the ground rising as he went.

After moving at a steady pace for about five minutes without finding smooth ground to sit on or shelter from the rain, Hamelin decided he would have to keep going, even though the ground continued to move upward. He was too far in to go back, and by now, he just wanted to get out of the cold rain. Then on top of the howling wind, there was suddenly a bright flash of lightning followed immediately by a loud clap of thunder. It sounded close—very close—and Hamelin panicked. Frantically pulling at the branches and bushes, he just kept going as quickly as he could.

He knew that he was climbing up, which, he thought, might not be so bad if he could come to a spot with some protection. The ground began to feel rocky under his feet, and his climb got even steeper. On occasion, he even had to make sure he had a good toehold against some stones while his arms were pulling on the brush that now seemed to be thicker and even closer to his face than his feet. At one point, he pulled himself through a brushy area where the branches sprang back on him and slapped the side of his face. The cold switch fortunately missed his eyes, but he felt a sharp sting on his forehead and realized he'd probably scratched himself pretty good, but he leaned forward and kept climbing.

The wind slowed some, and the rain let up a little, but it was still steady. Hamelin wanted desperately to find shelter from the wet cold. For a moment, he thought that his bed back at the children's home would feel warm and snug. Then just when he thought he couldn't climb anymore, he felt, first with his hands and then his elbows, a flat area in front of him. He climbed up on it, one leg at a time, and then, from his knees to his feet, he carefully stood upright. Feeling around the darkness with his hands, he slowly walked forward.

He was either on top of the hill or had come to a level spot, maybe a ledge of some sort. A fierce crack of lightning branched in the sky and lit the area all around him, giving him the answer: it was a small area cut into the side of the hill, and it provided a level surface that ran from the edge back into the hill. Based on his brief look, Hamelin figured the covered ledge was about ten big steps wide and about four to five steps deep from front to back. To his right, in the farthest part of the ledge, was a large, dark shape. Another flash of lightning revealed that it was a somewhat rounded boulder three or four feet higher than his head, with a foot or two of space above it, up to the ceiling of the ledge. The huge rock was some six feet wide and was nearer the back of the ledge than the front, but it was not all the way back, because just behind the boulder, between it and the inner wall of the ledge, was something dark, though he hadn't been able to see exactly what.

It was still raining, but the boulder and hill provided Hamelin with some shelter from the elements. He was high above the last cluster of trees and bushes, and the clouds moved enough to allow the moonlight to help him take in his surroundings. He crept carefully toward the boulder. When he reached it, he felt his way along it to his left, toward the back. He then discovered, more by feeling than by seeing, that the dark area he had seen earlier was a narrow opening in the hillside.

Hamelin figured that the opening would provide him with more shelter from the rain and would move him farther away from the edge of the hill. But he didn't want to go too far into the opening because he didn't know what he might find there. By feeling all around him, he could tell that, by stooping slightly, he could move into what felt like a doorway in the side of the hill.

He decided he would stop there, just barely into the opening, since he had no light. He kneeled down with one hand on each side of the opening. For balance, he kept his left hand on the inner wall of the hillside, while he reached up with his other hand to take the strap of his backpack off his right shoulder. But it was late, wet, and dark, and Hamelin was tired. He never was sure exactly how it happened, but somehow, as he shifted his weight, his left hand slipped, and he lost his balance and bumped his head on the rock face of the hill. It hurt. The dark night got even blacker as he found himself dizzy and just wanting to lie down. And to make things worse, even though it was summer, his clothes were soaked through, and he was cold. So, dizzy and afraid to stand up—plus wet and cold—he lay down for just a second and closed his eyes.

Later on, when he thought about it, Hamelin wasn't sure whether he had fallen asleep or momentarily passed out from the hard bump on his head. Anyway, there he was, sleeping half in and half out of the opening between the hillside and the rock, with his backpack hanging off his shoulder. How long he was out, he didn't know, but later on he guessed that it may have been an hour or more. However long it was, somewhere in his dreams, he heard a noise. It sounded like a deep, bear-like growl close to his head. Then, in the same dream, he heard what sounded like a violent flapping of wings and a loud, high-pitched, powerful shriek.

Hamelin opened his eyes but didn't budge an inch. He was still hearing things, but now it sounded like the padding of big feet running away down into the dark space in front of him. He still wasn't fully awake, but as he slowly began to lift his head and look in the direction of the cave, he had the full light of the moon at his back. His head was throbbing. He took a deep breath. And then, as he looked into the blackness of the cave, he saw two small eyes, closely spaced, reflecting the moonlight—and looking straight at him. The eyes were about three feet off the ground, belonging to whom or what he didn't know. Hamelin raised up and sat back almost at the same time, trying to get a little space between him and the pair of eyes. He leaned back but couldn't get his feet under him quickly enough to move as fast as he wanted.

Then the eyes came a full step—or was it a hop?—toward him. And there, in the light of the moon, standing in the entrance to the cave and looking out at him, was a black and white and gold creature. It looked ready to attack . . . and at the same time beautiful. It was an eagle, but larger, more majestic, and more defiant looking than any regular eagle he had ever seen. In this part of Texas—just like earlier today, with Marcie!—he had seen his share of eagles. They were beautiful, powerful birds soaring and circling in the sky. He remembered telling Marcie that some of them were strong enough to carry off small sheep, and now he believed it.

But the creature Hamelin saw before him, though it looked like an eagle, was more than an eagle. It had a silky white head and chest and great wings that, even folded at its side, looked to be massive feathered arms of flight and power. The beak was golden and beautifully curved, but it looked sharp as a sword at its downward point. And the eyes . . . they were yellow gold in the irises with ebony pupils, and they flashed with moonlight as they shot around to scan quickly in several directions. And yet, Hamelin also felt as if the eyes never left him.

He was so afraid that he thought he could feel his insides shake, especially in his throat and chest. But at the same time, he somehow thought—and hoped—deep down that the Great Eagle wouldn't harm him. Inching back even farther on his hands and knees, trying to get a little more space between him and the majestic bird, Hamelin stood up. Even when he stood, though he was taller than the eagle, he still felt smaller. At the same time, the eagle extended itself up on its legs even higher and simultaneously opened its wings slightly. This partial unfolding thrust the eagle's breast out in a feathery flex that lifted and expanded its entire body even more.

Hamelin and the eagle looked at each other. He desperately wanted to run, but he wasn't sure that he could move at all. He just stood still and looked at the bird.

"Welcome," said the Great Eagle, with a voice that sounded like wood on wood but ended with a small throaty screech. "I see you have come. You have found the cave."

Hamelin's first thought was, *What? Did this huge bird just talk?* The eagle stared. Finally, Hamelin dared a whisper. "Found the cave? Wha . . . what do you mean?" he stammered.

The eagle's small eyes rounded with a flash, and he breathed out heavily as he said, "I was sent here to meet you. You have now found the cave, and the journey must begin."

"What journey?" Hamelin asked. "Where are we going?"

"I am only your guide. Where you are finally going is not mine to say," said the great bird. "But I do know that you have been summoned to this place and that you are to follow me. But we must hurry. The appointed time is near."

Hamelin hardly knew what to do. It was late at night, he was cold and wet, his head hurt, and now there was a big, talking eagle telling him that he had been "summoned." Was he dreaming?

"Come along," said the eagle.

"But I still don't know where we're going," said Hamelin.

"I told you," said the eagle, "that's not for me to say, though it is yours to *refuse.*"

Hamelin felt a deep wave of dread pass over him. Somehow he knew he was supposed to follow the eagle, but he was terrified to do so. On the other hand, he was afraid *not* to. The bird tilted his head slightly to the side, watching him with a searching, surprised look, as if astonished that Hamelin would even dare to question his words.

Then the eagle turned and, with a step and a quick hop, moved along in front of him. Hamelin, very reluctantly, took a few steps toward the opening of the cave.

Chapter 17

The Journey in the Cave

THE EAGLE DISAPPEARED INTO THE BLACKNESS OF THE cave and seemed to bear right just inside the opening. First Hamelin stretched his neck, leaned forward, and peered in. Then he slowly entered. Though he expected to be enveloped in darkness—and was for a short distance—almost immediately a light was visible just a few feet in front of him. He followed the light, but it momentarily faded. Then after first moving several steps to his right, Hamelin, feeling forward with his hands and his feet, took a short step to his left and suddenly emerged into a large, bright area. There was so much light in the cave that his first instinct was to look for its sources. But then it became obvious: it was emanating from the eagle himself. As majestic as the eagle had looked at the mouth of the cave, he was more glorious now—even radiant.

As Hamelin walked in, it was as if he had walked through a door of blackness into a large illuminated cavern. The area was wide and spacious all around. As far as the light from the eagle would shine, that was as far as Hamelin could see. He could make out the edges of the walls around him, and he could even see stalactites of varying lengths.

But then his eyes were drawn back to the great, resplendent bird.

"This way," said the eagle. "Follow close behind so you don't fall out of the light." And off he went.

The radiance that seemed to come from the very center of the eagle continued to light their way. If Hamelin got too far behind, he would find himself falling back into the shadows. If he stayed close to the eagle, he could even see quite a few paces ahead of the great bird. After some distance, however, he learned it was best to stay five or six feet behind and, of course, to keep a steady pace.

The light from the eagle allowed Hamelin to see the lower parts of the cavern walls. At first they walked in the middle of the cavern, but before long it was obvious that the eagle's path was bringing them closer to the wall on the left. Eventually they walked close enough that Hamelin could reach out and touch it. What was on their right he couldn't tell beyond the space of a few feet, as the light seemed to focus more and more around the eagle and leave everything else, except for an area about six or seven feet around the great bird, in blackness.

They walked on until Hamelin's legs began to ache, and the eagle sensed that the boy was tired: "Looks like you need a little rest."

"Yeah," said Hamelin. He wished he could go home.

"Running away can be exhausting," said the eagle.

"How did you know that?"

The eagle stared. Hamelin suddenly felt very uncomfortable and looked away from the great bird's gaze. Maybe the big eagle didn't like questions . . .

After a few moments, the eagle said, "We must move on. The hardest part is still in front of us."

That didn't sound very encouraging to Hamelin—the path had already been hard. In the darkness, however, he had no choice but to follow. He pulled his backpack up high on his shoulders, stretched his arms, and said, "Okay."

But before starting off, the eagle slightly unfolded his right wing and reached down just below his chest, deep within a layer of feathers in the lower part of his enormous white breast. As if from nowhere, he pulled out a pair of ordinary looking gloves. "Here," he said, "you'd better put these on. You'll need them for the journey ahead."

After the eagle's earlier stare, Hamelin decided to hold his questions. He reached out and took the gloves. They were too big for him, but he slid them on anyway, even though he had a hard time getting all his fingers to spread wide enough to fit into the gloves, which were also a little stiff. Even then, his fingers and thumbs would go only about halfway up inside, which made it hard to keep the gloves on his hands.

The eagle watched and seemed to squint quizzically at the oversized gloves. After a barely noticeable moment of hesitation, he said, "Let's go." He then turned and strode off down the path, and Hamelin followed. The light continued to shine from the eagle, and they stayed close to a path that ran along the wall on their left.

The path within the cavern wasn't severely rocky, but it wasn't smooth either, which meant Hamelin often stumbled slightly, stepping a few inches farther down than he expected. Or because there were small, loose pebbles on the path, his feet sometimes slipped. So far, he hadn't come close to falling, but he put his left hand on the wall for balance. All the while, the path continued to descend gradually.

Hamelin felt his own pace slowing, but the eagle kept on. Then the path seemed to take a long, slow curve to the right. Hamelin kept his eye on the great bird, but at one point, when he let the eagle get a little too far ahead of him, he couldn't see the path at his feet. He paused and let out a breathy sigh. He let his hand drop from the wall, and a split second later his foot slid sideways on some loose rocks and dangled with nothing under it.

Hamelin fell to his hands and left knee and grabbed the path. The gloves helped as his fingers dug in. He had no idea that the path had grown so narrow. Fear shot through his body in a sudden jolt. Breathing quickly, he slowly leaned as far left as he could and carefully put his left hand back on the wall. He pulled his right foot back up and slowly stood. He now realized that he was walking on a path that measured only about three to four feet wide, and there was no telling how far down the drop-off went.

The eagle briefly paused, glanced back, and then kept on.

It all began to feel so odd to Hamelin, like a terrible dream. He never recalled seeing a hill this big out north of the children's home, and now it felt like they had been walking for at least two hours inside the cave. Apparently the cave was only the entry to a huge set of underground caverns. But how much farther?

And then, for the first time, he began to notice the smell. It was like the smell of dirt in a plowed field, only stale and moldy. And it was definitely getting colder. The path continued to descend and gradually curve to the right. Hamelin kept his left hand on the wall and occasionally stretched out his right foot to the side to check the width of the path. He did his best to keep up with the eagle and his light, but it wasn't easy.

The path now occasionally moved upward, but the general trend was down, which made it all that much harder for Hamelin to keep his balance. His steps were short, and his feet slid with each step. His left arm ached from being raised up constantly, and he felt his stomach and leg muscles growing tighter and more tense, as he feared falling. Once again his right foot slipped, but he stayed standing, and this time he heard some small rocks and gravel slide and bounce off the path. He paused to hear the rocks hit bottom. After waiting several seconds, he wasn't even sure he did hear them, but if he did, the noise was faint and very far away. The eagle paid no attention and strode, or hopped, on.

To make matters worse, it now felt to Hamelin that the ceiling of the cavern was getting closer. The wall on his left curved above his head, as if they were walking through a low archway. He had to lower his head and soon found himself stooping, as the curve of the ceiling came closer and closer while the path at his feet got narrower and narrower. What he could still see from the eagle's light showed he was walking on a ledge no wider than three feet now.

In fact, Hamelin was hardly walking at all. He was slowly shuffling along, sliding his feet forward instead of picking them up. His knees and back were screaming for a break. Finally, as the ceiling got lower and the path narrower, he got on his knees and began to crawl. That helped his back, but only a little. If only he could return to the children's home. But he was too scared to even think about turning away now from the only light he had.

He was glad to have the ill-fitting gloves, as they protected his hands against the rocks and even seemed to help his grip on the rock path. His knees began to burn as he crawled along on all fours, every part of his body tired. The eagle was still just ahead of him, but now the great bird was eight or nine feet ahead instead of the usual four or five. Hamelin was increasingly afraid and so tired that he couldn't go on.

"Please," he called out. "Please, Mr. Eagle, can't we stop?"

"Not here," the great bird said, "just a short distance more and then there will be a place where we can rest." Hamelin took a deep breath and kept going.

Finally, the ledge they were on took a very sharp turn to the right, and he looked up to see the eagle facing him. The path had widened somewhat, but the area above Hamelin's head opened up dramatically, as if he had emerged from a tunnel.

The great bird leaned down and stuck his beak right next to Hamelin's nose. They were eye to eye. Hamelin at first thought he was looking past the little dots of light in the middle of the eagle's eyes right back into the great bird's head, but then he realized that the eagle was gazing long and hard at him—with the look that adults get when they are about to ask you a hard question.

Hamelin blinked. He couldn't look at the great bird anymore. Instead, with the eagle still facing him, he looked past him and saw a large, open space. From Hamelin's vantage point, it appeared bottomless and uncrossable, except for a small footbridge. The bridge was maybe two feet wide and stretched out behind and beyond the eagle for a distance farther than the light shining from him could reach.

All of the bridge that Hamelin could see appeared to be made of four ropes, two on each side. It was suspended over a drop-off that was now directly in front of him and extended ahead into the darkness beyond. The two lower ropes were horizontal to the path and parallel to each other. They were set some two feet apart and were connected by wooden planks, which served as the footpath across the black chasm below. The two ropes at the top had nothing to hold them together but looked like handrails for anyone who tried to walk across the bridge.

Hamelin gulped, and his back shuddered. He hoped that the eagle wouldn't expect him to walk across that flimsy-looking footbridge over the pit of darkness below. He was still on all fours, and now he began to feel a rising, almost smothering heat coming from the blackness in front of him—and a smell like burning rubber. Almost immediately, his whole body was flooded with fear.

Chapter 18

Charissa, Daughter of Carr

THE TWO GIRLS FINISHED PUTTING ON THE ROUGH-MADE clothes they had borrowed from their servants and quietly slipped out of their quarters. It was about eleven o'clock at night, and their father, the king, had already gone to bed and assumed that they too were asleep.

"I wish we weren't doing this," said Sophie to her sister Eraina. "It's wrong to deceive Father."

"Sophie," responded Eraina, "we've got to find out what's going on among the people in the campgrounds. Our father is withdrawing, and we've got to know what people are saying."

"I know, but I hate leaving him alone. He's still so sad because of Mother's death." Eraina looked down as if to acknowledge Sophie's statement.

The two girls now looked nothing like princesses, and before long they had made their way from their father's luxurious tent over to the far side of the campgrounds, to their favorite spot for hearing the latest gossip. Though they obviously were young, no one paid any attention to them as they eased their way into the big tent that served as the central tavern for what was now Carr's kingdom in exile. They found a spot where they could see a lot of the crowd but also easily slip out the back if any trouble started.

Many conversations were going on in this big, loud place, but the voices of two women near the front rose above the others and before long commanded the attention of everyone there.

"Well, it's true, I tell you," said one large woman seated at a table with a big mug of ale in front of her.

"I know, Tela," her companion replied, "but there's no point talking so loud."

"Who cares who hears what I have to say? All of us in here know it!" The room got quieter still.

"I tell you, it was her own fault that she was captured by Landon's army! She may be twenty-three years old, but I tell you that oldest daughter of Carr—what's her name? Princess Charissa? She should have *stayed* in hiding with her father and her two sisters! Gittin' herself caught like that put *all* of us in danger!"

"Ya can't argue that, Hazel," said a tall, skinny man wearing a round hat and sitting at the table next to the two women. Apparently he knew Tela and Hazel, and they didn't mind his joining in the conversation. "All of us have been put in danger just lookin' for the girl."

"Well," Tela started in again, "if she hadn't been so . . . so high and mighty, and *vain*, she wouldn't *be* where she is now—wherever that is!" You could hear the men and women seated nearby growl a kind of general consent.

Another man, with a round face and a thick brown beard, spoke up from a nearby table, "Well, I know I'm sure tired of having me and my boys dragged out on special duty just to look for the king's daughter. She shouldn't have gotten herself caught."

"Now, now," said the man who served the drinks. He stood behind a long table with lots of flasks and bottles. "Let's don't get out of hand here. All of us have had our share of misery since Landon and his crowd came around here."

"That's for sure," said Tela, "but Carr should have *known* that that Landon was up to no good from the start. I remember telling people that all those wolves that were prowling around the countryside, killing our animals and threatening our children, were no accident."

"Well, of course not," said the tall man with the round hat. "All of us know those wolves were just scouts and forerunners."

"But still," said Hazel, "I have to admit it was hard for me to see at first. We were having all that trouble with the wolves and then along came Landon—and he was so handsome and strong—and he introduced himself as a great warrior, the prince of a distant kingdom. He was the hero of that big battle *against* some of the wolf packs. Remember? Who'd have thought then that they were working together?"

Everyone was quiet. After a few moments, Tela spoke again. "Yeah, but you didn't have to look at him long to see that something wasn't right. He had a certain look in his eyes that put him in the mind of those wolves. And I saw it myself one time."

She stood and stuck her finger out and gazed into the distance, and heads from all around the tables picked up. "I saw it myself . . . It was like he was sending his thoughts to the wolves. I tell you, he was communicatin' with 'em. He could move his head or stare into their eyes, and they would just do whatever he wanted."

The host spoke again. "Yeah, it's a wonder any of us escaped. I suppose we should be glad to be out here. By the time Landon and his men and all those wolves took over the city, it was all we could do to get out."

"That's what I'm sayin'," said Tela. "Why didn't Princess Charissa hurry out when everybody else did? Carr, his daughters, his household, his armies—everybody ran. It was obvious that Landon had the best of us. I heard they almost got Charissa that very night because she went back to get her favorite string of pearls and one last gown!"

Sophie had heard enough and got up to leave, and Eraina quickly followed her out.

"Where are you going?"

"I can't take any more of that," said Sophie. "All they're doing is criticizing our father and our sister."

"Well, it's *true*, isn't it? You know good and well that you and I both heard Father almost yelling at Charissa when he found out that one of the soldiers had to go back to get her, and all she could say was that she couldn't leave her pearls. She put *all* of us in danger."

"I know," said Sophie slowly and reluctantly. "I know. Charissa is so beautiful—"

"Oh, she's *beautiful*. But it's a shame she doesn't have any humility to go with it," snapped Eraina. "Always fretting over her hair and skin, taking forever looking for the jewels she's going to wear that day, staring at herself in the mirror."

"But," Sophie began, "she's our *sister*—"

"Yes, and our beautiful sister was constantly complaining about everything. Of course, the conditions out here aren't the same as back in the palace. But that's true for you and me too. And what about Father?" Eraina insisted.

"I know," said Sophie. "I know."

"Please, Sophie. I don't like sneaking around at night and listening to these conversations any more than you do. But we've got to know everything we can about what's happening. I'm not sure we can even trust the people around Father."

"Well, you can certainly trust Fearbane," answered Sophie.

"Well, yes, I do trust him. But being too trusting is what got Father into all this mess. Trusting Landon and . . ." Eraina stopped. "Look," she said softly to Sophie, "I'm going back in. Please come with me."

Sophie sighed and followed her back into the tent, and once more they settled into their spot. And it was obvious that the talkative woman up front was still holding court.

"—that's right, that's right! We all know what happened," continued Tela. "While all the rest of us have to endure the grit and grime of living out here, those princesses still live in luxury!" Sophie glanced at Eraina.

"And *that's* the problem," came another voice from several tables over, and everyone turned to look. The woman who spoke was not new to the tavern, but no one had ever heard her say a word.

"What do you mean?" asked Hazel.

The fair-haired woman began again with a voice of one who probably had a little too much to drink, "I mean just what my sister told me. She is one of the ladies-in-waiting for the princesses." The room got very quiet.

"Yes. And?" prompted Hazel.

"Beautiful Princess Charissa had to have her 'special bath' every morning. With her ladies-in-waiting beside her and guards stationed some distance away, they made a little processional to the waterfall just outside the edge of the camp. Charissa would spend nearly an hour in it every morning, washing away the grit and dirt of these campgrounds."

"Go on," said Tela.

"Well, one night, according to my sister, Charissa just couldn't wait until the next morning to get the 'sticky feel' of the campground off her 'delicate skin.' She complained that her clothes were just clinging to her body and that she felt 'suffocated.' She grabbed a towel and her robe and headed out without a guard detail or anyone else. My sister saw her leaving and begged her to stop, but she ignored her. Well, we all know the rest."

"Yeah," began the tall man with the round hat, "it wouldn't have taken long for Landon's dogs to smell her presence."

Everyone fell quiet again. The girls silently agreed that they had heard enough, so they walked out of the tavern. However, once outside, the two princesses paused silently, listening a little longer to the tavern crowd continue the story, loudly repeating all the details that everyone already knew.

One soldier added that he had been rousted out to give chase to Landon's dogs and men: "I could hear the princess screaming. Even got a good look at her while those soldiers pushed her through the crowd. I had to hang back with my group of men—we were no match for that lot. But we followed for as long as we could. You should've heard Landon's men mock her, laughing as she clutched at her robe. We had to turn back when they got to Landon's quarters."

The crowd fell silent, and even though they had the typical resentment of poor folk against the king, they still really loved King Carr and his family and felt sorry for the beautiful

princess, who was now in the clutches of Landon. The two
girls then continued their way back to their father's tent.

———⊷———

In the suffocating blackness, Charissa had lost track of the
days. The dark place that she was locked in had not a single
pinprick of light to relieve it. She was no longer in the dungeon in her father's castle, that much she knew. She was
now held in a very small space, and the dampness of the
floor and the moldy smell made her think she was underground, maybe even in some kind of cellar. When she was
first taken here, she had felt her way along the walls looking
for any change in their surface, but there was nothing but a
cool wetness that dripped along her hands and arms down
to her elbows.

There were some small concrete steps in one corner that
led straight up to a fastened door—perhaps a cellar door—
and the room she was in was no more than four or five paces
in each direction. The only human contact she had, if it was
human, was when the door above her, at random moments,
would briefly lift and a small flask of water and crust of
bread would be thrown down. The water was barely enough
to last each day, so she was always weak.

She wore only the dirty and torn robe from the night of
her capture. For hours at a time, she lay on the floor and
feared that the darkness would finally smother her. She soon
lost all track of the days and either slept or dozed in a weak
unconsciousness.

Finally, she sat up one day—as if something rose up
within her—and said out loud, "I must try to live." From
that point, every day, she made herself try to recover every
memory she had of home and family, of her father, mother,

and sisters. And every memory she could possibly draw up she used to feed her mind and spirit. She practiced seeing her life and her entire collection of memories, as much as she could, in their proper order. From birthday to birthday, she would relive her years, or from holiday to holiday, she would think about the things she had done with others, her friends and her sisters, and try to reconstruct the conversations during all the parties and festivals they had enjoyed.

She also remembered that, as her father's oldest, she had been trained to be strong, to be a warrior, as if she were a son. And she had loved the training and his attention and that of her father's chief commander, Fearbane. But perhaps it was fear of always being treated like a boy that one day had made her tell her father, "No more training"—that her interests had turned to being "a woman," which at the time had really meant clothes, jewelry, and fashions. Even now, her mind easily drifted back to her beautiful things, and she could see herself standing in a soft evening gown in front of a full-length mirror. But when those memories of her beauty came back, she would breathe deeply and tell herself, "You must not dwell on those things. It's your vanity that landed you here." And then she would feel guilty again for what she had done and cry for her father and sisters and ask for their forgiveness.

And then there were other memories. She couldn't stop them, and finally she decided that maybe it was best that she kept them, to remind her of her conceit and folly. She remembered being captured by Landon's soldiers just as she had emerged from the bathing pool. Though she had fought and screamed, she was no match for them. She remembered hearing for the first time iron doors clang behind her when she was taken by the rowdy soldiers and pushed through the jeering crowd to her father's castle—this time not to her rooms but to the dungeon below the castle. And now in her mind, almost audibly, she could hear again what she heard that night, soldiers and guards laughing on the other side of her prison door and whispering through the cracks in the door what they would soon do to her.

She originally hoped that her imprisonment would not last long and that her father and Fearbane would rescue her, but Landon must have counted on that too, because early the next morning, before the sun had even come up, the dungeon door was thrown open, and she was roughly bound and gagged, tossed into the back of a horse-drawn wagon, covered up with blankets and other objects, and taken away.

Once the wagon was safely out of the city, she was tied to the back of a horse and taken, judging by where the sun was, northwest of Parthogen, her father's city. After another hard day of riding, they had arrived at a two-story cottage hidden in the woods. Here they pulled her off the back of the horse and threw her into this dark prison.

She longed to see the light and to have someone to talk to. And she constantly felt in that darkness a suffocating fear, which was often even worse than her fear of what lay outside her cell.

Then one day there was a slight change. With her food and water, something else was thrown down into the cellar. It was a small towel, moist with water. She grabbed the towel and with it washed her face, arms, and legs, scrubbing them over and over to get the musty smell and the dried mud off.

The next day they threw her another moist towel, and again she washed. Two more days of darkness went by and then again another towel, but this time also what felt like a dress. The fabric was plain, she could tell by its feel, but it was a certainly a dress. And after washing herself from head to toe, she put it on. The next day, the door opened just slightly, and though the light hurt her eyes at first, she tried to look upward. Once again, bread, water, and a moist towel were lowered, but this time a brush was wrapped in the towel. She washed, brushed her hair, and waited.

Clearly they were up to something, and Charissa knew it. If they wanted to manipulate her, then it was obvious they needed her—her death was not their immediate plan. *If they need me alive*, she thought, *then there is still hope of escape.* She knew she must keep her wits about her; she must remember her training in horsemanship, archery, and hand-to-hand fighting.

The next day brought about a dramatic change. Two guards led her out of the cellar, but even walking up the steps was painful. She put both hands to her forehead to block the light. Not only was she unaccustomed to it, but the room into which she stumbled was magnified in its brightness. It was filled with mirrors on every side. She stood in the middle of the room, trembling, her head down, and she sensed another person walking into the room. She slowly took in the dark figure that stood next to her, beginning with the feet, and gradually lifted her head. She encountered a slender, almost beautiful, yet oppressively stern woman looking at her. The face was pale. The hair was jet black, well-groomed, and fell evenly to the woman's shoulders. Her eyes were narrow and dark, and her very presence made clear to Charissa that the woman was in charge. She knew she must do whatever the woman said.

The woman slowly walked around her, and though Charissa wore the only dress they had given her and had brushed her hair, the woman's every look suggested disdain for her appearance. "Follow me," she said. And Charissa slowly, with halting steps, followed the woman as she walked over to one of the mirrored walls and proceeded to go around the room in front of each mirror. She didn't move quickly, but neither did she stop. The pale woman traversed the entire perimeter of the room, with Charissa following.

From that point on, Charissa's every move was ordered and watched. She was given a small, straight bed in the corner of the mirrored room and took all her meals on the floor. She was made to walk around the room several times a day, and after many days was finally allowed, under guard, to walk just outside the cottage for brief periods. She never entered other areas of the house or grounds, though it was obvious that the stern woman stayed on the second floor above her in the cottage and that there were barns and stables not far from the front of the house.

Slowly her strength returned. But most of the time she remained indoors, where she was surrounded by the mirrors, and she could tell that the lack of good food and fresh air was taking its toll. Her face and hair were no longer softened by the smooth creams and luxurious oils that her father had provided. And the cheap fabric of the dresses she was being forced to wear was a constant humiliation that was reflected in all the mirrors.

But Charissa was determined not to forget what was happening. She knew the woman was working to control not only her behavior but also her mind and will. And though the stern woman began to soften her ways a little—and even allowed Charissa to bathe regularly and eventually added oils and cosmetics—Charissa worked to maintain her inner strength. She reminded herself often that it was her selfishness that had led to her capture in the first place, and she knew that the woman was toying with her vanity again.

Charissa spoke little and then only when spoken to, but never of her family. She showed no thought or hope of getting home but regularly looked for her chance to escape.

One day the pale woman came to her and announced that a visitor was coming. "Today you must make yourself beautiful, because a great prince, Prince Tumultor of Osmethan, is coming here to visit."

The idea of a visitor was a great surprise.

"May I ask who he is?" she said softly.

The woman stared at her in a way that made Charissa lower her eyes, as if she had been impertinent even to ask the question. Finally, the woman responded, "He's the brother of Landon."

The very name of Landon brought a shudder to Charissa, and the woman noticed it. She quickly added, "He is ashamed and embarrassed at his brother's cruelty. He has heard that you are a daughter of Carr, and he hopes you will forgive his family for his brother's malice." And then the woman abruptly turned and strode away. Charissa was given a beautiful dress to wear that afternoon, and the woman sat her in front of the mirrors and applied cosmetics and brushed her hair for hours.

Late that evening, Prince Tumultor, with a small band of soldiers, arrived at the cottage. His men were given rooms adjoining the barns, and the prince was taken upstairs. He washed up but wasted no time coming downstairs to greet Charissa. It was obvious that her beauty overwhelmed him.

Within minutes, her bed was taken away, and a table was quickly placed and set in her room. Before long, it was filled with rich foods and drink and two candelabra for light. Though the woman sat between them, it was obvious that the prince's attention and conversation were focused on Charissa. By the end of the meal, she held his eyes for a moment longer than the stern woman liked, and then Charissa smiled for the first time in weeks.

"Shall we go for a walk?" Tumultor asked.

"I don't think that would be wise," the woman said in a clipped voice.

"But surely a walk on this beautiful moonlit night—"

"No," said the woman, her voice rising in volume. "You know very well—"

"What I know well is what I want," said the prince, staring at the woman. They held each other's glares.

"Madam," said Charissa, "perhaps I should be excused."

The woman jerked her head toward her, obviously angry that she dared to speak.

"Since my bed is not here, I'd be glad to go downstairs again," Charissa said as she looked to the door that opened onto the cellar steps.

"No," said Tumultor, who suddenly stood and walked toward the staircase. "I'm going upstairs to get my cloak for our walk!"

"You mustn't!" shouted the woman at the prince's back. She quickly turned to face Charissa before following Tumultor up the stairs. "You stay right here!" she said firmly.

Charissa tiptoed over to the foot of the stairs, where she could hear their loud exchange.

"My lord! This is not the plan!"

"Well, I have my own plans!"

"I daresay you do! But you know you're supposed to wait."

"I don't like waiting!"

"Your father's plans require it! The plan requires marriage. The absorption of Parthogen—"

Charissa moved away from the steps. She had to act, and this might be her only opportunity.

She doused the candles on one of the candelabra but grabbed the other one. She stepped quickly to the cellar door, opened it, and hurried down the steps with the one branched candle holder. She set it down, candles still lit, and raced back up the stairs. The room was now dark except for the light coming up the stairs through the open cellar door.

She could still hear voices upstairs. She grabbed a chair from the dining table, threw it down the open door, and screamed as it clattered to the bottom. She then stepped into a dark corner while the prince and the stern woman came rushing down the stairs and ran toward the lit opening.

"This is your fault!" yelled the woman.

"My lady!" yelled the prince as he first stood at the top of the cellar steps before running down, followed by the woman.

Cries of "if she's hurt . . ." and "my lady!" were shouted at the same time, and the captors never heard Charissa running behind them, slamming the door, and jamming the lock with a table knife.

Charissa then rushed out the front door toward the barns and the soldiers' quarters.

"Help!" she half shouted and half gasped. The soldiers rushed out of their rooms, wide-eyed.

"The prince!" Charissa said breathlessly as she pointed toward the house. They all rushed to the cottage.

She then threw open the doors of the barn and swatted the backsides of all the horses except Tumultor's, spooking them into escaping their stables. She quickly mounted Tumultor's horse, and with all the skills of horsemanship she had learned from Fearbane, she rode away into the night like a highway bandit.

Chapter 19

The Footbridge and the Amazing Flight

"**S**TAND UP," SAID THE EAGLE, "AND FOLLOW ME. THIS IS the path you must take. You must cross this bridge." Then, seeing the look on Hamelin's face, the radiant creature added solemnly, "It is a task you must accomplish to reach the Atrium of the Worlds and beyond."

With that, the eagle faced Hamelin and backed up several steps onto the bridge. Stretching out one wing toward him as if it were a great arm extended to help, he said, "Get up. Use the top ropes at the sides of the bridge for support and walk forward." The eagle backed up another step. He was almost like a father wanting his child to walk.

"Come on now," said the eagle. Hamelin crawled forward to the bridge. He rose up on his knees and, with the gloves still on his hands, slowly reached his right hand up to the top rope on the right. He then placed his left hand on the upper rope to his left. The two ropes, with Hamelin on his knees, were just about at his head level. He slowly pulled himself up on two feet but stood there awkwardly leaning over at the waist.

The gloves, though large, now felt good on his hands. His grip was strong, but his lower back was shaking, and his legs were stiff. He looked at the eagle, and the great bird gave him a slow, deliberate nod. Hamelin raised his right foot and barely got it on top of the first wooden plank. Before he could put any weight on it, however, he looked down at the black emptiness below. A wave of heat wafted up, and with it a hint of a rotten, burning smell. Hamelin's nose stung, and his throat—already dry—got even drier.

He tried to put a little weight on his right foot, but the portion of bridge under his foot began to wobble. His hands were holding tight, but the more he tried to put weight on his right foot, the more sideways the bridge swung, making it wind and twist snakelike off into the distance.

"I can't do it," cried Hamelin.

"Yes, you can," said the eagle with a steady tone. "I know you can," he added, "and I know you will."

"No, I *can't!*" Hamelin cried, and this time it wasn't the whine of a little boy. It was a cry of fear and defeat. "I can't! I can't!"

The eagle's voice rose to another level of strength and firmness: "Yes, you *can!*"

Hamelin looked up. He saw the eagle. He saw the eagle's wing extended to him. He desperately wanted to take that step, but every time he tried to lift his left foot, more weight fell upon his right foot, and the footbridge veered even more wildly to the side.

Finally, with one last push on his right foot, Hamelin thought he could perhaps get his other foot up, but it was no good. The footbridge veered violently to his left. He began to lose his balance in the other direction. His right elbow started to bend, and his whole body pitched to the right. His left foot came up off the rocky path. He then lost his balance, and his right leg, still on the footbridge, began to bend at the knee, while his left leg stretched and pawed wildly for the ground. He clenched the ropes even harder, but the whole bridge twisted and waved left to right across the darkness in front of him. At that point, deep inside, Hamelin felt himself giving up.

Again he yelled, "I *can't!*" And this time his voice had not only fear but also a defiant anger in it. Believing that any second he would fall to his right through the ropes and into the chasm, Hamelin pushed himself backward, using his hands against the ropes to throw his body away from the bridge. He was surprised at how much energy he had as he pushed. He flew several feet onto the rocky ledge behind him and grabbed for the ground. He hit on his bottom first and then rolled onto his back, which was somewhat cushioned by the backpack, but his head kept going, and he felt it bang hard against the rocky path.

Hamelin gripped the ground as hard as he could, fearing that he would slide off what was still a narrow path to his right. His whole body was shaking violently, though his hands felt strong, like they were digging into the rock floor to give him support. His right hand found a bit of rock that was sticking up out of the ledge, almost like a smooth knob, and he clutched it fiercely. With his left hand, he found a small crease in the path and dug his fingers down into that crack in the rock.

He lay on his back looking up, panting for breath and afraid to budge. Suddenly the eagle appeared suspended above him. Scooping the air, the great bird held himself three to four feet over the prone boy, his wings extended to their full range and his golden feet and talons stretched downward. The eagle's wings, powerful enough to have brushed him over the edge of the abyss like a mouse, suddenly seemed to Hamelin like huge arms of protection surrounding him. The boy's eyes filled with tears, and his face burned with sweat and shame.

Then almost as quickly, the eagle dropped to the path at Hamelin's feet. He looked up desperately at the eagle, who looked back with those strong eyes. At first Hamelin thought he saw anger in them, but he soon realized it was more pity—and he knew he had failed.

"I told you I couldn't do it," he cried. "I told you! Please, let me go home."

"You can't go home," the eagle replied. "There is too much to lose. You must try again!"

"No!" Hamelin wailed.

"You don't realize what you are doing. She is waiting for us! Besides, there's Ren'dal, Chimera—even your own—" But then the eagle paused.

Hamelin, confused, started to ask, "My own *what*?" But his fear overpowered his mind, and he pleaded, "Please, *please* don't leave me here. Please help me!"

The eagle shut his eyes, as if thinking what to do. Many seconds passed before the bird said, with a resignation in his voice that Hamelin did not expect, "Very well. You have chosen—not well, but it is your choice. Now you—and many others—must live with the consequences."

Hamelin had no time to think about the eagle's words. Suddenly the great bird was above him again, with wings outstretched, facing the boy as he lay sprawled on the ledge, still on his back looking up. The eagle, with his massive body, then stretched out his legs and grasped Hamelin just under his shoulders. His talons were so powerful that Hamelin at first feared the great bird was going to rip his clothes and flesh. But then he realized that, like a cat sheathing its claws, the eagle was holding back the sharp ends of his talons. The great bird lifted him, slowly at first, and at the same time Hamelin cautiously loosened his grip on the rocky path, expecting the eagle to set him upright on his feet. But with a frightening speed, the bird plunged off the ledge that Hamelin had worked so hard to grasp.

They dropped into the chasm itself. The smell of burning trash and the waves of heat increased with every inch of the descent. Hamelin's nose and neck could feel it immediately. But just when he thought they would surely hit bottom, the eagle stretched his wings, and with a few muscular strokes, the powerful bird and his passenger shot forward on a level plane.

The eagle was flying forward, but Hamelin, who had been lifted off his back and was still held by the great bird's talons just under his shoulders, had his face buried in the eagle's chest, which protected his face and eyes from the heat. And even though there was some light shining from the bird, Hamelin could see almost nothing. He remembered again that eagles could carry off lambs before killing them for food. Where was he taking him? He could sense that there were objects whizzing by all around him. Perhaps they were flying close to the walls of underground caverns. Or maybe the eagle was darting around the stalactites and stalagmites. Once Hamelin thought he heard animal noises from below. Another time he felt a sudden draft of cool wind, almost as if someone had left open the front door on a windy winter day.

Then just as quickly, the flight seemed to be ending. The great bird had not yet landed, but he slowed down to what felt like a circular glide. And then, just as Hamelin thought the ride was over, the eagle shot straight up in a burst of speed that left Hamelin's breath in his stomach. The sudden change up, from what felt like the bottom of a tower, lasted only seconds before the eagle plummeted in a nosedive that thrust Hamelin's feet out above his head. Then before he could anticipate what would happen next, the eagle quickly made several sharp turns and landed on a flat surface, where, without ceremony, he plunked the boy down—not all that gently either.

Hamelin, breathless, rolled over on all fours and looked around. Was this the eagle's nest? No—he found himself in the area just inside the cavern where he had originally entered. He faced the opening and could see some light on the other side of it.

"You said you wanted to go home, so go. Better not to run away when you don't know where you want to run to, and better not to run at all if you can't finish."

"I . . . I couldn't . . ." Hamelin stammered without knowing how to finish the sentence. But he quickly added, "What do I do now?"

"Now?" said the great bird impatiently. "Your moment to act has passed. Go back to your bed!" And he turned away as if to leave. Then looking out at the opening, he turned back and said, almost grudgingly, "Don't forget your gloves."

"But could I—?"

It was too late: the Great Eagle took flight out the opening of the cave. He was gone so quickly that Hamelin had no time to follow.

He tried to scramble to his feet and get to the opening to see where the eagle had gone, but it was no good. The beautiful, terrifying bird had vanished. He almost wanted to yell, "Come back!" but he didn't know what he would do if the eagle did. He turned around and looked back momentarily into the cave and saw that the entry space extended farther to his left than he had seen the previous night. It even looked like there was another path he hadn't noticed. But there was no point in thinking about that now.

Weary and feeling crushed, Hamelin removed his backpack, which was still muddy from last night's rain and now slightly torn from his fall at the edge of the chasm. He unzipped it, took off the gloves, which were also muddy, and jammed them into the pocket. The zipper was hard to zip back up, but finally he got it halfway closed, where it stuck completely. He gave up on the zipper and in frustration slung the backpack onto his shoulders and started down the hill.

His mind was racing. *Who are Ren'dal and Chimera? And what did the eagle mean by "your own"? And who is the "she" who is waiting?* And what was wrong with him? He had made it so far . . . why couldn't he just make it across that bridge? *Oh, and what else did the eagle say?* From there he would go to the Atrium of the Worlds and beyond? He really wanted to tell the eagle how sorry he was and maybe even ask for another chance. But the amazing bird was gone.

It was a lot easier going down the hill than it had been climbing it the night before. The sun would be up before long, so Hamelin had some gathering light. He slipped and slid some hundred and fifty feet down the hill to the road, and this time he managed to cover the distance without getting stung by any low-hanging branches.

Once he reached the bottom of the hill, he crossed the road and entered the woods on the other side. He headed back south, half walking, half jogging, and before long made his way to the edge of the woods that broke into the clearing just opposite the screened delivery porch.

It was now close to sunup, but he slipped into the front door—not the side porch, because the kitchen staff got up early—and made it upstairs without being seen. The stairs made a little noise, and he heard one of the adults downstairs holler, "Who's that?" But Hamelin just kept going.

He tiptoed back into the boys' bedroom, quietly got all the way down to the end of the room, and sat down on his bed. He removed the two comic books and *Robinson Crusoe* from his backpack, put them away, and then quickly pulled off his damp and dirty clothes and stashed them and the muddy backpack under the bed. He got out his toothbrush and underwear and, as if he had decided to get up early, went into the bathroom and started the water for a shower.

It wasn't much longer before Mr. Stephenson yelled into the boys' room that it was time to get up, and some of the usual early risers headed to the bathroom. They noticed that Hamelin was already in there, but nobody really paid him any attention. He finished his shower, brushed his teeth, returned to his space, and got dressed. By the time everyone gathered for breakfast, no one had any idea that he had been out all night and certainly not a clue as to what he had been through.

Of course, no one would have believed him had he told them. Hamelin could scarcely believe it himself. But he knew that it had all happened. Fortunately too, no one noticed, or at least no one bothered to ask about, the scratch on the side of his forehead. But more than the scratch, what Hamelin remembered was being so scared—of acting like what older boys and bullies would have called "a chicken." And what especially stayed with him was the feeling that he had failed somebody who was waiting for him, that he had been too afraid to do something he was really supposed to do. Something for somebody, maybe several people, on the other side of that bridge.

Chapter 20

Charissa: The Escape, the Lion, and the Pool

C HARISSA KNEW SHE SHOULDN'T TRAVEL SOUTHEAST TO her father's kingdom, since that's what her pursuers would expect. So her plan was to go south as far as she could and then head east and thus make her way back to her family.

But she had never traveled so far north or so far west, and though she was clever to ride hard due south, she had no idea what the terrain would be like. She rode all night through dark woods and a grassy plain, but before she realized it, she found herself in a barren area. By late afternoon, she could find no source of water for either herself or her horse. To make matters worse, as she walked over a particularly rocky spot holding the reins of Tumultor's horse, he jerked away, and she couldn't get him back.

By the time evening fell, she was parched, lying against the side of a giant boulder, unable to see any sign of water or vegetation in any direction. As she lay there, she heard wild, catlike cries followed occasionally by doglike howls. She was sure that she would not live much longer, dying from either exposure or wild beasts, or both. But if she did die tonight, at least she had escaped the darkness, the mirrors, and the stern woman. She fell asleep and dreamed that she was running from Tumultor and his band of soldiers. In the dream, she strung her strongest hunting bow, the one given to her by her father. However, when she reached for her quiver, the one given to her by Fearbane, it was empty.

Her whole body ached, and if she hadn't been so dehydrated, she would have been sweating: the sun had already risen, and the ground and rocks around her had already started to bake in the morning heat. She didn't know if she had the energy to continue on her journey. She thought of her family—her mother, who had died just a few years ago, and now her father and sisters, who were, no doubt, frantically looking for her. She closed her eyes and tried to think of them, but her burning thirst made it hard to focus her mind. But then a sound interrupted her wandering thoughts. She heard a soft padding just above her. It sounded like it was at the top of the boulder she was lying against. Then, not sure whether she was dreaming, she bolted wide awake when this time for sure she heard something—like the soft purring of a cat—but if it was a cat, it was the purring of a very big cat.

She jumped up, turned around, and there at the top of the boulder just four feet above her head was a huge mountain lion. The massive cat was not in a pouncing position, but he nonetheless looked at her intently as if he could jump at any moment. She looked at the giant animal as he watched her, his tannish-yellow skin covering a smooth and muscular feline body. The mountain lion stared. Charissa stood frozen in place. And then the cat blinked, lazily.

And then the strangest thing happened. She knew, of course, that animals can't talk, but she could have sworn she heard the huge creature say, or maybe it was in her mind, "Follow me, and I will get you out of here."

Suddenly the cat leaped over Charissa's head and landed ten feet behind her. She spun around quickly, and then she fainted. She wasn't sure for how long, but she remembered dreaming that the nurse who tended her when she was three years old was scrubbing mud off her face with a rough, scratchy cloth. She was looking up at the old nursemaid in her dream when she opened her eyes to see the mountain lion licking her face. Charissa screamed but quickly stifled it. She instinctively grabbed for her bow, which wasn't there. The mountain lion backed away at a slow, catlike pace, started to turn away, but then turned back to her once more and said, this time clearly out loud, "Come along."

Am I dreaming? Is this a fantasy? she thought. *Or am I dead already? Either way, I might as well follow.* She got to her feet and followed the cat—though maintaining space between them.

They moved slowly south. After some distance, Charissa suspected the lion was heading for what looked like three large boulders.

When they got there, she moved closer as he walked around the right side of the boulders. There, shaded from the hot morning sun, was a small, damp spot on top of what looked like a flinty rock surface. The cat scratched the moist area, and a little pool of water gathered. He drank, scratched the area again, and it filled up once more with water. Then he looked at her, tilted his head sideways, and purred deeply, "Aren't you thirsty?"

Charissa stumbled forward, buried her face—stomach to the ground—in the water, and sucked the little pool dry, not once but twice. She rolled over, looked at the lion, smiled, and said, "Thank you." The big cat let out a soft, throaty roar.

Then the great lion led her from that point southeasterly until they came to a wide expanse of grassland. He always seemed to know where to find a small pool of drinking water or some small shrub with edible berries. Finally, after a full day of traveling, they came to a rise in the grasslands, which turned into a smoother rock surface. Once on top of this rocky tableland, the lion led Charissa toward another prominent physical feature, a curved, almost dome-like elevation on the upper part of the rocky plateau. The lion continued, with catlike jumps, to the top of the dome, and when Charissa finally reached the same spot, she saw that, at the very top, was a big hole. The hole looked to be seven paces in diameter and was almost perfectly circular. It led straight down into what appeared to be the lush bottom of a vast cavern.

"Now we climb down," said the lion.

"I can't climb down there," said Charissa. "There's nothing to hold on to."

"Then you had better hold on to *me*," he said.

With that, the mountain lion crouched down on his haunches, making himself as low as he could get, and Charissa climbed on the back of the great cat.

She was a good horseman, but this was like no other ride she had ever had. She straddled the cat's back, gripped his shoulders with each hand, one on each side just behind his head, and tucked her head down on the lion's left side just as low as she could get it. At first she closed her eyes, but then she shook her head, opened her eyes, and took a deep breath.

What she saw was the cat as he jumped through the hole and landed some ten feet down on a very tiny ledge barely inside the surface of the opening. From there, the agile creature pulled his front feet back toward his rear legs, arched his back even more—with Charissa squeezing his back even harder with her hands, elbows, and knees—and started down the ledge.

When Charissa realized after the initial jump that they weren't falling, she looked around to take it all in and saw—in the fading daylight that still managed to glance through the skyward opening—her descent atop the magnificent lion, step by sure-footed step on a circuitous trail that spiraled ever downward along the inner walls of an underground cavern.

When they finally reached a wider place on the ledge near the base of the cavern, the lion leaped the final few feet to the floor and, without letting Charissa dismount, raced through that room and out a door on the opposite end. She had not been able to see much in the room, but she thought she saw flashes of color, maybe even the tiny reflection of a pond. The lion scampered down a short hallway and into another great and massive area, which was far enough removed from the room with the opening to be almost completely dark. There he stopped and tilted his body so that Charissa could dismount.

"You must wait here," he said.

"What?" she replied, her voice shaking. "Wait here? How long? Surely you won't leave me?"

"It will not be long," replied the lion. "You must wait here for a boy and an eagle. They will come soon. When they do, go with them. You will know what to do after that. If you need something to drink, then you may go back to the room where we first entered. Just as you enter that room, to the right, you will hear the sound of water coming down from the wall.

There is a pond there. You may drink from it. But—I warn you—drink from that water only when it is night. *Do not* enter that room during the day."

"But how long will they be?"

"They won't be long. The eagle is on his way to get the boy, and they will be here soon. But again, remember my warning: only when you are thirsty may you enter that room, but even then, you must *never*, under any circumstances, enter that room while it is light."

She nodded, and suddenly the lion was gone. And then, with no gradual buildup, it started again—the fear, the smothering claustrophobia, the heavy darkness, the isolation, and the thirst—all the things she had felt in the cottage cellar.

That night, Charissa did exactly as the lion said and entered the first room only when it was dark, found the pond, and drank. She stayed away all the next morning and afternoon, remaining in the cavern where the lion first left her, hiding in the dark and afraid to enter the large, dome-like room as long as she could see any light coming from its entryway.

But after several days, there was no sign of an eagle or a boy. The darkness began to fall on her in waves, holding her down and stealing her breath. Finally, one morning when she could endure the dark no longer, she crawled through the corridor and into the room, looked into the pond as the light was full, took a drink, and looked again.

She saw her reflection and was surprised to see her beauty restored. And weakened by despair, her will was no longer strong enough to remember, much less heed, the lion's warning. The more she looked, the more desire she had to continue looking. She stared and stared and was captured by what she saw.

Chapter 21

Changes

THE VERY DAY HAMELIN GOT BACK FROM THE CAVE, THERE was a birthday card in the mail for him from Layla and Bryan. He didn't show it to anyone else because he was too embarrassed to make a big deal that his birthday had been forgotten. Besides, he didn't want to think about all the strange things that happened after he ran away. But he did feel better knowing that Layla and Bryan remembered.

For several days after Hamelin got back, he worried that some of the grown-ups would somehow figure out that he had been gone all that night, but they never did. Of course, he couldn't help thinking about what had happened to him that night at the cave, even if he didn't want to.

With no one to talk to about his experience, he stayed to himself for days. He wondered what would have happened if he had crossed the footbridge and what, or who, the eagle said was waiting for him on the other side. He was so ashamed of his failure—he wished he could see the Great Eagle one more time to make up for it.

Once or twice, Hamelin even wondered whether his adventure had really happened. Was it all just a dream? But then he'd touch the left side of his head. He could still feel a little sore spot there, and he remembered how he had slipped at the mouth of the cave, bumping his head.

And there was more evidence that it was all real: his clothes had since been washed, but there was still the crumpled backpack under his bed covered with dried mud. He had had that scratch on the side of his forehead for days. Even his hands were sore from gripping the ropes and the path. It had happened. All of it. And the churning feelings in his stomach were still there every time he thought about the black chasm and the bridge—and his breakdown in courage.

The rest of the summer went by in the usual way at the children's home. Since there was no school, the children had more freedom to play, but Hamelin kept to himself. Marceya noticed and finally got him to talk to her, though he still kept quiet about the eagle, the cave, and the footbridge. She knew he was holding something back, but she had secrets of her own, so she let Hamelin keep his. But at least they were talking again.

Some of the older children were involved in different activities in Middleton. David Rivers had a car, and he often drove kids into town to meet friends or play summer sports. He was sixteen years old and had a job, so he saved up his money and managed to buy the car for almost nothing. It had apparently broken down, and the Middleton police had found it abandoned on the side of the road, so they sold it to him. David was clever and hardworking, and by buying junk parts cheaply and even having some people give him things here and there, he had managed to get the car running.

Hamelin admired David's ability to get things done. He was decisive and positive. He was also really good about watching out for the younger kids. That summer, word got around that he had seen Patton in town one day and warned him that he had better stay away from Hamelin and the other younger boys at the children's home. David's warning made a big difference in Hamelin's life.

The next school year was much more enjoyable for Hamelin. He made better grades and learned a lot. He was able to check out books from the school library, and one of his favorites was a book called *It Must Be Magic*. There were all kinds of exciting stories in it about seven-league boots and flying carpets, and Hamelin often dreamed of being in those magical places and doing the courageous things that Hercules or Jason had done. *But you had your chance*, he reminded himself. Since he had failed to cross the footbridge, those kinds of exciting things would never happen to him again.

But Hamelin continued to read about great adventures. He went to the library whenever he had a chance, though it was never fun to be around the librarian, Mr. Albert Litchie. None of the students at the school liked Mr. Litchie. His main communications were glares and sharp shushes. And he seemed to be everywhere, constantly patrolling, appearing when least expected. And he was endlessly staring with his round, closely placed eyes. Hamelin could feel his eyes even when he didn't hear his steps.

The kids called him "Litchie the Snitchie," or sometimes just "Mr. Snitch," because he frequently turned in the names of children to the teachers or, worse, the school principal, saying that this or that child had made a disturbance in the library and ought to stay after school.

Hamelin was usually quiet and almost never had to stay after school, but it was bad when he did, since the children from the home who were kept after school would miss their bus and have to walk the two long miles back, where more questions would have to be answered. That would usually mean not getting their chores done on time, which would also mean more chores to do the next day.

Third grade had a lot less trouble from Patton. Even though he occasionally glared at Hamelin, he didn't come close enough to bully or threaten him the whole year, thanks no doubt to David Rivers.

Near the end of Hamelin's third-grade year, another surprising development took place. One night after supper, Mr. Stephenson stood up and announced, "We're leaving."

The children looked at each other, but no one said anything.

Finally, looking rather embarrassed at everyone's silence, Mrs. Stephenson stood up and added—as if the children needed, or wanted, an explanation—"I'm going to have a baby of *my own*."

She smiled and waited for a response, but everyone stayed still until David Rivers stood up, looked around quickly, and said, "Okay guys, who else washes dishes tonight?" And that was it.

Within a few days, Mr. Stephenson rented a trailer and loaded up their things. Then, without lengthy good-byes, they drove away.

Hamelin watched them go. No one stood around for very long. He looked around for Marceya, who had been standing next to him when the Stephensons drove off, but she had vanished. He walked around the side of the house looking for her and thought he saw her by the old shed.

As he walked away, he heard some of the older boys talking.

"I wonder who'll replace them," one said.

Someone snickered. "Who cares? Anybody would be better than them."

Another added, "Yeah, now that there's nobody, it's already better!"

The boys laughed, but Hamelin didn't think it was funny. And he was more interested in finding Marceya anyway.

When he got to the old shed, she wasn't there, but he heard a noise, like someone taking a deep breath and then holding it. The shed door creaked in the wind, and Hamelin stepped inside. He looked around. It was silent until he heard a big explosion of breath.

It was Marceya, huddled in a corner of the shed. She didn't want Hamelin to hear her crying, but she couldn't hold her breath any longer, and she burst into sobs. He went to her quickly and kneeled down beside her.

"What is it, Marcie? You okay?"

She stayed in the corner with her arms around her bent legs, her face buried in her knees. She cried. And Hamelin waited.

"They left me," she sobbed. "Just like that. Their truck and trailer all loaded up and they just left . . ." Marcie cried and cried. And Hamelin knew she wasn't talking about the Stephensons.

He wanted to tell her not to worry, that they would come back to get her someday. But he couldn't promise that.

They both sat there for a long time. Finally, Marcie spoke up. "One day I'm going to be free like that eagle we saw. Maybe just—whatever . . . just get away from here."

Hamelin looked at her face and was afraid he knew what she was talking about. She glanced up at him and smiled. Marcie almost never smiled, but Hamelin had noticed that whenever she did, she was pretty.

"Don't worry, Hamelin," she said. "If I go find my parents, I'll come back and get you. They will probably adopt you, or at least I think I can get them to." Then her face clouded up again, and she looked down. The smile vanished, and her eyes narrowed as she seemed to be remembering something.

"You can't leave, Marcie," said Hamelin. "I know you want to real bad and so do I—"

"Don't tell me what I can't do," she said. "I can think or do whatever I want!"

"But you don't know where they are!"

"Oh, yes I do! I told you before, they're in California. And I think I know what part of California they went to. My mom's boyfriend—I mean, my dad—is a bricklayer, and he said there's lots of things being built in Los Angeles."

"But Los Angeles is a big place!"

"Doesn't matter. I'll find them. Just don't you worry about me finding them. I heard them talking, and he—yeah, that's right, my mom's *boyfriend*—mentioned Los Angeles." Her eyes began to well up again with tears.

"Marcie—"

"I'll find them. And I'll get my mom away from him. I heard them talking one time. He told her they couldn't afford me anymore, and she said, 'No, I won't do that.' So I know it wasn't her idea. They packed the trailer up one day, and then when I went off to school, they just left."

"But Marcie—"

"No! I know my mom didn't want to do it, and I'm going to go find her and rescue her from that guy." Then Marcie looked directly at Hamelin and said, "Look, I know you don't know where your parents are, but if you did, you'd do exactly what I'm planning on doing. You'd go look for them."

After some time, Marcie got up, kissed him on the cheek, and walked away.

Hamelin watched her go and wished he had known what to say. Especially the next day.

Chapter 22

Marcie

WHEN HAMELIN GOT UP THE NEXT MORNING, IT WAS obvious something was going on, and whatever it was, it wasn't good. The older boys and girls were rushing around the house, and he could hear them call, "Marcie! Marcie! You in here?"

Every room, closet, and potential hiding place was being searched. Obviously, Marcie was missing. As soon as Hamelin hollered out, "I saw her in the old shed yesterday," two boys rushed off in that direction. When Hamelin got outside, there were two sheriff's cars driving up and people from the town starting to gather.

"Okay, we'll have to go through these woods," said a man in a sheriff's uniform who looked like he was in charge. The outdoor search soon started, and in the meantime, Hamelin told David Rivers about Marcie crying in the shed after the Stephensons drove away in their trailer. That her parents had just left her. David told the sheriff and some other adults, so they talked to Hamelin to hear the story from him, but there wasn't much more to tell. Except he forgot to mention California, which he was later glad about.

Even the county commissioners came out to search, but nothing in the houses, sheds, or woods gave them any clues. There was no note, and her few clothes were still there, except for what she had worn yesterday. Marcie had just vanished.

By late afternoon, more people from Middleton had come out, including people from the school, like Mr. Burleson; Mrs. Eastland, a fourth-grade teacher; and even Mr. Litchie, who didn't go into the woods but did look very concerned. When night came, the searches were stopped. The word from the sheriff was that she appeared to be a runaway—no signs of foul play—and that he had already put out her description to other law enforcement officers and agencies. "She'll turn up," he was heard to say, but Hamelin wasn't that hopeful. Marcie was tough—tougher than he was—and if she ran away, as he figured, she wouldn't be easily found. And she certainly wouldn't come back on her own.

That night, Hamelin went back to the boys' room when it was bedtime, and long after everyone else had gone to sleep, he sat on the side of his bed, thinking about Marcie.

Finally, he put on his pajamas, pulled the covers back, and got in bed. He lay on his right side and patted the pillow under his cheek and neck, but as he did so, he felt something under the pillow. It was a piece of paper. He reached under the pillow and pulled it out. He fished around for a small flashlight that he kept in the apple crate of stuff by his bed. He pulled the covers over his head and clicked on the flashlight. It was a note. From Marcie.

Hamelin,

By the time you read this, you'll know I'm gone. Please don't tell anyone what we talked about or where I said I was going to go. It'll make it easier for them to find me. I'll miss you, and I won't forget what I said, that I'll try to get my mom to adopt you. I really think she would, and I can talk her into it.

Please don't be sad. I hope to see you again. And please don't be mad at me. You're the only one here I'll really miss, and I hope you'll miss me.

But I know you'd do the same thing if you knew where to find your own parents. I think I know where my mom is, so I've got to go rescue her.

Love,
Marcie

Hamelin lay awake in bed a long time that night. He knew deep down that he couldn't tell anybody about the note. Marcie had asked him to keep it a secret, and he would. But that wasn't all he thought about. It was the way she put it. What she had said to him twice now—that he would do the same thing if he knew where to find his own parents.

He remembered the eagle's words. Was that what the eagle was referring to when he used the words "your own"? Hamelin stared into the darkness, wondering.

A rumor went around later on—some said it was started by Ken Tomson at the Dairy Dream—that a girl matching Marcie's description had been seen early on the morning she disappeared getting into a '49 Chrysler just north of the children's home, but nothing ever came of it. Marcie was gone, and there were no other clues. Hamelin hoped she found her mom.

Chapter 23

A New Couple Arrives

FOR ONCE IT SEEMED THE COUNTY COMMISSIONERS DID something right. Instead of there being no one who would come to work at the Upton County Children's Home, the county had scarcely placed its ad looking for new house parents when the job was filled. A middle-aged couple (he was fifty, she was forty-eight) by the names of John and Margaret Kaley quickly appeared on the scene. The Kaleys' very presence immediately brightened the faded colors of the children's home.

Mrs. Kaley's hair was light brown, showing a few streaks of gray, but stylishly wavy and almost to her shoulders before curling up slightly. Her clothes were colorful, and she almost always wore dresses, not slacks. She no longer looked as thin as she probably had been at a younger age, but she was still lovely, and her face was softened by her daily touches of makeup.

Mr. Kaley was tall with slightly rounded shoulders and big hands that were either shyly stuffed in his pockets or busy patting someone on the back. His gray hair, quick smile, and easy sounding voice went well with his large, happy eyes. Unlike the Stephensons, the Kaleys appeared really glad to be at the home and eager to work with the children. They were talkative and quick to learn everyone's name, and the kids were surprised—and at first didn't know what to do— when Mrs. Kaley suddenly hugged them or Mr. Kaley patted them on the shoulder or offered a friendly handshake.

By the second week of June, the Kaleys had moved in, and the whole atmosphere of the children's home had changed, from the food to how things looked. The Kaleys made everything better. The children noticed that the furniture they brought with them was very nice. "They must have some money," whispered one of the boys. And the Kaleys didn't mind at all having the children see their apartment (some of the kids had never seen it when the Stephensons lived there) or help them move in. And when two of the boys were carrying a big piece of wooden furniture (Mr. Kaley's chest of drawers) and accidentally bumped the edge of it on the threshold of the apartment door, Mrs. Kaley acted as though she didn't even notice the scratch they left on the chest. "That's all right, just put it over here, boys," she had said.

But that wasn't all. From the day they arrived, the Kaleys worked to fix up the home. They enlisted support from one of the women's clubs and two of the churches in town, and soon there were several teams of adults from Middleton painting inside and out, rewaxing the floors, putting new linoleum in the kitchen and bathrooms, installing new cabinets in the kitchen, replacing most of the old chairs and tables in the dining room, and generally cleaning the main building and the two girls' houses. Everything got reorganized, and a lot of things were stored or even thrown away in the process of cleaning out closets and spaces beneath the beds.

It was an amazing change. By July, everything was finished. In fact, the week before, the Kaleys had already begun to plan a celebration, a Fourth of July party at the children's home with ice cream, hot dogs, barbecue, and hamburgers, and all the people from the town who had helped fix the place up—plus quite a few others—were invited. It was a big party. When it got dark, they set off some firecrackers and Roman candles. Hamelin and all the other children laughed and cheered and enjoyed themselves so much that, for maybe the first time ever, they were proud to be there.

But that wasn't all. That night, right after the fireworks ended, Mrs. Kaley, who was already putting away the leftovers, saw Hamelin and said, "Well, Hamelin, I hope you've had a good day."

"Yes, ma'am, I have."

"That's good," said Mrs. Kaley. "I'm so glad. And I see you have another big day coming up soon."

"Uh, yeah, I guess so," said Hamelin. He shrugged because he had no idea what she was talking about.

"My goodness, Hamelin," she said, seeing his reaction. "I'm talking about your birthday! I see from my list that you have a birthday next week. You'll be nine years old!"

"Oh, yeah, I . . . I know," Hamelin said, thinking how stupid his reply sounded.

"What a wonderful age!" she said with hardly a pause.

Hamelin almost couldn't believe his ears. Mrs. Kaley was still talking, but his mind wandered to last year, his forgotten birthday, running away—and his failure. He looked down and started feeling small inside, but Mrs. Kaley just kept talking. He tried to pull his thoughts back to listen—

". . . We'll have lots of fun too," she said cheerfully. Then she suddenly got quiet. He noticed and looked up at her. She stared at him, her lips pulled in and her eyes narrowed, as if she was searching his face for something. The silence felt strange, but Hamelin was afraid to say anything, afraid he might say the wrong thing or accidentally say too much about last year's birthday. But just as quickly, Mrs. Kaley smiled, her eyes widened, and she turned away with a nod and continued to put away the leftovers from the barbecue while Hamelin walked off to help the boys put up the chairs that had been used for the celebration.

That night, as he lay in bed, his mind was full. The Kaleys were nice people. Though they were older, Hamelin couldn't help thinking that they were like the parents he had often wished for. The Fourth of July party that day had been fun, with families from the town coming out to the children's home, and now even the home itself looked and felt better.

He was almost asleep when he remembered that Mrs. Kaley was planning a birthday party. And then his mind wandered back to the events of his birthday last year, and he fell asleep thinking about the cave, the eagle, and the bridge.

Chapter 24

Hamelin's Big Surprise

THE NEXT SIX DAYS PASSED SLOWLY FOR HAMELIN. THE Fourth of July had been on Monday, so his birthday, July 10, would be the next Sunday.

Every day between the fourth and the tenth, Hamelin got up early and did his chores and whatever else he could to help around the home. He was glad for every opportunity he had to be around Mrs. Kaley. She seemed happy to see him too. He kept hoping she would talk more about the party, but she was more interested in other topics.

She asked Hamelin questions about the children's home, about its routines, and also about the other children. He told her about David Rivers, Marceya, and of course Bryan and Layla. But on Wednesday, Mrs. Kaley's questions turned to Hamelin.

"How long have you lived here?" she asked. "How'd you get to be here?"

Hamelin told her everything he knew, the story Mrs. Frendle loved to tell about finding him on the porch, or the stoop, as she had called it, along with a note.

"And your family?" she asked. "Do you know anything about them?"

"No," said Hamelin. "There's nobody. At least nobody I know of . . ."

"Oh," she said, "I see. And how do you know that July tenth is your birthday?"

"That's the day Mrs. Frendle found me, so that's the day she counted as my birthday."

"So you must have been a newborn baby when they found you."

"That's what everyone says. Why?"

Mrs. Kaley shrugged and smiled, but it seemed to Hamelin that she was trying to act like she was just curious. He noticed her interest, but he didn't think about it much, since she went on to ask him about the kinds of food and cake he liked. He figured she was asking for his birthday, so he was glad to talk about that.

When he woke up on Friday morning, July 8, he got excited that the countdown was nearly done. Only today and tomorrow, and then the next time he would wake up, it would be his birthday. He had never looked forward to a birthday so much, and especially now that the Kaleys were there and everything was so much better.

It turned out that his biggest birthday surprise actually arrived at seven o'clock that evening. It was just after supper, and the children were clearing away the plates and other dishes from the dining room when Hamelin heard a car pull up in front. He heard somebody at the door and then some excited voices. He thought for just a moment that he recognized those voices—he was almost sure he did. He ran from the dining room area to the small foyer at the front door.

He could hardly believe what he saw. Standing next to Mr. and Mrs. Kaley, with their overnight bags already on the floor and big smiles on their faces, looking straight at him to see what his reaction would be, were Bryan and Layla!

Hamelin stopped. Everyone standing around was quiet. Then Layla broke the silence: "Hamelin!" she screamed as she held out her arms. He ran straight to her. He didn't even hear Bryan say a second later, "Hey, Buddy!"

Hamelin buried his face on Layla's shoulder, right into her curly brown hair, as she bent down to get his hug. He had never hugged anyone so tight in all his life—until ten seconds later, when he turned to Bryan, who stood there smiling. Bryan kneeled down on one knee so that he and Hamelin were about the same size, and Hamelin hugged him as hard as he could.

For a second, he felt his eyes burn, and he was afraid he was going to start crying. But Layla said quickly, "Oh! We surprised you, didn't we, Hamelin?"

"Yeah, you did," he said. "How did you get here?"

"We drove in my car," said Bryan with excitement in his voice. "Come see."

Everyone rushed outside, and there in the driveway in front of the children's home was a blue sedan, almost as old as David Rivers's car, but it looked as shiny and wonderful as any new car.

"Where'd you get it?" asked Hamelin with excitement as he ran toward the car and looked inside the driver's window at the interior.

"Back in Abilene," said Bryan.

"Bryan's been saving his money for two years," said Layla. "He just got this car about two weeks ago, so we decided that for our first road trip, we'd surprise you and come back here to celebrate your birthday."

"So you're staying for my party on Sunday?"

"Well," said Mrs. Kaley, "that's another surprise. We thought we'd have your big party *tomorrow*, because of some special surprises we planned for Saturday."

Hamelin's eyes got big.

"We know Sunday is July tenth, but since Layla and Bryan could be here tonight and tomorrow, and because"— Mrs. Kaley looked at Mr. Kaley, whose eyes widened— "we have some *sur-pris-es*," she said in a singsong voice, "we thought we'd have your party *to-mor-row*! Is that okay?"

"Sure!" he said with no hesitation.

"Hey, Hamelin," said Mr. Kaley, "seeing these two is a pretty good birthday present already, right?"

Hamelin's face was his answer. He hardly knew what to do, so to do something, and maybe also just to make sure they stayed, he grabbed Layla's bag and tried to get Bryan's too before Bryan got it. The Kaleys, who had known ahead of time about the surprise visit, had already made plans to have Bryan and Layla spend the night in their apartment. It had a small guest room, and the Kaleys had arranged the double bed for Layla and an extra rollaway bed for Bryan. They would get to be with Hamelin that evening and all the next day for his birthday before leaving early Sunday morning.

That evening was the real start of Hamelin's birthday. Hamelin, Bryan, and Layla, plus the Kaleys, sat downstairs in the living room and gathered in a circle around the coffee table. The kitchen staff brought out some cakes and cookies for everyone. They poured Hamelin a big glass of cold milk, while Bryan and the Kaleys had hot cups of coffee. Layla didn't drink coffee, but Mrs. Kaley offered her hot tea, and the ladies in the kitchen were glad to brew it for her.

Hamelin had never before understood how adults could enjoy just sitting around and talking, but that night he wanted it to go on forever.

"Well, Bryan and Layla," began Mrs. Kaley, "we are learning a lot about Hamelin, but tell us about yourselves."

"Yes," added Mr. Kaley, "and if you don't mind, please tell us how you came to live here at the children's home."

It was a story that Hamelin knew only a little about, so he listened, but Bryan gave few details. He told briefly how he and Layla and their parents were driving to their aunt's house and that there was a terrible accident in which their mother and father both had died.

Bryan grew quiet and looked down into his coffee cup. He shook his head very slowly, as if saying no, and Hamelin thought there must be some things he couldn't, or wouldn't, tell.

When Bryan didn't continue, Layla picked up the story as he continued to stare into his cup. "Afterward, we lived in Alpine, Texas, with our aunt, our mother's older sister. But she developed health problems and grew too frail to take care of us. She hated giving us up, but eventually we came here to the children's home. She's still alive, but . . ."

Layla stopped there, and the thought crossed Hamelin's mind that his story wasn't as sad as theirs—although he had never known his parents, at least he hoped they were still alive.

Mrs. Kaley shifted in her chair and smiled softly at Layla. Mr. Kaley was sitting close enough to Bryan to reach out and pat him on the shoulder.

"I'm sorry to hear that," said Mrs. Kaley. Then she folded her hands and said, "So, what can you tell us about your time here? The staff and children."

Bryan and Layla told them stories about the children who had come and gone during their years at the home and about Mrs. Regehr, Mrs. Frendle, and Mr. Moore, who was still there. And, of course, they talked about Hamelin. They told with laughter—and lots of interruptions as they kept adding more and more details—how excited everyone was the day he was found and about how Mrs. Frendle had told the story over and over of how she had found him in a tomato box out by the milk bottles on the side stoop. And they described in detail—because the Kaleys kept asking—how he was cared for as a baby, that he had stayed at night with Mrs. Regehr and during the day in the kitchen with Mrs. Frendle.

For Hamelin, hearing Bryan and Layla tell those stories gave him a warm feeling—maybe he did have a home and a past and a family after all.

And then the Kaleys asked him about his memories of the home and the people there. The words tumbled out so quickly that he didn't even think about them. He told Mr. and Mrs. Kaley how Bryan and Layla had taken care of him, how they had been like a big brother and big sister to him, how Bryan used to watch out for him and let him tag along when he was playing with the bigger boys, and how Layla used to read him books.

And, without planning it, Hamelin added, "And Bryan and Layla never forgot my birthday, even after they left." He paused and then just blurted out, "Even last year they remembered my birthday and sent me a card." No one really knew what Hamelin meant when he said "even last year," but they all glanced at one another and realized that last year's birthday must have been difficult for him.

Everyone was quiet for a few moments. Then Layla, wanting to brighten the awkward silence, said, "Well, Hamelin,

I know tomorrow is your big birthday party, but I have a present for you that I want you to open tonight, since you've mentioned how much we used to read together."

Hamelin knew as soon as she handed him the brightly colored package—it was wrapped in blue-and-red-striped paper with a red bow on top—that it would be a book. But still he couldn't wait to see it, because a book from Layla would be special.

He ripped open the package, and sure enough, inside was a book titled *The Princess and the Goblin* by George MacDonald.

"It's a wonderful book," said Layla. "I've read it myself many times. It's all about a boy who has to find his way in life and who meets some wonderful friends and has exciting, magical adventures. You'll love it."

"Thanks, Layla," he said, and before he even thought about it, he hugged her neck. Hamelin didn't know what else to say, but when he stepped back and looked at Layla and saw her wide, glistening eyes, he knew that she knew how grateful he was.

"Hey, let's not get too excited here," exclaimed Bryan with a coy look. "I've got a present for you too, but you're not getting it 'til tomorrow. Because I follow the rules of birthday presents." He winked and jabbed Hamelin in the side. They all laughed.

"Well," said Mrs. Kaley, "maybe it's time for Hamelin to go to bed."

Hamelin knew that it was already well past his normal bedtime, so he didn't complain. He hugged Layla again and tried to give Bryan a jab in the ribs, which Bryan easily blocked while quickly giving him a soft pop on the head.

"Gotcha," said Bryan.

"Hey!" said Hamelin. "I'll get you tomorrow."

He headed to his room, but then he turned, waited for a second, and hugged Mrs. Kaley. Then Mr. Kaley patted him on the back. Hamelin hardly knew what to think—he had gotten probably the best hugs of his life all on the same day. He held his new book in both hands and ran up the stairs to bed. He put the book away—he would read it as soon as Bryan and Layla left. In the meantime, as he undressed, he felt quiet on the inside. He thought about trying to say a prayer because he had the feeling you feel when you want to tell somebody thank you. But except for the blessing for the food that Mr. or Mrs. Kaley usually gave before the evening meals, Hamelin didn't know much about praying, so he just lay quietly in bed thinking. As he lay there, he thought he could hear Bryan and Layla still talking with the Kaleys downstairs. He wondered what they were talking about, but it didn't really matter. Tomorrow would be a special day.

Chapter 25

The Big Day: Hamelin's Birthday Party

THE NEXT MORNING, HAMELIN WOKE UP MUCH EARLIER than usual and almost jumped out of bed. But to his surprise, he was not the first one up. As he dressed, he could hear men working outside.

"Over here!" someone shouted.

"Where? A little more over here?" came the reply.

"No, no, back up, back up a little . . . *there*."

"Okay, okay."

"That's it! That ought to be about right."

Every now and then, he thought he could hear Mr. Kaley's voice too: "No, a little bit to the left, a little bit more . . . whoa! That's it! Good job, boys. I think right there should do it. Okay, let's get 'er put together!"

Hamelin raced down the steps to see what was going on. Somehow he knew it was going to be something special.

And special it was—in the big yard on the south side of the house, three men were hard at work, with Mr. Kaley busily supervising and Mrs. Kaley occasionally offering some advice.

The Kaleys both waved at him, but they were too busy right then to talk. Hamelin stood nearby and watched, but he wasn't sure what the workers were doing. They were driving wooden stakes in the ground every few feet, and, as it began to appear, the stakes were being put in a large circle, some thirty-five feet in diameter.

With the stakes in the ground, the workers went back to their truck to unload something big. The Kaleys then quickly walked over to Hamelin with big smiles on their faces, and Mr. Kaley said, "Well, what do you think?"

"I don't know. What is it?" he asked.

"You'll have to wait and *see-ee*," Mrs. Kaley said in a sing-songy voice, just as she had done the night before.

This had to be the other special surprise Mrs. Kaley had mentioned. The men placed a tough plastic floor on the ground and replaced the ordinary wooden stakes with perfectly round ones. The new stakes fit into some holes dug all around the outside circle of the blue plastic bottom. Then some stronger sheets of plastic were rolled out to create an outside wall, about four feet high, which went around the entire floor in a perfect circle.

Finally, it dawned on Hamelin what they doing, and he couldn't hold it back any longer. "It's a swimming pool!"

"It is!" said Mr. Kaley, beaming to see Hamelin's look of surprise.

"You're exactly right," said Mrs. Kaley with a big smile. "It's for your birthday party."

"Really?"

"Yes," she said. "Of course, it's not just for you; it's for all the children. We'll all share it, especially on these hot summer days. We just thought that your birthday would be the perfect time to get it—especially with Bryan and Layla here."

It took almost no time for the men to get the walls of the pool put up. Then they placed a ladder on the side and a small pump so that small amounts of chemicals could be added and the water could be circulated to keep it clean. The workers also started emptying a large tank of water they had brought with them into the pool. To help things along, Mr. Kaley, Hamelin, and David Rivers also rigged up all the garden hoses they could find and hooked them to the five outside faucets of the children's home. Before long, water was pouring into the pool from the hoses as well.

"Well," said the head worker, a man named Bill, "we know our tank ain't near enough to fill that pool up, but it'll give her a good head start. You've got good pressure out here, so with all them outside faucets turned on all the way, that thing will fill pretty quick, soon enough for the kids to start splashin' around sometime today."

Mrs. Kaley looked a little concerned. "Today? I sure hope so! What time today?"

"Well, ma'am," Bill said slowly, "let's see here . . ." He squinted one eye and cocked his head. "Since that pool holds about twenty-five thousand gallons of water . . . with all them hoses going, I'm guessin' it'll be 'bout midafternoon."

But no matter how long it would take to fill the pool, it was already the most exciting thing going on at the Upton County Children's Home.

The older children wondered how the home got the pool, since they'd never been given nice things before by the county. One of the ladies who worked in the kitchen whispered to some of the older girls that she was pretty sure the Kaleys had paid for it out of their own pockets.

Whoever provided it, the children were all laughing and talking with excitement. By the time the men had loaded their truck and were driving away, all the children and most of the staff were watching it fill up.

"Hey, Hamelin, what a great party *you're* going to have!" said a thirteen-year-old boy by the name of John Felix. Of course, Hamelin knew what Mrs. Kaley said about the pool being for everyone, but he also thought maybe the Kaleys wanted to make him feel special on this day, and they certainly had.

If possible, things got even better. Bryan and Layla were also up. The Kaleys had told them about the pool the night before, so they were standing in the front yard, smiling at the fun that Hamelin and all the other children were having as they watched the pool being filled with water.

Then Mrs. Kaley appeared again on the front porch. "Okay, everybody. Come inside for *break-fast!*" And Hamelin heard her do it again—she used a sweet singing voice to say the two syllables, "break-fast." And she clapped her hands and yelled, "A watched pool never fills!" She giggled at her own joke as she went back into the house.

Mr. Kaley rolled his eyes, shrugged, and then, with a wink and a smile, said to all the children still standing there, "Well, I guess we have no choice—it's time for '*break-fast.*'" He imitated the singsongy voice, and they all laughed as they hurried into the dining room.

They smelled it before they saw it, but what they saw were huge platters of eggs, pancakes, sausage, biscuits, and gravy. All of Hamelin's favorite foods were there, and Bryan and Layla just stared, amazed at how much the food had improved since they lived at the home.

As soon as the Kaleys had been hired, they had immediately looked for a new head cook. They wanted someone who would live at the home in order to improve the food

for the children. Mrs. Carroll, who had replaced Mrs. Frendle, was glad to remain as kitchen staff but have someone
else take over as head cook. Mrs. Daly had resigned, and
Mr. Kaley and the new head cook now took care of ordering
all the food.

The new cook, Mrs. Lorena Parker, was perfect for the job.
The Kaleys had found her in the little town of Paint Rock, which
was about a hundred fifty miles east of Middleton in Concho
County. Mrs. Parker was a widow who had raised several children and helped out with raising a lot of grandchildren as well.
But now even her grandchildren had grown up and moved
away, and, except for holidays, she didn't see them very much.
She was short and had a round face with wavy gray hair and a
smile that quickly displayed her front teeth and her wrinkled
cheeks. And everyone loved to be around her.

Mrs. Parker's sole delight in life was to cook and make others happy with her food: huge breakfasts, hot lunches, and,
when school started, big lunch bags for the children (always
with sandwiches, cookies, and a piece of fruit), not to mention the full suppers every evening. For breakfasts, the menu
would vary day by day. There were always boxes of cold cere-
als, but she often would have other things as well: sausage,
bacon, or ham; eggs or muffins; and pancakes or oatmeal.

For cooked lunches and dinners, she would rotate
the meals among roasts, hamburgers, tacos, big bowls of
chili and beans, chicken, fish (baked or fried), spaghetti,
lasagna, and, when Mr. Kaley's kitchen budget allowed it,
even sirloin steaks. And one of her real specialties, which
everyone loved, was chicken and dumplings.

There were always big bowls of vegetables—mashed
potatoes, green beans (she liked to mix a little extra ham in
with the beans), spinach, asparagus, broccoli (usually with

cheese sauce on the asparagus and broccoli), corn (whether still on the cob or shelled in the pan), baked potatoes, sweet potatoes—and always some kind of salad, whether a mixed salad, a potato salad, or a fruit salad. And if it was a special meal, she might add one of her bouncy green or orange congealed salads with fruit and flavors mixed together. The kids started calling it "green stuff" or "orange stuff." And they loved it.

And Mrs. Parker specialized in making (and sampling) desserts: chocolate layer cake (probably everyone's favorite), strawberry cake, chocolate sheet cake, vanilla cake with chocolate icing, chocolate cake with vanilla icing, and the best—and for some, the first—carrot cake the kids had ever eaten. Her pies made the whole house smell like a baker's shop. Coming into the house about midafternoon had become a special experience in new favorite smells for the children and staff. She made apple pies, cherry pies, chocolate pies, coconut cream pies (or coconut with meringue), special cherry cheese pies (with a vanilla cream pudding and cherry syrup on top, whipped cream optional), peach pies, lemon pies, and her all-time favorite, banana pudding.

By the time Hamelin's birthday weekend rolled around, Mrs. Parker had already been on the job for nearly two weeks and, meal after meal, had provided daily surprises with her food for all the residents of the home.

Since it was his birthday, Hamelin got to request his favorites for all the meals, so he had asked for pancakes with lots of syrup and hot butter to be added to the regular full fare of breakfast dishes. For lunch, he wanted hamburgers, and for supper, after his late afternoon party, he wanted chilidogs and baked beans, to be topped off with chocolate cake and ice cream for dessert.

He thought it was already an exciting day, and here it was only breakfast. Mr. Kaley even said a prayer before breakfast, giving thanks for the food and for Hamelin on his birthday. When Hamelin lifted his head from the prayer, he was a little embarrassed, but his world felt big.

After breakfast, he was allowed to skip chores for that day—a new practice for celebrating birthdays since the Kaleys arrived. He was glad since he was looking forward to spending time with Bryan and Layla. They walked all around the grounds of the home, and Bryan and Layla reminisced about their time there, talking about things they had done at different places, whether in the woods, at the pond out behind the house, or someplace else nearby. Then they asked Hamelin about school and his friends. He wanted to tell them about last year and his experiences in the cave, but he never could seem to get his mouth and mind together.

They caught Hamelin up on what they were doing. Bryan was working for a bank during the day and attending night classes at Hardin-Simmons, a small college in Abilene. Layla was a student at the same college. She was majoring in literature and guessed she would need at least five or six years to graduate, since she was taking small loads and working as well. They were sharing an apartment and making some new friends.

"Hey, Bryan," Hamelin said. "Do you have a girlfriend?"

"Umm, no, not really," Bryan answered, but he winked at Hamelin.

"How about you, Layla? I bet you have a boyfriend!"

"Not yet!" Layla answered. But she smiled even though she sounded like she was scolding.

Hamelin took them inside the children's home and showed them all around. Even though they knew every inch of it well, the Kaleys had done so much to change things that it almost seemed like a different place.

Layla especially was amazed at all the new touches. "I'm really happy for you and all the other kids, Hamelin. The Kaleys have done so much to make things better."

The morning raced by, and it wasn't long before it was lunchtime.

"Hey, Hamelin," said Bryan, "let's take another quick look at the swimming pool." The two of them raced off, saw that it was a little over half full, and went back to the house for lunch.

Mr. Kaley made a few announcements, explained to everyone about the new swimming pool, and gave out some important safety rules. He told them how many people could be in the pool at once and explained that there always had to be a "buddy system," since no one could swim alone. He also said there always had to be at least one of the older children or a staff member outside the pool watching when others were swimming. The children didn't seem to mind the rules; they were just thrilled even to have the pool.

Before long, Mrs. Parker brought out her hamburgers, and they dug into them. For dessert, she made her "cowboy" cookies—huge combinations of oatmeal and chocolate chip cookies, every one of them at least four inches in diameter and extra thick. She talked constantly while she passed the heaping plates of warm cookies around—"In my family, some like oatmeal cookies and others chocolate chip, so I just combined the recipes, made them big, and called them 'cowboy' cookies!"

"Yee-haw!" yelled Mr. Kaley as he grabbed two cookies. "Better give me some more!"

"Oh, John," said Mrs. Kaley, and everyone laughed.

After lunch, the afternoon flew by. Bryan spent some time talking with Mr. Kaley—probably, Hamelin thought, telling him more about how things were at the children's home back when he was there.

Layla and Hamelin sat in the small living room on the first floor.

"I miss reading to you, Hamelin," she said.

"Me too. I miss that a lot."

"Sometimes I wish you were with Bryan and me just so I could tell you about my classes and the books I'm reading."

"Really?" said Hamelin, his eyes wide.

Layla realized what Hamelin was thinking. "Oh . . . Hamelin, Bryan and I miss you a lot . . . but of course they'd never let you live with us now. We're too young, and we barely have enough money to take care of ourselves. I hope you understand."

Hamelin looked at the floor and tried to smile. She patted him on the shoulder.

"But things are better here now," Layla continued. "They're taking good care of you."

The two sat in silence. Finally, Hamelin asked, "So, what new stories have you read?"

"Wonderful new stories and new authors. I'm reading British authors like Chaucer, Shakespeare, and Milton—plus quite a few others." Layla went on to tell Hamelin about several American authors like Washington Irving, Mark Twain, and O. Henry. He was especially interested to hear about the strange tales of Washington Irving and the surprise endings of O. Henry.

She also told him about the book she got him, *The Princess and the Goblin*, but she gave him only a little taste of it;

she didn't want to spoil the story. It sounded exciting, and he couldn't wait to read about the magical events in it.

"Maybe one day you'll read *Lilith*, also by George Mac-Donald. It's my favorite so far," she said. "It's all about a man who follows a raven through a fireplace and ends up in another world."

Right then, Hamelin's stomach tightened. He knew he had his chance to tell Layla about his strange experience with the eagle, but just as he opened his mouth, David Rivers walked up and said, "Hi, Layla! Glad you and Bryan are here." They talked for a moment, and when David left and she turned back to Hamelin, he hesitated. *She'll probably think I'm just making it all up*, he thought.

"Let's go see what Bryan is doing," Layla said. They stood up, and the moment was gone.

The day wasn't over yet, but already Hamelin dreaded that it would end too soon. He tried not to think about that, but he knew, even on a wonderful day, that something was off. Whatever it was, it kept pulling at him. Like he was supposed to be somewhere else, but he had missed it.

Chapter 26

The Party Continues

AS HAMELIN AND LAYLA STARTED OUT THE DOOR, BRYAN was just coming in.

"Hey, Hamelin, I want to give you the present I have for you, without all the other kids around." Bryan pulled out a box about two inches wide and five inches long. It was wrapped in plain brown paper with a string around it. Hamelin could tell that Bryan had wrapped it, not Layla.

He took the gift, tore off the paper, and opened the box. Inside was a shiny new red Swiss Army knife. It had every kind of blade on it, plus several other attachments, including a small pair of scissors.

"It's great!" said Hamelin. The look in his eyes also told Bryan how happy he was to get it.

"Be careful with it," said Bryan. "You want to make sure that little kids don't play with it. And keep it in your pocket and always know where it is. You can have lots of fun with a knife like that, and it can come in handy when you least expect it."

Bryan showed him how to open and close it safely. When Hamelin tried, Layla said, "Hamelin, please be careful!"

"He knows how to handle it," Bryan reassured her with a wink.

Hamelin gave Bryan a big hug and then, just for good measure, gave Layla one as well. He finally said, in a rush, "Thanks for visiting me. I'm really glad to see you. I . . . I love the book and the knife and everything . . . and I . . ." He paused, finding it hard to say what he was thinking. Layla felt his struggle.

"We love you, Hamelin," she said, "and we miss you a lot." Bryan nodded and squeezed him on the shoulder. Hamelin realized he didn't have to finish his sentence.

They stood there silently for a moment longer. Then Bryan spoke up, "Remember, you always have to keep your pocketknife with you. You never know when you'll need it."

"I will," said Hamelin. "I'll remember what you told me."

Layla smiled and a tear formed at the edge of her right eye.

"Hey, let's go check on the new pool," said Bryan. "Maybe it's full by now."

When they arrived, everyone was standing around, watching them as they approached.

"Hamelin," said Mr. Kaley, "we're waiting on you! The pool is ready, but *you're* the birthday boy, so you get the first jump in the pool."

"Hurry and get your swimming trunks on!" yelled Mrs. Kaley.

Hamelin ran straight upstairs, put on his swimming suit as fast as he could, and raced back down to the yard. Bryan and Layla also hurried off to change and got back to the pool just a minute after Hamelin.

With everybody assembled and ready, Mrs. Kaley nodded at Hamelin. He climbed to the top step of the ladder and looked down at the water, which was softly rippling and shooting flashes of sunlight into his eyes. For just a split second, though, he thought he saw something dark and shadowy at the bottom of the pool, something waving at him, inviting him to come. Hamelin hesitated. He thought of the eagle and the darkness below the narrow footbridge.

Then he heard, or thought he heard, an older girl's voice whisper loudly—it was similar to Layla's—"*Please hurry!*" Then he heard another voice like it, but closer, and it was Layla's for sure—"Come on, Hamelin!"

And so he jumped; it was a magnificent cannonball with a huge splash and boom. He was quickly followed by fourteen other screaming children.

The afternoon could not have been more glorious. It was a hot July day in southwest Texas, and the kids jumped, swam, played games, and splashed one another. Mrs. Kaley rotated groups of fifteen about every twenty minutes so that everyone could get in. Hamelin had never had so much fun.

As he climbed out of the pool after the first twenty minutes, he noticed Mr. and Mrs. Kaley talking privately to Bryan and Layla.

"Hey, Hamelin, come here for a second," Bryan hollered. Hamelin quickly jogged over to where the four of them were standing. "Show Mr. Kaley that spot on your foot."

"Oh," said Hamelin, "you mean the clown's hat?"

"Yeah," said Bryan, "that's it."

With that, Hamelin lifted his right foot, and Mr. Kaley kneeled to inspect it. Bryan stood at Hamelin's side and gave him a forearm to lean on.

"That's a pretty unusual marking, isn't it, Hamelin?" asked Mr. Kaley.

"Yeah, I guess so," he said.

"Where'd you get it?" asked Mrs. Kaley.

"I don't know," said Hamelin, "it's always been there."

"At least as long as we've known him," said Bryan.

"It doesn't look like an ordinary birthmark," said Mr. Kaley. "It's almost like a tattoo, but not like any I've ever seen."

Hamelin shrugged as he hopped once and then put his foot down.

"That's interesting," said Mr. Kaley. He looked like he wanted to say more, but he just shot a look at Mrs. Kaley and then said, "Well, we were just curious, that's all. Bryan had mentioned it. Thanks . . . I hope you don't mind."

"Naw," said Hamelin, "it's always been there. Sometimes kids laugh at it, but mostly no one notices, since it's on my foot."

About that time, Mrs. Parker appeared at the front door and yelled, "Hot dogs will be ready in fifteen minutes!"

"Great!" said Mr. Kaley. "That'll give us enough time to finish this group in the pool before we eat. Then maybe another group or two can go after dinner."

"Hamelin," said Mrs. Kaley, "you're the birthday boy, so you'd better go get dressed. We want to make sure you're first in line for the . . ." She paused dramatically, and then sang, "*Chi-li-dogs!*"

Hamelin cheered and ran off to get ready.

Soon the party was ready to start. Hamelin was the first to build his chilidog, and he made a huge one. He started with a base of mustard and ketchup on the bun, then he added the hot dog, poured a big ladle of chili, and finally topped it off with a sprinkle of cheese. He decided to wait until his second hot dog to try out the green pickle relish and the chopped onions. Potato chips and baked beans finished off his first plate. By the time he and most of the other kids had finished off their second hot dog (a few even had three), Mrs. Kaley announced that it was time for the birthday cake.

At that moment, Mrs. Parker appeared, proudly holding the biggest chocolate layer cake any of them had ever seen. "And when you eat all this," she announced, "I've got three sheet cakes—vanilla cake with chocolate icing—to go with it."

Mr. Kaley lit the nine candles on the cake, and everyone sang "Happy Birthday." At the end of the song, Hamelin quietly made his wish and blew out all the candles in one big blow. Everyone cheered and then enjoyed the ice cream and cake. It was Hamelin's best birthday party ever.

He stayed up as late as he could that night, talking to Bryan and Layla, but the evening ended all too quickly for him.

"We'll come back as soon as we can," Bryan assured him. And Layla promised to write for them both. Then she and Bryan went to their room to pack. They had to make an early start in the morning.

As Hamelin lay on his bed that night, his mind was full of thoughts. It had been a day he would never forget. He kept thinking about the party, the new swimming pool, the pocketknife, and the book. And he thought about all the little things that Layla and Bryan had said. And the Kaleys. Somehow—Hamelin wasn't sure why—it all mixed in with his thoughts about last year and the cave and the eagle. But as good as the day had been, something was still missing. If only he could have told Bryan and Layla about last year.

He finally fell asleep. He dreamed of the eagle, a pool, and a big banquet room filled with food—and a boy and a girl in strange clothes. Who were they?

And there were others—but by the next morning the dream was mostly forgotten.

———

Hamelin rolled out of bed early to see Bryan and Layla before they left. Mrs. Parker had already fixed them breakfast, and he joined them. They were all quiet at first, especially Hamelin.

"Hey, we're going to see you again as soon as we can," Bryan said. "You're really growing fast, and we've got to keep up with you and all you're doing."

"I'll write you as soon as we get back," promised Layla. "And I'll let you know about all my favorite books."

When Layla mentioned the books, vague memories of his dream flashed across Hamelin's mind. He looked back and forth at Bryan and Layla. He really needed to tell what had happened last year, but they were now about halfway through breakfast, and then Mr. and Mrs. Kaley joined them.

"Thank you so much for coming and making it such a special birthday for Hamelin," Mrs. Kaley said.

"We really enjoyed it," said Bryan. Layla nodded, but she could see that Hamelin was troubled. He fidgeted at the table, desperately wishing everyone would go away so he could talk privately to his friends. Maybe they could sneak away for just a short while.

"Layla . . ." he started.

But at the same time, Mr. Kaley said, "Well, we wish you could stay, but we know you have to get going."

Just a few minutes more! He thought Layla and Bryan would understand. They wouldn't think he was just making it up. He especially wanted to know what Layla would think. She understood strange stories. She could have helped him understand what happened in the cave and the eagle's words at the footbridge.

But now they were standing out front, saying good-bye. Bryan and Layla each gave Hamelin a long hug and then climbed into Bryan's car. They waved good-bye outside the open car windows as they drove off. Hamelin and Mr. and Mrs. Kaley stood in the front driveway waving at them.

Hamelin ran all the way out to the road so he could see as far as possible as he watched the car disappear from sight. In the distance, Bryan and Layla were still holding their arms outside their car windows waving. Hamelin wanted to scream, "Stop!" But within a minute, they were gone from sight. And it felt like he had lost them forever. He closed his eyes.

He turned back to the house, his head down. But as he walked back through the gate that separated the driveway from the front yard, he had the feeling others were nearby.

He looked up and saw the Kaleys. They were still there, waiting for him. They walked with him into the house, one on each side, with Mr. Kaley's hand on his shoulder.

They sat down again at the table with Hamelin, and Mrs. Parker brought out a giant cinnamon roll with nine candles on it.

"Happy birthday," said Mrs. Kaley softly. "I know you're sad to see them go. But this is the day you usually celebrate, so we wanted you to know we haven't forgotten." She hugged Hamelin, and Mr. Kaley patted him on the shoulder.

Thoughts of last year flashed through his mind, and he wished more than ever he could have told Layla and Bryan. He said, "Thanks," and tried to smile. He closed his eyes, made a wish, and blew out the nine candles. The Kaleys cheered and seemed so happy to celebrate his birthday, which made him feel even worse, because he had silently wished that he could be as brave as Marcie.

Chapter 27

Time Flies By

EVERYTHING WAS BETTER AT THE UPTON COUNTY CHILdren's Home now that Mr. and Mrs. Kaley were the house parents and directors of the entire operation. The food was better, the house was cleaner, and there were more activities. And the children were happier.

There were now fifty-one children, a few less than when Hamelin first arrived. He knew that Mr. and Mrs. Kaley cared about all of them, but it seemed they had a special smile for him. At times, he thought he caught them looking his way but trying not to be obvious about it.

And things at school continued to go well. David Rivers kept bullies like Patton at bay, and Hamelin really liked his fourth-grade teacher, Mrs. Virginia Eastland.

Mrs. Eastland had moved to Middleton after the death of her husband and had one child, a daughter named Amy, who was older and was away at college.

Hamelin really liked the days when Mrs. Eastland read to the class, and he also especially enjoyed it when she would take the children to the library and help them find good books to read on their own. She didn't seem to pay any attention to Mr. Litchie when he gave her a list of the children he saw whispering.

"I think I can take care of this," she told Mr. Litchie, and she didn't whisper her reply. He didn't like it, but Mrs. Eastland didn't appear to be worried about his fussy attitude. As long as the children were reasonably quiet, she let them talk with their friends about what they were reading and rummage around the bookshelves.

Because of Layla, Hamelin had read a lot and was a better reader than most fourth graders. So when he showed up at school one day with his new book, *The Princess and the Goblin*, Mrs. Eastland noticed.

"Oh, a book by George MacDonald. Where did you get that?" she asked.

"A friend gave it to me," he responded. "For my birthday."

"Well," she said, "you have a wonderful friend, because that's a very fine book. Tell me when you've finished. I'd like to hear what you think about it."

Hamelin needed no encouragement to read the book, but Mrs. Eastland's comments made him even more eager to finish it. Every day after school, after he had done his chores, he went upstairs to read.

It was a wonderful story, all about a princess, her great-great-grandmother, a magic thread, goblins, and a boy named Curdie. Hamelin was so quickly taken in by the adventures of Curdie that he could scarcely put the book down.

Still, the book was more than two hundred pages long. It took him another two weeks to finish it. There were words he didn't know at first, but he was able to guess their meanings from the surrounding text. He followed most of the story, even though some of it didn't make sense to him, and he loved it. He finished it on a Friday night, so he had to wait until the following Monday to tell Mrs. Eastland.

When Monday morning arrived, Hamelin took the book with him to school and went straight to her. "I finished it," he announced proudly.

"How wonderful!" she said. "You must tell me all about it."

And so they talked for about fifteen minutes before class started, and Mrs. Eastland smiled as Hamelin retold the story. Once he got started, he could barely hide his excitement.

"I can tell you enjoyed it," chuckled Mrs. Eastland when he finally finished.

"Yes, ma'am, I did."

"Then I'm going to make sure you have plenty of books like that to read."

"You know other books that good?"

"Oh, yes," she smiled. "Worlds of them."

And so began a pattern that lasted throughout the year. Mrs. Eastland encouraged his reading and showed him exciting books to check out of the library. Occasionally she lent him her own books, especially the kinds she knew he would like.

Hamelin grew a lot that year too. He wasn't the largest boy in his class by weight, but he was one of the tallest. His body was stronger—maybe because of Mrs. Parker's good food—and he felt good about it.

The school year, though, was soon over. That summer, Hamelin had another fun birthday party, but nothing could compare with last year's. Bryan and Layla were not able to come, but they did visit for a day in the middle of August. Both had only a few days off for vacation, so they were going to visit their elderly aunt in Alpine, who used to take care of them. She was in extremely poor health, and they wanted to see her again. But since it was not far out of the way, they made a special effort to come through Middleton just to see Hamelin.

The first thing both Bryan and Layla almost yelled when they saw him was, "Hamelin, you've grown!"

"Wow," said Bryan, "you're really getting big." He grabbed Hamelin's arms and said, "Man, feel those muscles!" Hamelin liked hearing he was bigger. He could feel it himself.

They had time to talk and walk around together. "I can't believe I'll soon be starting my *sixth* year of college," Layla moaned.

"But you're getting close," said Bryan. "And how about me? I've been going a year longer than you!"

"But you've worked so many jobs," she said.

"True, but you've worked all the time too."

"I know," said Layla. "But—"

"And you haven't changed your major even once," said Bryan.

"Yep. Still doing literature. Lots of reading."

"I'll bet that's fun to get to read so much," said Hamelin.

"It is. But we're both ready to finish," she said.

Hamelin didn't care what they were talking about. He just enjoyed being with them. He wished they could stay longer, but they had to leave for Alpine after supper. He again wanted to tell them about his experiences in the cave, but there just wasn't enough time, and he didn't want to rush the story. Before he knew it, they were gone again down the road.

Hamelin's fifth-grade year was okay. His teacher was Mr. Waverly, an older man who had once been a high school principal. Mr. Waverly really wasn't a very difficult teacher. He encouraged the students to study hard, but he didn't give them much homework. He often told them stories about the war—"WW Two," as he called it.

Sometimes Hamelin went by Mrs. Eastland's room, and she almost always had time for him. She would ask him about the books he was reading. He didn't read quite as much that year just because it wasn't as easy to talk to Mrs. Eastland. Still, Layla continued to write throughout the year, suggesting books for him to read.

But he never could get his experiences in the cave out of his mind. Hamelin thought a lot about the Great Eagle and that dreadful darkness under the bridge. He also thought more and more about the other mysteries in his life—like where he came from; that odd mark on his foot, which Mr. and Mrs. Kaley seemed so interested in; and why he had been left on the porch as a baby. Didn't his mother and father want him? Why did they leave him?

By the time the fifth grade ended, Hamelin had made a decision: he would try to find the cave again. Sometimes he wondered to himself why he had never gone back there. Deep down he knew part of the answer was that he was afraid. He had given in to his fears before at the footbridge, but he couldn't let that be the final chapter of his story.

Besides, everything he ever wanted to know about his real name, where he was from, and why he was left on the porch could be answered by his parents. And Marcie's words about finding his parents if he could kept running through his mind—but now with a further puzzle. Marcie's words had matched the similar but unfinished comment by the eagle about "your own."

Now he was wondering if all his questions about who he was might be connected to the mysteries of the cave, the bridge, and why he was summoned to follow the eagle to the Atrium of the Worlds. He became determined to find out.

Chapter 28

Searching for the Cave

NEAR THE END OF MAY, HAMELIN BEGAN TO PLAN HIS TRIP back to the cave. This time, however, he decided he would not sneak out of the house; instead, he would just ask for permission to go on a hike in the woods—no one needed to know why or where.

So on the first Friday afternoon after school had ended, Hamelin went to Mr. Kaley and asked if he could explore the woods north of the children's home after he completed his chores early the next morning.

"Well," said Mr. Kaley, "I suppose so. Any special reason?"

"I just want to see what I can find."

"You want to go alone?"

"Yes, sir. But I'll be real careful, and I'll be back by supper-time. Can I go?" Hamelin spoke in a rush and then waited.

Mr. Kaley thought a minute and then said, "Well, sure. But promise me you'll be careful. Watch for snakes—and don't do anything that might get you hurt."

"Yes, sir," said Hamelin. "I'll be careful."

So that was that. The next morning, he got up, had breakfast, did his chores quickly, and got ready to leave.

Even though it was June and already starting to get warm, he wore blue jeans and some good hiking shoes. He decided, however, to wear a short-sleeve shirt and to carry as little as possible with him. He got a sack lunch from Mrs. Parker and made sure he had his pocketknife, which he always carried with him, and at the last second he put his small flashlight in his back right pocket. By eight forty-five, he was on his way out the door.

Hamelin walked steadily northward through the woods, staying on the right side of the road. He did his best to recollect and repeat what he had done nearly three years ago. His plan was to walk about the same distance through the woods before crossing the road and then try to find the hill that had led to the cave.

Of course, he knew that it wouldn't be the same, since back then he had made his way along in the dark. Plus, now he was older and better prepared, so he'd move at a faster pace.

Hamelin recalled that three years ago he had walked for a while, had paused to eat his sandwich, and once the wind had started blowing and the rain had started coming down, had hurried across the road. He had then gone through the bar ditch on the west side of the road and immediately found himself in a patch of very dense shrubs and brushy trees. He had climbed up the rather steep side of that hill in the rain.

So after he had walked slowly for about an hour, he decided it was time to turn left out of the woods, cross the road, and see what the other side looked like.

So far, so good: he saw that, not very much farther north, there was a small range of three hills, though none of them looked as tall as the one he remembered climbing as an eight-year-old. He decided to go to the middle of the three hills since it looked taller than the others and had more trees and thicker brush going up its side.

He got even with the middle hill and began to make his way up. It was a fairly steep climb, but not as difficult as he expected. He did have to pick his way along, occasionally even using rocks for a foothold.

After about fifteen minutes of climbing, he made his way up to what could have been the ledge he had found that night nearly three years ago. The ledge looked smaller than he remembered, but, as he kept reminding himself, he really hadn't been able to see much back then—all he had was moonlight and a few lightning strikes.

This must be it, he thought. But his hopes didn't last long, because there was no sign of any opening that led into the hill. And besides, the space within this outcropping of rock didn't seem as big. The ledge itself just wasn't wide enough.

There was nothing else to do but head back down. But Hamelin wasn't going to give up easily. When he got back down to the road, he went on farther north to the next hill. He then made his way up the side of that hill just as he had done on the first, but in this case, he was even less successful: he never found a ledge. In fact, he hardly found a place to stand anywhere on the side of the hill. Before long, he had climbed up nearly the entire side of the hill and was getting close to the top, but no luck. There was nothing that he could see anywhere, even from this higher point, that looked like a ledge or the mouth of a cave. Disappointed, he made his way back down to the road.

Well, he thought, *the only thing to do now is climb that first hill*. So Hamelin walked south a short distance to try the remaining hill. He followed the same routine, but the results were the same as the last. After climbing for about twenty minutes, he could see that there was no ledge to be found. He returned to the road and, with no other hills in sight to try, decided to stop for some lunch and think. He wasn't going to give up easily.

He crossed over to the east side of the road and went back into the woods. He found a clear spot underneath a thick, old mesquite tree surrounded by several smaller ones. He took out the sack lunch that Mrs. Parker had made for him, and as he expected, it was full. There was a ham and cheese sandwich, an orange, a banana, a cookie, and something to drink. But though he was hungry, Hamelin found it hard to eat. He had taken just a few bites of the sandwich when he stuffed it back into the bag. Why couldn't he even find the right hill? It had to be one of those three hills, and he was certain that he hadn't made it all up. The more he thought about it, the more frustrated he became. *It has to be one of them,* he thought. *The one in the middle had the ledge or was the only one with a ledge of any kind, so I'm going back. I must have missed something.* He closed up the brown paper bag, left it by the tree, and started back toward the middle hill.

But then something strange happened: on this very warm June day, a day that until then had had virtually no clouds, the sky suddenly changed. Some large, dark clouds formed quickly out of the northwest and seemed to hover right over the hills that he had just climbed. The wind didn't pick up much, but the cluster of storm clouds—dark, billowy thunderheads—had come out of nowhere.

He looked up and saw the clouds as they passed in front of the sun, casting a shadow across the ground. As Hamelin looked toward those dark clouds, which now completely covered the sun, he felt the same strange feelings that had come over him three years ago. He had almost forgotten how he had felt back then, but now he remembered.

And then he heard a strange sound. At first he couldn't make out what it was; it was low and sounded far away. But it got louder and louder until it was a high-pitched screech. Then, bursting from the dark thunderheads, a huge bird glided above the three hills. At first it appeared to be soaring away, but then it turned and, coming in his direction, began spiraling down from the clouds until, from Hamelin's point of view, it soared like a vulture in a slowly descending circle just over the middle of the three hills.

He stood frozen in his tracks. Was it the Great Eagle? The screech grew louder. The bird's wingspan was wide, and it continued banking, turning, and slowly dropping in large sweeping circles over the three hills. Then just when he thought the bird would disappear behind the tallest of the three hills, the center one, it pulled out of its glidepath and took a direct line right toward him.

Hamelin couldn't take his eyes off the magnificent creature, whose gold, black, and white colors shone like precious stones in the light of the now partly cloud-covered sun.

The huge bird sped straight to him, but just before it reached him, it banked hard to its left and shot away. At the same moment, the wind from the bird's velocity hit him in the face. He blinked. And when he turned to follow the beautiful bird's path, it was gone.

Chapter 29

Another Way In

HAMELIN RACED INTO THE WOODS TO FIND THE BIRD. HE was pretty fast, and he ran for all he was worth, but he knew that catching up to an eagle in flight was impossible. Still, he hoped that maybe the bird would land long enough for him to catch up.

Hamelin darted in and through the trees, ducking under some low-hanging branches of mesquites, scurrying around live oaks, and leaping over rocks, cactus plants, and other places where the ground wasn't even. At one point when he jumped, the spot where he landed turned out to be a little lower than he had expected, and he momentarily lost his balance. He fell forward on his chest but caught himself with his hands before his face hit the ground. He scraped his knees and his palms, and he felt the right-hand pocket of his jeans tear, probably because of his pocketknife.

He got up quickly and took off again, running in the direction the bird had flown, looking all around, hoping the eagle had landed either on the ground or in a tree. After running for several minutes in zigzagged paths, always generally eastward, Hamelin slowed down. He kept walking briskly, but then he slowed even more and finally came to a stop. Panting heavily, he looked around, but he knew deep inside that it was hopeless. The Great Eagle was not the kind of bird you could find. He'd have to let you catch him.

Hamelin stood still, his chest pounding and his hands clenched into fists at his side. He closed his eyes, wishing he could make the Great Eagle appear. That *had* to be the Great Eagle! But what was the point of flying right at him and then disappearing into the woods?

And why did the eagle circle over the three hills, especially the largest one in the middle?

That's it! he thought. *The eagle is trying to tell me something.* Hamelin stood there thinking it all over. He desperately wanted to find the ledge, and now he was more sure than ever that the huge bird had to have been the Great Eagle and that he was telling him to try the middle hill again. And then it started raining. *Just like before*, Hamelin said to himself. *Yes, the eagle is trying to tell me something. It's the middle hill. It's raining, and I'm supposed to go back!* It was just what he wanted to do anyway, so Hamelin rushed back to the paved road and headed north. He reached a point just below the middle hill, and the rain stopped. *That's a good sign. Yes, the eagle wants to make it easier for me to get there.*

He climbed up the middle hill again, through the brush and trees, and got to the ledge. But nothing had changed. The ledge still appeared smaller, and there was no opening over to his right, nothing but a solid wall of hard-packed dirt. The longer he stood there, the more frustrated he became. *I know what the eagle is trying to tell me*, he thought. *He's saying that it's the middle hill and I'm supposed to come back here. So what now?*

Hamelin wasn't going to quit. *Maybe there's another opening.* He then climbed back down the hill, almost to the bottom, and decided to walk around to the north side. *Now that I think about it, maybe the eagle didn't come directly over the middle hill. Maybe it was on the north side of it,* he reasoned.

Hamelin made his way around to the north side and started climbing. It was pretty easy going, as the ground was not as thick with brush and trees. He got about two-thirds of the way up the hill, about the same height as the ledge on the east side, and stood there looking around. And then he saw it. Just above him was not a ledge but an opening, a small hole big enough maybe to look into.

He climbed up to the hole and found that there was a place to stand directly below it. He was just tall enough to stick his head in. *Good thing I brought the flashlight,* he thought as he reached into his back pocket and pulled it out. He turned it on and peered into the opening. He was immediately struck by how large the space inside looked. Sure enough, just like the cave he had been in before, there were glistening walls and beautiful formations above and below. Hamelin's heart began to beat rapidly. *This has to be it,* he thought. *It's the cave, and the eagle has led me here to this spot. I'm being summoned again. I've got to go in.*

He took a deep breath and worked his elbows up into the opening. Luckily, there wasn't a long drop to the floor, so he was able, using the flashlight, to get his head and shoulders through and then lower himself down the few feet below him, hands and arms first. He got to his feet and shined the flashlight all around, and just in front of him, there looked like something of a path in the middle of the space and between some stalagmites. *This has to be the way forward.*

Though he was excited to be back in the cave and confident that he was supposed to be there, Hamelin was still cautious. It was a cave, and it was dark. He followed the path a short way, always keeping the opening and the light from the opening in sight. But still no eagle to guide him. He then decided that the best thing to do was just to keep moving. "If you don't know what to do next," he had always heard, "just keep moving." So that's what he would do. No need to pause or think anymore. This was it.

Hamelin walked on with the help of his flashlight for quite a few minutes, but he kept track of the way back toward the opening. Even after he rounded a corner and the light from the opening was no longer in sight, he was still sure that, with the flashlight, he'd be able to get back if he had to. But he was confident also that there was no going back. *Before long, the eagle will join me.*

He heard some noise ahead, and his excitement grew when he expected any moment now that the great bird would appear, lighting the cavern with his radiance. But, just to be sure, Hamelin kept the flashlight on. The noise was just in front of him, and though he couldn't hear the brushing of wings that he associated with the eagle, he did hear something that sounded like movement. And then he was pretty sure he saw a light.

He ran toward it but realized as soon as he got there, after he had turned another corner, that the light he was seeing in the next room was the glistening of the walls, reflecting the light of his own flashlight back toward him. He decided to turn the flashlight off and just stand there for a moment.

If the light from the flashlight had fooled him, then maybe turning it off would help him see the light from the eagle. Then a troubling thought hit him: *Is that really the eagle?* Once the doubt entered his mind, it grew.

What's happening? I'm in this dark cave by myself with only this stupid flashlight. Where's the eagle? And that's when he heard it. It was an animal sound, but it was nothing at all like the sound the eagle made, sometimes like wood scraping on wood, or a screech.

Hamelin was frozen. *What was that?* It came again, and then he recognized it, or at least realized what it sounded like—a cat, a big cat, with a very loud purring.

It got louder. Maybe it was getting closer, and Hamelin instinctively did what his fears dictated. He turned the flashlight on quickly, and it flooded the small room he was now in with light. And at the other end of the room, at a height just above his head, he saw two eyes—or was it more?—looking back at him. And then he remembered how a cat's eyes can glow in the dark, and he quickly turned the flashlight off and slowly backed up. He was pretty sure that whatever it was had seen him—it could probably see him in the dark—and now he was at a terrible disadvantage. But he had absolutely no idea where to run or where to step in this pitch blackness. The purring turned abruptly into a growl. Hamelin whirled around, switched on the flashlight to see the path in front of him, and ran as fast as he could.

He now had no clue where he was in the series of caverns he had come across and no idea where to find the opening. From this direction, although he was trying to retrace his steps, everything looked different. His mind was in a panic. He could hear noises behind him, like padded feet jumping

and loping toward him, plus something like a hiss—a loud
hiss.

He could see, just in front of him, something he didn't
remember from before, a turn in the path. There were now
two paths that he could take—one to the left and the other
a gentle curve back to the right. He didn't remember any
right-angle turns as he had come in, so he took the option
back to his right, but he couldn't run very far in the darkness
and had to turn the flashlight on again.

There was no point in turning it off now, because
whatever it was could surely see him—and who knows,
maybe even smell him. He couldn't outrun it if it was a
cat—he knew there were bobcats in this area of Texas—in
the wide open spaces, much less in this cave. He'd have to
find a place to hide if at all possible. He ran furiously, but he
could hear the sounds behind him growing closer. It was no
longer a hissing sound but a crying yowl that a cat makes just
before it's in a fight. Hamelin knew his situation was hopeless, but fear made him keep running, determined to fight
until the end. Maybe the big cat, or whatever it was, was just
chasing him off, trying to scare him. Well, that was working. The thought of just being chased off gave him a small
amount of hope, so he tried to pick up his speed a little more.

But even with the flashlight on, he couldn't avoid the
unevenness of the path, and he stumbled over several rocks.
He went flying forward on his stomach, the flashlight still
in his right hand. He was amazed that it hadn't broken in
the fall, but it was his chest and the undersides of his outstretched arms that took the brunt of his slide forward. Now
he heard a loud cry. It was the yowl again, but now it broke
into a roar. He rolled over on his back and shined the flashlight toward the sound.

And then he saw it. Or them. Whatever it was. It was so frightening that he was later on completely uncertain as to what he saw. But one thing he knew for sure—it was like a bobcat, with stripes and other markings like a bobcat, but it was huge. The flashlight shook in his hand, and the light bounced from every angle off the stalactites and narrow walls on either side of the path. The creature was now slowly walking toward him as if stalking a prey, like he had seen cats back at the children's home do as they crawled through the tall grass, ready to pounce on a mouse.

The light that hit the huge cat bounced off his chest and off the walls, and for a faint second, Hamelin thought the creature had more than one head, which he knew was impossible. But the sounds, the hissing and roars, sounded like more than one animal was chasing him. Did bobcats ever run in packs? Was this a mama and her cubs? Was she teaching them how to hunt? Just as his fears climbed into his chest and throat—and just before he screamed—he turned off the flashlight.

The second he did, he saw a light flash in front of him and heard a hard thud, almost like one body against another. There was something that resembled a screech, and he raised himself up on his knees, hoping to get to his feet and run again, but before he could turn, some large body hit him in the chest. Whatever it was, it locked its legs around him, and he even felt some claws digging into his back, though they didn't pull at his flesh and tear him apart the way he expected.

The next thing he knew, he was hurtling backward in mid-air, and he thought he was going to land on his back and then be mauled—but the forward momentum of the push just kept going. And then he heard it and felt the wind of it against his sweaty face—the stroke of powerful wings. That's when Hamelin closed his eyes and hoped against hope that he was in the clutches of the eagle.

He felt himself being pushed through the air in darting movements left and right. The flight lasted for a couple of minutes before he was plunked down in a sitting position with his back against a cavern wall. He was looking down at first, but he could tell there was a beam of light, an opening, just above his head. He looked up, and just in front of him, facing him, was the eagle.

"Leave!" screeched the eagle. "Why are you here?"

"Because... because... I thought you wanted me to come."

"No—you wanted to come."

"But... but I saw you flying over the middle hill and—"

"Yes, I was flying away from the hills to the other side of the road. I was leading you *away*. You weren't summoned. You just decided on your own."

"But I have to be here. I want to help the girl who's waiting, and you said something about my own—"

"It's too late to help her!"

"But can't I try again?"

"If you do, you'll need more than that!" said the eagle, glaring at the flashlight.

Hamelin looked at it, still clutched tightly in his hand. "But isn't there something I'm supposed to do?"

"There was."

"But... I mean *now*?"

"Yes. Leave—that opening is not the right way in, and it's not the right time."

"Will I ever come back?"

"Even if I knew, I couldn't tell you. I have not been told to get you, so go back. Go back through that opening and never enter this cave again until—if ever—you are summoned."

The eagle abruptly turned and flew away into the darkness. Hamelin was still sitting with his back to the opening, but the darkness and the memory of the monstrous cat suddenly made him scramble to his feet. He pulled himself back through the hole and managed to get down, even though it was head and arms first, onto the small level spot just below. Shaken and exhausted, he climbed down to the paved road.

He started walking south but then realized he couldn't allow anyone to see him in this condition. His clothes were a mess, his blue jeans torn, and his elbows and forearms skinned up. He crossed back into the woods on the east side of the road and stood there in a daze. His legs and arms were shaking. It slowly began to dawn on him what had happened—that he had nearly died and that the Great Eagle had had to rescue him from some wild, strange giant cat.

He stumbled farther into the woods and began slowly to angle back south toward the children's home. But he was still shaking and breathing hard. He needed to stop. He looked around and unexpectedly saw he had somehow made his way back to the big mesquite tree, and his sack lunch was still there right next to it.

He sat down, slowly ate the rest of his lunch, and realized that Mrs. Parker had put his favorite drink, a can of Dr Pepper, in the bottom of the sack. He drank it all. He leaned back against the tree and, from exhaustion and the food he had just eaten, dozed off.

As he slept, the pictures in his mind were all mixed up—there was Marceya, the eagle, Mrs. Frendle, and a giant four-headed cat, crouched and ready to pounce. There were other people he couldn't recognize. They all stared at him. Most were sad, especially one young woman. Slowly, others crowded into his mind—a terrible, laughing clown and a strange animal with the head of a lion, the legs of a goat, and a snake's tail. It roared a loud boastful noise that ended in a bleat. And then someone began to push Hamelin from behind. The eagle stared and did nothing. And the pushing began to sting, and it hurt so bad, Hamelin thought he had been hit with a bullwhip. He was about to be hit again—but he suddenly woke up.

His back was on fire! He jumped to his feet and ripped off his shirt and saw it had big red ants crawling all over it. He shook them off with several hard two-handed shakes. He looked at the tree and saw a line of red ants crawling around it from the other side, drawn to the crumbs in his brown paper bag. He gave the shirt another shake, and then he saw something else.

Right there in the bark of the big mesquite were initials, hand carved and not very straight, but still readable— "JSK + JSK." There were some other marks that weren't recognizable. The carvings had clearly been there for a long time, judging from the indentations and coloring.

But Hamelin didn't have time to think about that—his back was still stinging. He needed to put some cold water on it, so he quickly headed toward the children's home.

As he got near the home, he noticed that Mr. Kaley was standing at the side of the house, looking in his direction.

"How was the hike?"

"Okay."

"You look like you've been running." Mr. Kaley glanced down at Hamelin's untucked shirt and the dirt stains up and down the front of his shirt and blue jeans. "You skinned yourself up. You okay?"

"Yeah, I tripped and fell."

"Pretty hard fall. I'd say. Did you see anything interesting?"

"Oh, I . . . not really, I guess."

Mr. Kaley heard the hesitation in Hamelin's voice, so he waited, but Hamelin wasn't going to tell what happened.

"I mean, there was this tree," Hamelin finally mumbled.

"A tree?"

"Yeah, it was kinda interesting. Someone had carved initials in it. Like 'somebody plus somebody'—you know?"

"I see. Well, sounds interesting. Maybe you can show it to me sometime."

Hamelin wasn't sure how to respond, so he just shrugged. Why couldn't he just tell Mr. Kaley the whole story? But the words wouldn't come.

"Hamelin," said Mr. Kaley, "you know you can always come to Mrs. Kaley or me for help or anytime you want to talk, don't you?"

"Yes, sir, I do." Hamelin wanted to tell him, but what would he think?

"Well, it'll be time for supper before long. See you in the dining room. And . . . why don't you let Mrs. Kaley look at those jeans for you? They might need mending."

Hamelin ran upstairs and got in the shower. The cold water soothed his back and, though it burned at first, relieved his skinned arms and knees. He stood under the water a long time just thinking about what had happened. He *had* to tell his story. Layla had written in a recent letter that she and Bryan would be visiting on his eleventh birthday, which was coming up. This time he would tell them everything.

The next day, Mrs. Kaley handed him his blue jeans, all washed and mended.

"Thank you, Mrs. Kaley."

"Oh, sure! And by the way, the right pocket was torn pretty bad, so I ended up adding some material and making it longer. I know how you boys are always stuffing things in your pockets, so I figured you wouldn't mind." She smiled broadly.

Hamelin thanked her and smiled. He was glad to have his jeans back and also glad she didn't ask any questions about what he was doing in the woods.

The days from then until his birthday passed slowly. Now that he had decided to tell Layla and Bryan, he was looking forward to unbottling what he had kept inside.

Chapter 30

Hamelin Tells His Secret

ON MONDAY EVENING, JULY 9, BRYAN AND LAYLA ARRIVED, and Hamelin ran to their car to meet them.

"I'm so glad to see y'all!" he said before they could even get out of the car.

"Oh, Hamelin, I'm so glad to see you too," said Layla as she stepped out of the car and hugged Hamelin all in one move.

"Hey, Hamelin!" yelled Bryan as he came around from the driver's side. "Look at you. You're almost as tall as Layla!"

"Omigosh, you *are*," said Layla as she stepped back to look at him. Hamelin grinned, and Bryan bear-hugged him, lifting him a few inches off the ground.

"Yep, you've grown," he said, as if it was now official.

The evening meal was good, as always. Mrs. Parker knew that Bryan and Layla were coming, and so she had fixed one of her special meals that everyone liked—homemade pizzas. Mrs. Parker had her own recipe for the crust and always loaded the pizzas down with cheese, hamburger meat, olives, her own special tomato sauce, and any other favorite ingredients the children asked for, such as pepperoni, Canadian bacon, mushrooms, or onions. The pizzas were a big success, topped off by a big German chocolate cake with ice cream.

When everyone was full, Mr. Kaley leaned back in his chair and patted his stomach. "Mrs. Parker," he said, "we had to beat the Germans and Italians in World War Two, but we can't beat their cake or pizza!"

"Oh, John," said Mrs. Kaley as she swatted him gently on his upper arm. All the children laughed, and Bryan and Layla looked at each other and smiled.

The meal was great, but Hamelin could hardly wait to have some time alone with his friends. He had a lot to tell them. After supper, however, the Kaleys took the three of them to their apartment. They wanted to hear about Bryan and Layla, how their classes were going, and all about their work. Hamelin tried, but he had a hard time listening—he was too eager to talk to them alone. The evening stretched on, and he started shifting in his chair.

The old clock on the lamp table next to Mrs. Kaley struck nine and sounded a short version of the Westminster chime. Hamelin glanced at the clock and looked back at Mr. Kaley, who was in the middle of a story about his college days. Hamelin then noticed that Mrs. Kaley was looking at him. He looked down.

"Oh, John," she said suddenly. "These kids don't need to hear our old stories. Maybe Bryan and Layla would like to walk around the grounds a bit before bedtime. You could go with them, Hamelin." Mrs. Kaley gave him a wink, and he smiled back.

So the three said their good-nights to the Kaleys, walked out into the front yard, and slowly strolled around the grounds.

They walked along the fence to the backyard, where the two girls' homes were. Layla took a brief peek inside the house where she had stayed as a girl and then rejoined Bryan and Hamelin. "It looks so much better!" she said. The three of them stood for a while in the backyard and talked more about how things at the home had changed.

For some reason, even though Hamelin was determined to tell them his story, he just couldn't find the right words to start the conversation. They started slowly walking again and came to the other side of the house, where the delivery road ran alongside the main home and where farther to their right were the woods. They stood in the partial light that came from the kitchen windows.

All three of them seemed to linger at that spot for no particular reason, and then Layla said, "Well, Hamelin, just think. Tomorrow it will be eleven years since you were found right *there.*" She pointed to the screened porch.

"That's right," said Bryan. He glanced toward the porch and then from there to the woods across the road. "Hmm," he said again as his eyes narrowed. He looked like he wanted to say something but decided not to.

They all stood there, caught in their thoughts, when suddenly Hamelin just blurted out, "There's something I've been wanting to tell you."

"What is it, Hamelin?" asked Bryan.

"Well, it's kinda weird, but . . ." Hamelin just stopped. Now he wasn't sure how to go on.

"It's okay," said Layla. "You can tell us." She put a hand on his shoulder.

He took a deep breath and started again. "You remember back on my eighth birthday, when Mrs. Frendle had just left and the Stephensons were still here?"

Bryan and Layla nodded.

"They forgot my birthday that year."

"What?" said Layla. "That's *terrible*! I'm sorry. I hope *we* didn't forget too!"

"No. Y'all sent me a card."

"So what happened?" asked Bryan.

"Well . . ." His voice was shaky at first, but he took another deep breath and the words poured out. He told them how he ran away, climbed up the hill, and found the cave.

He paused, partly to see if they wanted to say anything, but also to see their reaction. They seemed to be listening, so Hamelin plunged on, hoping they wouldn't think he was crazy. It took a while to tell it all, but Bryan and Layla never interrupted when he told them about the Great Eagle, the gloves, his failure to cross the bridge, and the amazing flight back.

Right then someone turned on the porch lights, and Hamelin could suddenly see the faces of Bryan and Layla. They were looking at him intently. No rolling eyes. No embarrassed looks. No faint smiles. Layla seemed to be holding back. She looked at Bryan, as if he should be the one to speak.

Finally, Bryan said, "So what happened then?"

"Well, I left the cave and walked home. I got home just before the sun came up and sneaked back to the bedroom and got out of my muddy clothes. No one ever knew that I was gone."

"Did you ever see the eagle again?" asked Layla.

"No," said Hamelin, who hadn't wanted to tell yet about his most recent experience. But a second later, he added, "Well . . . sorta."

"What do you mean 'sorta'?" asked Bryan.

"I mean, I did."

Bryan and Layla waited. Hamelin looked down.

Bryan seemed impatient. "So the eagle . . . you did see it again?"

Layla glanced at Bryan, and her eyes widened. She could obviously hear the urgency in his voice. Hamelin looked down again.

"Yes," he said. "But I was just trying . . ."

"It's okay, Hamelin," Layla said almost in a whisper. "Take your time and tell us what else happened." She looked at Bryan as if to tell him to calm down.

Hamelin then explained what had happened a few weeks ago. He told all about climbing the three hills but not finding the ledge. Then in a rush, he described the rain, the soaring eagle that dived right at him, and then his botched efforts to make the journey again—facing the big cat and everything. He ended by saying, "The eagle was really mad. He sent me away and said to wait for the right time, if ever. That I have to be summoned."

At this point, he felt drained, like he was totally out of words. He remembered the initials on the tree, his dream, and the ants, but they didn't seem important, and he figured he had said enough. Bryan and Layla didn't say anything.

"I know it all sounds weird, but it really happened. I promise."

"Hamelin," said Bryan, "we believe you." He paused, looked at Layla, and then said, "You know, Layla and I once had a strange experience with an eagle."

"Really?" said Hamelin. "An eagle?"

"Yeah, but . . . we can tell you all about that some other time."

"So you don't think I'm crazy?" asked Hamelin.

"*No,*" said Layla firmly. "You're not crazy." She hugged him. "I'm glad you told us. We'll keep your secret as long as you want."

The three friends walked back to the front of the house in silence. As they started up the porch, Bryan put his hand on Hamelin's elbow and gently pulled him to a stop. Layla stopped too and looked at Bryan, who was staring at Hamelin. "Would you like to show us the cave where you saw the eagle?" he asked.

"I don't think I should. I mean, the eagle said—"

"But we just want to see—"

"Bryan, let it go," said Layla. "Hamelin's not supposed to go—"

"Look, we wouldn't go in. I promise. We would just look. Just see if we know where the right opening is."

"I don't know, Bryan," said Layla. She looked at Hamelin.

Hamelin was starting to shake his head, but before he could answer, Bryan said quickly, "Look, why don't we all get up early tomorrow, and first thing after breakfast, we'll tell the Kaleys that we want to go for a walk. Then we'll use the morning to let you show us where you first met the eagle. It shouldn't be a problem as long as we're back here in time for your birthday lunch." He turned to Layla. "What do you think?"

Layla pressed her lips together and was obviously thinking it over.

Hamelin took in a deep breath, waiting to hear what she would say.

She finally nodded.

Hamelin let out his breath. He wasn't sure, but he trusted Bryan and Layla.

Chapter 31

The Three Friends Search Together

T HEY HAD NO TROUBLE WAKING UP THE NEXT MORNING because loud crashes of thunder and heavy rainfall hit just before dawn, making it difficult for anyone to sleep. By the time they got dressed and met in the kitchen, the thunder and lightning had let up, but there was still a steady sprinkle outside. Mrs. Parker was already busy at work preparing breakfast, and as soon as she spied the three early risers, she offered them a sample of the first homemade biscuits out of her oven. And since they were already started on the hot biscuits and butter, she of course quickly rustled up some scrambled eggs and cheese—"Just the way Hamelin likes 'em, since it's his birthday"—and enough bacon for the three of them.

Just as Hamelin was biting into one of her giant biscuits, with butter and jelly oozing out the sides, Mrs. Parker asked, "So what's got you young'uns up so early? Goodness gracious, Hamelin, it's your *birthday*! You should still be in bed. 'Course I never could—"

"Oh, we decided we want to take a morning walk," Layla said.

"In *this* weather?"

"Oh, we'll wait for it to stop raining."

"Well, don't be late for Hamelin's birthday lunch. I'll serve it up about twelve thirty. I've got—"

"Wouldn't miss it for anything," said Bryan. "We'll be back in plenty of time for one of *your* lunches." Bryan smiled at Mrs. Parker and winked at Hamelin, and they all resumed eating.

The two young people and their now eleven-year-old friend did watch through the windows to see if the rain would prevent their planned adventure, but by the time they had finished the breakfast Mrs. Parker kept adding to, the rain had stopped. It was still overcast, but it looked like the summer storm had passed.

They set out on their search. Bryan thought it best not to go through the woods. If they wanted to search for the cave itself, they should just walk north up the road. They could make better time, and, besides, the woods would be muddy and a lot tougher going than the paved road. As they walked, they silently took in the land and the trees, and the smell of rain, mud, and the wet pavement all mixed together. Hamelin was quiet, not really eager to go back, but Bryan had promised they would just look. And he wanted to be with these special friends.

Before long, they had walked about two miles, and Hamelin pointed out the group of hills that were now coming into view. Bryan commented—remembering his college geography class—that what they were seeing was really the beginning of the first hilly patches that eventually stretched on into the western horizon and, much farther away, led into the great Rocky Mountains.

As they walked the final stretch up the road, he asked Hamelin to reconstruct his original adventure at the cave three years ago, and Hamelin retold the whole story in detail.

"So," Layla said, "one of these hills right here has to be the one."

"Yeah, 'cause it wasn't far from the road," said Hamelin. It felt good to hear Layla talk like she had no doubts about his story.

As they got closer, they paused to look at the three hills, the two on the sides dominated by the one in the middle.

"Look," said Bryan, "since the middle hill is the one that had an opening on the north side, and since it's also the only one that you found any kind of ledge on at all, I say we should start our search right there. Besides, didn't you say it was the middle hill that the eagle circled around before he came flying at you?"

"That's right," said Hamelin. "But he was trying to lead me away."

Layla frowned and looked like she wanted to say something, but she stopped. She glanced at Hamelin with raised eyebrows, waiting for him to say more, but when he was silent and looked away, she mumbled softly, "The middle hill it is."

By this time, even though it had not rained on them during their more than two-mile walk, a dark, imposing front of thunderheads gathered quickly on the northwestern horizon. Just as suddenly, while they were about to walk toward the middle hill, a powerful bolt of lightning struck right out of the northwestern sky. From their vantage point, it seemed to strike near the top of the middle hill.

The thunderclap that followed came within only two to three seconds, so the lightning was still some distance away. But it happened so quickly and so dramatically that they all looked at each other with wide-open eyes.

"Ooh," said Layla, "I just had a big chill all the way up my spine. Bryan, are you sure—" But before she finished her comment, she looked at Bryan and got quiet.

Bryan didn't say anything, but his look showed he felt something strange too. All three were captured by the drama of the moment. Then hardly thirty seconds later, the three noticed that a dark, driving thunderstorm was fast approaching.

"Whoa!" hollered Bryan. "We'd better take cover. That looks like hard rain coming right at us."

They scrambled quickly off the road and sought cover in the woods. They knew not to get near a single big tree in a lightning storm, but the woods were full of trees, and they certainly didn't want to be standing out alone in the middle of the road if any more lightning should hit.

Fortunately, there wasn't any more lightning, but the rain was hard and fast, and it was cold. They found shelter under the canopy formed by several trees that had grown close together. Although some rain trickled through, they huddled together and protected themselves from the brunt of the cloudburst.

It rained hard for about ten minutes, but the downpour ended almost as abruptly as it had started. The driving rain passed quickly into a moderate rain, then to a light sprinkle. Finally, the rain vanished entirely, and the dark thunderheads above rolled away to the east.

"I think it's over," said Layla. "Are we still sure we want to do this?"

Bryan seemed determined, though Hamelin gave only a faint shrug. But when Bryan stepped out, Layla and Hamelin followed him back out of the woods. They crossed the road and came to some dense shrubbery.

"You think this is the spot, Hamelin?" Bryan asked.

"I think so . . . I mean, it could be."

"Well then," said Layla with a sigh, "here we go."

Hamelin was surprised that Bryan and even Layla were willing to keep going in spite of the rain and mud. But he was starting to feel better about it.

Bryan took the lead, Hamelin followed, and Layla was third in line. Bryan stepped across low places, over rocks, and around bushes and the occasional cactus plant and frequently gave out warnings about what to expect.

The overnight rains had already made the ground muddy, but the last hard rain had fallen so fast, it hadn't soaked in as much as it had run off. The bar ditches on each side of the road were now running with water, and the ground where the three walked was slippery. The bottoms of their shoes quickly caked up with mud.

By the time they made it partway up the hill, the sun had broken through the clouds at their backs, and the sky in the west had cleared up.

"It's gonna end up a steamy day today," said Layla as they kept picking their way through the shrubs, rocks, and scrubby trees.

It wasn't long before Bryan pointed to an outcropping of rock just above their heads. "That could be the ledge," he said with noticeable excitement in his voice. The underbrush began to clear out enough to allow the three to spread out a little. Then they climbed the last distance side by side.

As Bryan had said, they approached what appeared to be a rock ledge jutting out from the hill. Layla came from the left, Hamelin from the middle, and Bryan scrambled up on the right. The three friends stood on the ledge and looked back down at the road below. After inspecting the area for a few moments, Layla asked, "Well, Hamelin, you think this is the place you came to?"

"It's definitely the ledge I got to a few weeks ago, but it seems too small to be the one I found years ago. Besides," he said looking around, "I still don't see any opening."

That much was clear. The ledge had a depth of ten to twelve feet, about what Hamelin remembered. Its width, however, was less than he recalled, and there was certainly no opening to a cave.

"Okay," said Bryan, "but let's don't leave yet. Why don't we rest for a minute and think about this."

"Good," said Layla, "and let's sit over here. It's drier." So they all moved over to Layla's side of the ledge and sat down, looking back out over the side of the hill and taking in the view.

After a couple of minutes, Bryan spoke up. "Okay, Hamelin, as best you can remember, where exactly was the opening?"

"Well," Hamelin said slowly, "I remember I came up the hill in the dark and found my way to a spot like this. I was still facing the hill, and I felt along the back of the ledge, maybe over here." He pointed to his left. "And then I moved that way, to the other end there."

"Okay," said Bryan, "but obviously there is nothing over there. I know it was dark, but what do you remember about it? What did it look and feel like?"

"The main thing I remember is that there was a huge boulder over to my right, as I faced the hill, and the opening was just between the back of the ledge and the left-hand side of the big rock, the side closest to the hill."

"I remember you said you slipped, fell down, and bumped your head," said Layla.

"Yeah," said Hamelin. "I felt my way along the ledge and came to a little opening where the rain couldn't hit me. I was kinda crouching down, sort of on my knees, and I was trying to take off my backpack. Somehow, I slipped and bumped my head. I think I was out for a while. Then I remember hearing some sounds, like something running away. When I woke up, there was the eagle, and he was staring at me from just inside the opening of the cave."

"So," said Bryan, "if this is the ledge, the opening to the cave would have to be over there somewhere, and obviously there's not one."

"Right," sighed Hamelin. "Besides, this ledge just seems so much smaller."

"But," Layla reminded everyone, "when you're small, everything seems bigger."

"I guess so," Hamelin conceded. "But that was only three years ago."

They were all wondering if they should admit defeat when something caught Bryan's eye. He stood up, walked forward a few steps, and then turned and looked up at the rest of the hill above the overhang of the ledge. He noticed that the side of the ledge they sat on was drier even though there was a steady stream of muddy water still coming down from the hill above them. And now he could see why—the water flowing down from above their heads wasn't falling evenly onto the floor of the ledge. Instead, as it reached the area of the hill just above them, it turned a little sideways to the north before spilling over onto the other end of the ledge. It was

splashing down over where Hamelin thought the opening
to the cave should have been and creating a muddy buildup.

"Say," said Bryan, "you told us that there was a big rock
over there and that just behind it was the opening, right?"

"Yeah."

"Well, what if the rock you saw and felt three years ago has
been covered up with mud?"

"What do you mean?"

"Yeah," said Layla, her eyes widening as she understood
what Bryan was thinking. "Look . . ." She stood, turned, and
pointed above them to what Bryan had noticed. "The rain
water coming down from the top of the hill is washing soil
from the hilltop right down to that side over there. Maybe
your big rock, Hamelin, is now covered up behind a wall of
dried mud."

"There's one sure way to find out," said Bryan. "Let's
scratch away some dirt and see what we find."

They didn't have anything to dig with, but with the help of
Hamelin's pocketknife, Bryan cut and trimmed some sturdy
branches from the underbrush just below the ledge. He then
scrambled back up with several good sharp sticks to use for
digging.

It was messy business, digging mud and dirt away from
the hillside, but the three of them worked quickly. And
because the earth wasn't packed and the rain had softened
it even more, it was easy to dig out.

"It feels more like we're digging in a garden than through
hardpan," said Layla.

"I think that's a good sign," said Bryan as he pulled large
clods of dirt back on himself and the others. "It may be
messy, but we might as well dig close to each other, because

we just need a narrow spot to see if there's a boulder here, like Hamelin saw."

After pulling away what looked like about two feet of mud and soft dirt, Bryan said, "Okay, now step back for a second and let me try something." With that, he resharpened his stick with Hamelin's pocketknife and jabbed it straight into the dirt wall in front of him as hard as he could. Then with his weight behind him, he pushed it straight in. The stick penetrated the soft dirt almost up to his hands. Then it stopped.

"I think I hit something!" he said. He pushed again as hard as he could, but the stick would go no farther into the soft earth.

"Maybe we're onto something here," he said with a note of excitement. He pulled the stick back out, and the three of them began to hack and chip away at the soft wall with renewed energy. They all took turns digging away at a small hole that was only about one foot in diameter and grew narrower the deeper in it went.

Sure enough, when they got the hole dug out to a width of about two feet, there was clearly hard rock on the other side.

They worked hard and no one stopped. Layla began to widen the hole toward their left. Not only did the dirt peel away more easily from that side—maybe because it was farther away from the direct rays of the eastern sun—but the hole they had created got deeper, curving inward the more they moved to the inner wall of the ledge.

After another thirty minutes of work, they had cleared out a huge area of mud and soft dirt. It was obvious that the ledge at one time had been longer. More than that, there definitely was a rock surface or maybe a large boulder on the other side of the earthen wall, just as Hamelin remembered.

By then it was about ten o'clock, and the three of them, though excited by their discoveries, were tired. The sun, now higher in the east, was beating down on them, and the air was steamy from a combination of the wet ground and the rising July temperature.

Though it was nowhere near lunchtime, they decided to take a much needed break. Of course, Mrs. Parker had not let them leave without provisions: a bottle of water, a piece of fruit, and a big biscuit with a piece of cheese for each of them. "I like a midmornin' snack myself," she had said as she handed Bryan a brown bag with the supplies in it.

But only fifteen minutes later, they were all ready to get back to their project, and after another forty-five minutes of hard digging, they found it: a huge rock boulder. Between the left-hand side of that huge boulder and the back of the ledge, there was clearly a small opening.

The opening was toward the bottom of the boulder, just below where it and the back wall of the ledge came together. It wasn't large enough to crawl through, and so it wasn't as big as the opening that Hamelin had described from three years before. Still, there it was, somewhat triangular in shape and about a foot wide at ground level.

They took turns looking into the opening and found that even though the sun shone into it, there was nothing to see except blackness.

"If this really is the spot where you went into the cave," said Bryan, "then maybe the boulder has just slipped or shifted its place back toward the wall of the ledge. Maybe all three of us can push it forward a little bit and create more space."

"It looks too big to me," replied Layla, "and besides, since we're not going in, why make the opening bigger?"

"Well," said Bryan slowly, "I promised we're not going in, and I meant it. But you agreed we could try to find Hamelin's cave, and we can't be sure this is it unless the hole is bigger."

Layla stared at Bryan and gave him a scolding, raised-eyebrow look. "Okay, I'm willing to try, but we're not going in, even if we make more space."

"I promise," Bryan said quickly. "What do you say, Hamelin?"

"Okay," he said.

So the three pushed and pulled with all their strength. But though the boulder rocked forward about an inch, it settled back. After several groaning efforts, they quit.

"Well," offered Layla, "I think it budged a *little*. So there's gotta be some more space somewhere around this rock. I mean, if it moved, it can't be just a continuous part of this outcropping on the hill. Right?" She looked at Bryan.

"That's right," said Bryan. "I'm pretty sure I felt it move too, but it'll take a lot more power than the three of us have to move that thing."

"We could get Mr. Moore's tractor," said Hamelin. But as soon as he said it, he knew they'd never get a tractor up to the ledge, and he wouldn't ask anyway. "Never mind. Forget that."

And that's when a strange sound rumbled over their conversation. And odder still, it seemed to have come from the darkness within the small opening.

Chapter 32

The Music
from the Deep

"WHAT WAS THAT?" HAMELIN WHISPERED.
Another sound rumbled up, something loud
and groaning from deep below the opening. It
wasn't the sound of rocks falling or boulders crashing, which
would have been natural to suppose, since they were standing halfway up a hill on a rock ledge. If there hadn't been
a pop to it, they might have thought of an earthquake. But
the sound wasn't completely natural. It sounded more like
a giant metal spring releasing its tension or maybe the crank
on a piece of rusted machinery being turned. It had a deep,
scratchy, metallic quality to it—almost a groan.

Bryan got to his knees and turned his ear to the opening.
Layla and Hamelin did the same—all of them now squeezing together and leaning toward the small opening. Again
they heard it, something deep and grinding that sounded
like it was clawing its way up. Strangely enough, they could
feel the noise vibrate through the ground.

Layla put her hand on her brother's shoulder. "Bryan, what is it?" Hamelin heard something in her voice he had never heard before.

Bryan shushed her.

"*Bryan*," Layla said again, but a little louder. Bryan didn't answer. He only leaned closer.

The sound continued. It was unlike any of the sounds they were accustomed to. Though it wasn't loud, the volume grew. It continued its harsh, rasping notes, like the sound of a great girder of steel being drawn against a brittle pile of iron. But then new sounds floated up to join the first rumblings. At first an almost familiar instrumental voice, like a piping flute or piccolo, chirped a note that danced in and around the rasping and scraping of steel. But then another sound, maybe a horn of some sort—or an oboe?—came underneath the dancing pipe and raised it up, suspended and sustained upon the grinding metal.

"Layla, do we have to keep listening?" Hamelin whispered. She shivered but said nothing. *Maybe she can't hear me*, he thought, and right then he noticed another sound within—or maybe underneath—the grating metal and the reedy horn. Hamelin's first thought was of drums. He detected a wooden clack of sticks, like drummer's sticks, as they thudded and clicked against one another and on the sides and tops of what could have been dozens of snare drums.

As grating as the sounds were, Hamelin knew they weren't just random. As odd as they were, they blended into a musical mix.

The volume continued to increase, and he noticed that Layla's hand slid down from Bryan's shoulder, and her head seemed to drop lower, even closer to the opening. At the same time, Hamelin felt changes within himself. The music started to feel like it was inside him. And as he closed his eyes, he realized the sounds in his ears were making pictures in his mind, as if he could see where the music was coming from.

The sounds continued to grow, and Hamelin could now see the groaning, scraping metal, the rhythmic sticks, and howling, airy pipes. It was a marching band of instruments so big that he couldn't see who was playing them. And then new pictures and sounds piled on top of the others—sounds like the twanging of rubber bands, the clattering of kitchen pans, and an off-beat padding of webbed feet on muddy sand.

And he could feel the music coming toward him. Especially the flute. It floated above and maybe even carried all the other sounds, yet it was pulling him into itself, suspending and holding him. And he could see people—young people, even children—skipping and jumping after the sound. A parade, a march of a frenzied dance toward a dangerous cliff at the edge of a mountain. Hamelin wanted to shout at them to come back, but the warning sounds wouldn't come out. He saw a bridge—if only they would take the bridge to safety!

And then Hamelin could feel himself falling but still hearing the music. He remembered, as he fell, his first flight through the dark caverns with the eagle. But now there was no eagle. And he could hear the grating noises and the flute-like sounds, as if they were bouncing off cavern walls as he fell, tumbling around and past rocky formations in the abyss. Suddenly the sounds were smothered by others closer and louder.

Hamelin opened his eyes, and he, Bryan, and Layla were still crouching near the opening by the boulder. No one spoke, but Bryan and Layla looked distant. Now they heard more familiar sounds that overtook the strange, distant ones. It was an explosion of wings, the flurry of not just dozens but hundreds of small wings furiously beating the air, like the sound Hamelin had heard before when he and Mr. Moore had suddenly come upon a huge covey of bobwhites in the pasture near the tank.

Not only did the beating of the wings cover up the sounds from the deep and break the trancelike spell upon the three friends, but the sudden pounding felt so close that it made them quickly scramble to their feet and move back a step from the opening. Bryan sensed a potential danger and put his arms in front of Layla and tried to cover Hamelin too. Just then, two or three small, winged creatures buzzed out of the opening, flying just past them, and disappeared immediately around the corners of the ledge.

"Yi!" yelled Layla. "What was that?" She swatted the air with both hands as if warding off a swarm of gnats.

"I think it was bats," said Hamelin. "Do bats hum?"

"Maybe it was locusts," said Bryan.

"Pretty big locusts," Layla said, shaking her head.

The three friends moved with short, quick steps to the far side of the ledge, the drier part where they had rested earlier. They sat against the wall. They were breathless, dazed, and exhausted.

After several minutes, Bryan abruptly stood up and said, "Let's go." No further explanation was needed for Hamelin or Layla. They quickly descended from the ledge and made their way to the bottom of the hill.

Layla looked at her watch and said, "Omigosh, it's ten minutes 'til noon. We've got to get to your birthday lunch, Hamelin. If we hurry, we can make it on time."

They walked fast and over the next forty minutes covered the distance back to the children's home. They were so frazzled from their experience and so rushed to get back that they hardly talked along the way. They reached the home, washed up quickly, and joined the others.

Their minds raced with the memories of what had happened at the cave. And what they had felt and seen and heard. They didn't say so, but they all knew that they would have to talk these things over later that afternoon.

Chapter 33

What Next?

HAMELIN'S BIRTHDAY PARTY HAD LOTS OF ACTIVITY. IT began with lunch and ran all the way through a swimming party in the afternoon. After that, there were hot dogs and hamburgers, a birthday cake, ice cream, and presents. All of that would normally have been enough to occupy Hamelin, but not this time. The same was true for Bryan and Layla. The three could not stop thinking about the strange events of that morning.

Every now and then, they would share glances or grim looks, silently acknowledging that each knew what the others were thinking about. The events that morning had left them tired, puzzled, and scared.

In fact, when they finally had a chance to slip away and meet, it was easy to tell that their feelings of fear were not going away easily. They walked out back and sat down on the shady side of the old shed, Layla sitting between the boys.

"Hamelin," began Bryan, "I'm pretty worried about everything that happened this morning."

"I am too," added Layla quickly.

"But, first of all," Bryan said, "I'm sorry. I pushed both of you to go there, and then . . ."

"It's okay," said Hamelin. "I agreed to go—and at least we didn't go in."

"I'm still sorry," said Bryan.

"Me too," said Layla. "We shouldn't have pushed you. It's just that we—" Bryan looked at her and shook his head. "Well, anyway, we're sorry."

"But what was it? I mean, I don't get it," said Hamelin.

"I'm not sure," replied Bryan, "but we've got to see if we can come up with any answers."

"Okay," Layla began, "what do we know?" She expected Bryan to answer, but Hamelin spoke first.

"I think we found the cave and the ledge I was at three years ago," he answered. "At first I didn't, but Bryan's idea about mud covering the boulder was right. After we dug some of it away, I could see the ledge was big enough to be the one I remembered."

"Yeah," replied Bryan, "it was all there—a wide ledge, a boulder, and an opening."

"But," said Layla, "the hole we dug out certainly wasn't big enough for Hamelin to go through back then."

"True," said Bryan, "but we were able to move the big boulder a little. So maybe the boulder somehow slipped back and covered the opening."

"What would make it slip?" asked Hamelin.

Layla shrugged. "Maybe the ground could have moved?" She looked at Bryan. "Like a little earthquake? Couldn't that make the boulder settle back?"

"Sure," said Bryan. "The ground could've shifted a little, just enough to change the balance of that boulder and make it slide back. Wouldn't take much, I guess."

"Or," said Hamelin, not looking at either of them, "since some pretty strange things go on in that cave, maybe something spooky happened to make it slide over."

"I guess that's a possibility too," agreed Bryan.

"Speaking of spooky, what about the lightning?" asked Layla.

"Don't know," said Bryan. "I mean, it could have just been a coincidence that lightning appeared to strike right over the middle hill."

Layla squeezed her lips over to one side and tilted her head. "I doubt it. There are too many odd things going on here to just call it coincidence."

"There was no sign of the eagle this time," Hamelin said. He paused for several seconds and stared into space.

"But there were lots of other very unusual things," said Layla. "Like those sounds we heard . . ."

Layla looked at Bryan and Hamelin, but they were silent. That was the one thing none of them really wanted to talk about.

"It wasn't just noise," she continued. "It was too patterned to only be noise. It was an awful harmony. It grated on me. I kept waiting for the notes to move, to settle, to—as my music appreciation teacher at the university says—*resolve*."

"Yeah," added Hamelin. "I know what you mean. It was sort of like music, but not something I want to hear again. But . . . I couldn't stop listening to it, even though I really didn't like it."

"That's the part that *really* bothers me," said Bryan. He glanced at Layla and Hamelin and then ducked his eyes. "Do you realize that all of us were crouching down as close to that hole as we could get? At first I just wanted to know what the sounds were, but the longer it went on, the closer all of us leaned in toward the hole."

They all looked at one another, knowing Bryan was right. He went on. "Something was happening . . . it was . . . it felt like something bad. I think if that hole had been big enough . . . or if it hadn't been for that rush of bats or whatever they were, I wouldn't have pulled myself away."

Layla got quiet, her head down.

"I don't think those things were bats," said Hamelin, "though I did at first."

"Yeah," said Bryan. "They were different from any bat I've ever seen."

"They sounded like locusts," said Hamelin. "But they were too big for locusts."

"What do you think, Layla?" said Bryan. He noticed a big tear that rolled down her cheek. "Hey, what is it, Lay?" He put one arm around her and gave her a hug.

Layla looked at Bryan and took a deep breath. "I don't know, Bryan. It's . . . it's like I don't know what I did wrong, but I feel ashamed of myself. The music from that cave disturbed me, yet I was attracted to it. And more than that, I didn't like myself while I was listening to it . . . but I couldn't stop. It was like I had given in, but instead of enjoying it— like I do when I give in to a big piece of chocolate cake—I *hated* myself for listening. But the more I listened, the more I couldn't stop. And I could see things . . ."

Hamelin immediately wondered if she saw the same things he had seen, but he didn't want to ask.

Finally, Bryan did.

"So, what'd you see?"

"I saw some older people. They were very sad. They were . . . like Mom and Dad." Layla took a deep breath. Hamelin thought she was going to burst into tears, but she didn't.

"You saw Mom and Dad?"

"No, it wasn't Mom and Dad. But they made me think of them. I wanted to get in, to run toward them, but . . ."

"But what?" Bryan asked.

Layla just shook her head and wouldn't say more. She sat quietly but then looked at Hamelin with a questioning look, and he knew she wanted him to speak.

He told them about the marching, dancing children, the cliff, and the bridge. Everyone was quiet again.

"What about you, Bryan?" Layla said softly.

"Oh, nothing,"

"Don't tell me that!" she said as she jabbed him in the ribs with her elbow.

He smiled faintly and said, "No, really!"

Layla turned to face him. "Don't give me that! I know you. Besides, you said you saw things too!"

Bryan shrugged. "Well, I'm not sure what I saw."

"Just try," Layla insisted.

"Okay. I saw a boy. A big, strong boy—older than me—and I was drawn to him, like I knew him. I wanted to be with him, to play or just hang out. He . . ."

"He *what*? I'm not letting you stop there!"

"You stopped."

"Bryan . . . I'll tell you sometime. But you better keep talking now."

Bryan almost smiled, but a cloud came over his face. "The boy . . . he looked like Mom."

Layla nodded, and all three of them fell silent. Then Layla suddenly spoke again. "I almost wish I hadn't seen these things . . . maybe we shouldn't . . ."

"I know . . . I know what you mean," said Bryan. "I should've at least fought it off and gotten all of us out of there. But I couldn't tear myself away."

Hamelin sat quietly, watching Bryan hug and comfort his sister. There were things between them that only they knew. Layla was looking down while Bryan patted her shoulder.

"One thing I do know for sure, Hamelin," Bryan said after a few minutes, "I don't want you going back to that cave . . . at least not by yourself."

Hamelin didn't respond, except to twitch his mouth to one side. Bryan knew he hadn't agreed, so he tried again. "Hamelin, would you at least promise that you won't go without telling Layla and me first?"

"Hamelin," Layla said very solemnly as she looked straight into his eyes, "will you promise us that?"

He knew when he looked at Layla and saw how she looked at him that he had no choice. He couldn't deliberately do anything to disappoint her. Or Bryan. "I promise," he said slowly.

Hamelin then turned to Bryan. "But will you and Layla promise me the same thing: that you won't go without telling me?" Before they could reply, he added, "Because you had something weird happen with an eagle too, didn't you?"

Bryan glanced at Layla, and she shook her head slightly. He took a quick breath. "Yes . . . but it's complicated. Look, we can't tell you our story yet. But we will someday when we understand it better ourselves. But we promise you that we won't go near that cave again either, at least not without talking to you. Deal?"

Bryan held his hand out toward the others, and one at a time they all stacked their hands on top. They looked at one another, smiled, and all at once said, "Deal."

And so Hamelin's eleventh birthday ended. Bryan and Layla went back to Abilene the next morning. Having shared so much with one another, they all felt closer than ever. When they said good-bye, they were already looking forward to the Christmas holidays, when Bryan and Layla would come back.

Hamelin felt partly relieved. At least some of the burden he had felt for the last three years had been lifted. Telling others his story had helped. Still, in the back of his mind, he felt unsettled.

He hoped he wasn't done with the cave, but he also feared going back. Anyway, it would probably be a long time—if ever, according to the eagle—before he did.

Chapter 34

Paul, Thanksgiving, and a Strange Book

OR THE REST OF THE YEAR, NO MATTER WHAT HE DID OR how normal things were, Hamelin couldn't shake the feeling that he had left something unfinished. He spent a lot of the summer outdoors, and he also took the opportunity to read. And Layla kept writing and recommending books to him, and occasionally he would have a small surprise package in the mail, a book from her, but even in his reading, he felt something was going on.

He read all kinds of books: biographies of early American heroes, collections of short stories, and even the Hardy Boys and Nancy Drew mysteries, though he got tired of them quickly. But he never seemed to get tired of adventure stories or fantasies. He read *King Solomon's Mines* by H. Rider Haggard and several stories by Roald Dahl. Layla even persuaded him that *Alice in Wonderland* was not just for girls, so he read that.

But all the time he was reading or walking through the woods around the children's home, he felt it. The nagging fears about the cave, or thoughts about the meaning of "your own," or the feeling that he was supposed to be somewhere else. That was the worst. Would he ever see the eagle again? What would have happened if he had crossed the bridge? And what was the story that Bryan and Layla were holding back on?

Hamelin hated to see the summer end, but on the first day of sixth grade, as he walked into the classroom, he was surprised to be greeted by Mrs. Eastland! Just prior to the start of the school year, one of the three sixth-grade teachers and her family moved away from Middleton, so Mrs. Eastland, who had taught Hamelin in fourth grade, volunteered to take a class. Hamelin was thrilled when he saw her.

Mrs. Eastland started off as her usual stern self, but as she stressed all the rules of her classroom, she gave Hamelin a little wink. He knew she really wasn't as tough as she sounded. Even with everything on his mind, it was good to be around her regularly again.

At the beginning of the year, he realized he had grown over the summer. Some of the children in his classroom who had before been bigger than Hamelin were now the same size or smaller.

Things went along as usual at the children's home. The new school year brought a few new children to the home. There was one boy in particular that Hamelin noticed: Paul Thomas. He didn't know a lot of Paul's story, but he knew that the children who came to the Upton County Children's Home usually didn't have a happy story to tell.

Paul was a first grader and above average in height for his age. He had big, gray-green eyes, light-brown hair, and no doubt would have had a pleasant smile, but he seldom showed it. Paul was awkward, unsure of himself, and, as with many of the children, especially when they first arrived at the home, lonely and shy.

But Mrs. Parker's cooking and some special attention from the Kaleys helped.

"Hamelin," said Mr. Kaley, just before the bus pulled up the first day of school, "I want you to keep an eye out for Paul at school. You know what I mean. Don't let anybody bother him."

"Sure, Mr. Kaley." Hamelin was glad to do that, since he remembered his experiences with Patton McBoggerson.

As for Patton, Hamelin still saw him around, but Patton wasn't much interested in bullying Hamelin any more. Not that he had turned from being a bully, because he still was. David Rivers had graduated from Middleton High the previous May and wasn't there to stop him. But Hamelin had grown a lot, and Patton knew he couldn't push him around as easily as before, so he went after easier targets.

Hamelin looked out for Paul on the bus, during lunch, and after school. And he also managed now and then to sit next to Paul on the bus and talk to him a little.

At first Paul didn't seem to care that Hamelin was trying to befriend him. But after a few weeks, he began to come out of his shell. He was still shy, but it was obvious he was glad to have Hamelin sit with him. And he also seemed to find ways to hang around Hamelin a little at the children's home. So even though there was five years difference in the ages of the two boys, Hamelin liked Paul and was happy to help him get used to life at the home.

The fall semester went by quickly, and soon it was Thanksgiving. Mrs. Parker and the Kaleys made the holidays memorable for everyone. The Kaleys had long since changed the design of the dining room. No more long tables for everyone to sit at. Now there were eight round tables with eight chairs at each. The room was just big enough to bring in another table of eight, if it was needed. The Kaleys sat at different tables for each meal, and wherever they sat, that table usually had the loudest laughter and talk. Usually after a sudden burst of laughter, everyone could hear Mrs. Kaley say, "Oh, John!"

And as for Thanksgiving dinner that year, Mrs. Parker outdid herself: a turkey at every table, to say nothing of endless platters of dressing—Mrs. Parker's old family recipe, made with cornbread and special spices—sweet potatoes, mashed potatoes, green beans, fruit salad, glazed carrots, brussels sprouts, corn, and squash. And of course, there were several kinds of homemade breads.

Her voice, with stress on almost every other syllable, could be heard as the dishes came out, "*Now*, you *have* to *try* some of *every*thing!" Which was no problem, even for the vegetables, since they always had plenty of spices or cheese sauce or a little extra butter.

And the desserts were so many that everyone's favorite was there somewhere amid the pies and cakes and puddings of every flavor.

By the time Hamelin got back to school the following Monday, he realized that he had a lot to be thankful for—having a good, safe place to live with kind people to care for him; good friends like Bryan, Layla, and Paul; and a really good teacher like Mrs. Eastland. All of which made him feel guilty that he was so restless.

That very day, Mrs. Eastland asked him to stay behind for a few moments after school, as she had something for him. He suspected, and hoped, it was a book.

"Have you read any more of George MacDonald's books?" she asked.

"No," said Hamelin, "but I'd like to."

"Well, I just happen to have one for you." With that, Mrs. Eastland reached over to the corner of her desk and picked up a volume titled *At the Back of the North Wind*. "I think you'll like this."

Hamelin took the book with both hands and thanked her several times before she sent him away. "Hurry, I don't want you to miss your bus!" she said. He made it to the bus, sat next to Paul, and started reading right away. He was expecting something like the Curdie books he had read earlier, but *At the Back of the North Wind* was very different. It had strange and wonderful characters, just like the other two, and it also had a magical, even dreamlike feel to it. But it was different. Hamelin couldn't put the book down. He used every spare minute to read and finished it within three days.

The main character was a little boy by the name of Diamond, who was very ill. And though Diamond was not an orphan, Hamelin understood how different Diamond was. He found himself feeling some of the same things that Diamond felt and wanting to ask the same kinds of questions that Diamond asked. Why do people suffer? Why do bad things happen? And is there a reason for it all? Hamelin knew that the back of the North Wind and the mysterious cave with the eagle were different. But when he finally put the book down, he was restless. *Maybe*, he thought, *I'm like*

Diamond and need to go someplace else to understand these things. But where? The cave?

So, although he tried not to think about the cave, especially because of his promise to Bryan and Layla, the drive to go back became even stronger in his mind. And he couldn't shake it.

Chapter 35

A Sad and Unexpected Visit

HAMELIN'S RESTLESSNESS GREW. HE DESPERATELY wanted to tell Layla and Bryan what he was thinking, especially since he had promised them he wouldn't go to the cave without talking to them first. But he wasn't sure he could wait until they came back at Christmas. As it turned out, he didn't have to.

Bryan and Layla's aunt died on the Wednesday after Thanksgiving. As soon as they were contacted by her minister, they drove hard from Abilene to Alpine in one day. They arrived in time to make arrangements for her funeral services and to visit with her close friends there. Their aunt was their mother's only sister, and her death brought back painful memories of the sudden death of their parents.

After the funeral and burial early Saturday afternoon, they were sorting through her things when Layla sobbed and said, "Bryan, please, can't we just close up Auntie's house and come back later, when we'll have more time?"

Bryan thought for a few seconds, let out a loud breath, and said, "Sure. We can do that. Since she's left everything to us, it's our choice. We'll come back here over the holidays and settle her estate. We can go through all this stuff then." And so they left. But since Middleton was generally on their way from Alpine back to Abilene, they decided to stop there to see Hamelin and the Kaleys. They would spend Saturday night there and then leave Sunday afternoon.

Hamelin and the Kaleys were surprised to see them Saturday evening when they pulled into the driveway. But their happy shouts of hello quickly stopped when they saw the sad faces and especially Layla's red eyes. Bryan quickly told them where they'd been and why.

"You dear children," said Mrs. Kaley. "You must be exhausted!"

"Come in," added Mr. Kaley. "There's still plenty of food from Saturday's supper, and Mrs. Parker will gladly warm it up."

The Kaleys and Hamelin sat with them as they ate. Layla and Bryan talked quietly about their aunt, the years they had lived with her, and how close she and their mother had been. They didn't talk much about their parents, but it was obvious they were thinking of them.

Layla cried occasionally as she described her memories of so many things, and Bryan's voice was unusually soft. Once, Hamelin saw a tear fall from his cheek, even though his face was almost completely still. Mr. and Mrs. Kaley were able to offer comforting words to them, but mostly they just listened and occasionally patted one or the other on the shoulder or forearm. After some time, the Kaleys excused themselves.

Mr. Kaley patted Hamelin on the back as they left. "You can stay up late with them as long as you want," he said quietly.

The three friends put on their jackets and walked outside. It was early December, and the air was cool. About a year earlier, the Kaleys had placed a bench swing underneath one of the two oak trees in the front yard. Hamelin and Layla sat in the swing, and Bryan sat on the ground facing them, with the collar of his blue jean jacket turned up and his arms around his knees. Hamelin knew that this wasn't the time to bring up his problems, so he told himself he should stay quiet and let them talk.

But then Bryan said, "So, Hamelin, how are you feeling about the cave?"

Hamelin was surprised at the question. "Well," he began, "I've been thinking about it a lot recently. I really want to go back."

Bryan and Layla glanced at each other.

"We knew you'd feel that way," she said.

"Yeah," said Bryan, "we understand . . . when your family . . . I mean . . . when weird things happen, it's a hard thing to let go of. Layla and I have talked about it a lot, especially the last few days. We knew you'd want to go back before long."

"It's really been bothering me lately," Hamelin said. "I mean, sometimes I'm sorta afraid to go back because of what the eagle told me when I climbed in at the wrong spot and the things that happened the last time we were there together. But some other things have happened that have made me think more about what the eagle said the first time I went."

"Remind us," said Bryan.

"He mentioned a girl who was waiting and some names I can't remember. But he also said something about 'your own' and then he just stopped. I've been thinking maybe he was going to say 'your own *parents*.'"

Layla's eyes widened, and she looked intently at Hamelin. "Your *parents*?"

"Yeah, I've been thinking about them. Of course, I never knew them, but I keep wondering about them. And now I'm thinking that maybe crossing the bridge would lead me to them. Maybe they're just on the other side of what the eagle called the 'Atrium of the Worlds.'" Hamelin looked at Layla and then at Bryan, but he especially noticed that Layla kept looking at him, as if she was thinking hard about what he had said.

Finally, she said, "Hamelin, there's something I probably need to tell you. I never told you before—in fact, even Bryan doesn't know."

"What?" asked Bryan.

"It's something Mrs. Frendle told me. I wasn't supposed to tell anyone about it, and for all these years, I've figured it wasn't any big deal."

"So what is it?" Bryan asked. "Can you talk about it now?"

"Yes, I think so. Actually, I'm supposed to."

Bryan and Hamelin looked at each other, confused.

"What did she say?" Hamelin asked.

"Well, really, it's more something she gave me."

"Okay, start over," Bryan said. "Give us the whole story."

"Well, after you left for college, I had one more year here at the home. That's when Hamelin and I really spent a lot of time together, and Mrs. Frendle knew it. So after graduation, when I was all packed up and leaving, I was telling everyone good-bye and feeling terrible that I was about to leave Hamelin."

Hamelin nodded, remembering when Layla left.

"Anyway, right as I was getting into the truck, Mrs. Frendle comes out and hands me a letter. She said it was something she wanted me to give to Hamelin someday. She figured, I guess, that in case she left or died or something, it was something she wanted to make sure you got." Layla looked at Hamelin.

"What is it, Layla?"

"Honestly, I don't know much. All I know is it's a sealed letter from Mrs. Frendle. She said it contains the note from whoever left you on the porch."

"The note? I heard her talk about it some. She usually mentioned it whenever she told people the story of finding me. But I thought she always said you couldn't read it because the milkman—well, she always said he 'put his blamed bottles down right next to it,' and water from the cold milk bottles soaked the paper and made it so that you could only read part of it. I heard her tell somebody one day that's how I got the name Hamelin, that it was one of the few words you could read on the note."

"Yeah, I remember that too," Bryan said. "I thought she gave it to the sheriff, who even checked out the little town of Hamlin in West Texas."

"That's right," said Layla. "That's the story she used to tell. But apparently she either kept the note or somehow got it back from the sheriff. I do remember her saying one time that it was in a woman's handwriting, and she always figured it was your mother, but of course no one knew. Anyway, just as I was leaving, she told me if you ever started asking about your parents, I should give it to you. So I've got a letter you should look at."

"Anything else you know about it?" Hamelin said.

"No. It's in a sealed envelope, and it was for you, so I never opened it. I know right where it is back at our apartment. It's in a box of special things I've kept. But I think now's the time I'm supposed to give it to you."

"I'd really like to have it if it might be from my mother, but there's probably not much there to read. Mrs. Frendle always said a lot of people tried, but the writing was too messed up."

They were all silent for a moment. Then Bryan said quickly, "Hey, I just thought of something. I've got a buddy who graduated from college a couple of years before me. We got there at the same time, but it's taking me a really long time to finish. Anyway, he's had a really cool job with the police for a couple of years. He's always telling me about the things they do, especially working with other law enforcement teams. He says they even have ways to read old letters, notes that you can't see anymore. That they use special microscopes and chemicals or lights or something. I don't really know. Maybe I could get him to take a look at it or get somebody with the police who does that kind of thing to look at it."

"Sure," said Hamelin. "That might be pretty neat."

"We could do that," Layla said, "and bring it at Christmas, but—remember, it's your letter. You may want to wait and open it yourself."

"That's okay. I'd show it to you anyway. And I'd like to know as soon as possible if there's more to know from it. Maybe you could mail it to me after you try to read it?"

"Well, sure, but I really wouldn't want to do that because I would hate for it to get lost in the mail. Even if we can't read it, it's got a few words on it you can see, and it could be from your mother. At the very least, it would be a keepsake."

Hamelin's face showed his disappointment at a delay, but he nodded with a slight shrug.

"You know," said Layla, "if you're sure you don't mind us opening it, we'll go ahead and ask Bryan's friend to have a look at it. Who knows? If it's something important, maybe we can figure out how to get it to you quicker."

Hamelin's face brightened a little. "Thanks."

"But, Hamelin," Bryan said, "even if we get some new information for you, I'm still worried about you going back to that cave."

"I know," Hamelin said. "Like I said, sometimes I don't even want to go back, especially after I messed up the last time I tried and the eagle was really mad. Not to mention the spooky things that happened when all three of us were there recently."

"So, maybe you'll not go back at all," Bryan said.

"Maybe . . . but . . . well, there's something else that's got me thinking."

"What?" said Layla.

"Well, Mrs. Eastland gave me a book by George MacDonald." He looked at Layla, and she smiled. "Anyway, ever since I read it, I've been thinking even more about the cave, like something really big is going on, more than I know."

"Which book did you read?" she asked.

"*At the Back of the North Wind.*"

"I think I understand," she said.

"The book has really made me think about some things, about life and death, those things. Diamond thinks about them but also still talks about his parents and his family. Anyway, it's made me want to go back and try again."

"But," Bryan said, "remember what the eagle told you, Hamelin—that you shouldn't go back unless you are summoned."

"I know. But how am I supposed to know that? The first time, when he said I was summoned, I had no idea. I was just running away. And this last time, the eagle had to save my life, and then he sent me away. He said I wasn't summoned, and I thought for sure all the signs said I was. I think I'm supposed to go, but how am I going to know when?"

"Maybe looking for signs isn't the right way to go," Layla said. "When I have big decisions, I just try to be quiet and think. But probably people are different. I just know you can't force it. That never works."

"Yeah, I think that's what I was doing the last time. I wanted to go back so bad I wasn't thinking straight."

Everyone sat quietly, but finally Layla spoke again.

"Hamelin," she said, "here's a thought. Since you really trust Mrs. Eastland and since she's the one who gave you the book by George MacDonald that has you stirred up, maybe you should talk to her and get her advice."

Hamelin was surprised at the suggestion. They had all kept this among themselves. Tell someone else? It had been hard enough to tell Bryan and Layla.

"I think maybe Layla is right," Bryan said. "There are still some things we have kept to ourselves for years, and now we wish we had told someone else, maybe gotten their advice."

"Like what?"

Bryan looked at Layla, who nodded. "Like how our parents died and the strange experience we had with an almost magical eagle who guided us. Layla and I wish that *we* had talked to someone . . . like our aunt. We wonder if she could have told us more, or at least helped us understand why certain things happened. But now it's too late."

"Like what things?" Hamelin asked.

"Oh, Hamelin," Layla began, "we really want to tell you . . . but . . . it's just too much to go into now. But we promise we'll tell you some day, at the right time."

"Yeah," added Bryan, "it's getting late, and we need to fig-ure out for now what *you* should do, if anything, while you still can."

"What about talking to the Kaleys?" asked Hamelin.

"I thought of them too," said Layla. "But I'm not sure. We know they really care about you. It's obvious from all the questions they've asked us about you and also just from some little things we've noticed. But . . . it's like there's some-thing they know but can't say."

"So maybe I *should* ask them."

"You could try," said Bryan. "But I think they would just tell you to stay away from the cave to keep you safe."

"And I wouldn't blame them," added Layla quickly. "They're wonderful people, but all this is so odd . . . and dangerous. Sometimes—like with us—strange things hap-pen and you need someone who can understand, or at least try to understand, what you're talking about. And not just take the safe way out. So that's why I think Mrs. Eastland would be a good place to start. She seems to like stories of adventure and strange places, and . . . there's just some-thing about her. Bryan and I never had her for a teacher, because we were in junior high when she came to Middle-ton. But I remember her, how she . . . anyway, I think she would listen to you. And, of course, you can always talk to the Kaleys later . . . I mean, if Mrs. Eastland doesn't believe you or understand."

Hamelin listened. Maybe talking to Mrs. Eastland was a good idea.

"Look, just think about it," said Bryan. "You'll know what to do. And we can talk more over Christmas."

By then it was late, and Hamelin could see that they were tired, so they all went inside to their bedrooms.

The next day, after lunch, Bryan and Layla prepared to leave. The three friends and the Kaleys hugged each other good-bye more than usual. It was a sad departure, but they promised they'd be back for the holidays, right after settling matters with their aunt's house and possessions in Alpine. The last thing Bryan said was, "Hamelin, we'll talk soon." Layla smiled, winked, and hugged him again.

For now the next steps seemed clear: think about talking to Mrs. Eastland and wait for Bryan and Layla to come back at Christmas. At least the next three weeks or so would be simple.

Chapter 36

Mrs. Eastland's Advice

LMOST THE SECOND HIS FRIENDS DROVE AWAY, HAME-lin's restlessness hit him with full force. All he could think about was the cave and the eagle. He paced around the grounds of the children's home, thinking about everything he had talked about with Bryan and Layla. And especially their advice to talk to Mrs. Eastland, somebody who might understand his amazing story. Of course, the Kaleys would be glad to listen to him, but the more he thought about it, he knew he just couldn't bring himself to tell them. That left Mrs. Eastland. So late Sunday night, Hamelin decided to talk to her the first chance he got.

The next morning, he told Paul that he might not be riding home on the bus that afternoon. He asked him to tell the Kaleys not to worry, that he needed to stay a little bit after school and that he would be back to the children's home before supper.

When the school day finally ended, Hamelin slowly gathered up his books and papers while the other children were

leaving the classroom. Mrs. Eastland noticed that he seemed
to be waiting around, and so, when all the others were gone,
she asked him if he would like to talk about something. This
was his chance.

"Well, I have something to tell you that you may not
believe."

Mrs. Eastland smiled. "Try me. I've seen a few strange
things in my life . . . most teachers have!"

"Okay, but this is . . . well, pretty odd."

"Good," she said. "I *love* a good story."

"Well, I hope you like mine."

She laughed, which helped with his nerves, but he was
still afraid she would think he was crazy. It was too late to
back out now, though.

Mrs. Eastland pulled a chair for him near her desk. They
both sat, and Hamelin began his story. He told her about
everything: running away, the cave, the Great Eagle, the
footbridge, and even the two times he went back, including the episode with Bryan and Layla and the hypnotizing
music. Mrs. Eastland kept her eyes fixed on him the whole
time, and she didn't interrupt him even once.

When Hamelin finished his story, he glanced down at the
floor and then, looking up at Mrs. Eastland, waited for her
to say something. She appeared very thoughtful but didn't
say a word. Finally, he asked anxiously, "Well, pretty crazy,
huh, Mrs. Eastland?"

She tilted her head slightly and twisted her mouth to one
side. "Well . . . I . . . I wouldn't say crazy, but it is a very *strange*
series of events."

"So you don't think it really happened?"

"Oh, I didn't say *that* at all! I just said that it was all very
strange. But then . . . well, Hamelin, there *are* some unusual

things in life, things that are sometimes hard to explain—but just because they're hard to explain or understand doesn't mean they aren't true." She paused and closed her eyes nearly shut, as if thinking, or remembering, but kept her face toward him. Finally, her eyebrows moved again, and she asked, "What do you think?"

"I really don't understand it," he said, "but I know for sure it happened. And now I'm thinking about going back. Back to the cave, back through the opening. It's all I can think about. I don't know if I can, because the eagle said it's not up to me. But I know I really want to. I talked to Bryan and Layla, and they thought—me too—that we should find out what you think."

Mrs. Eastland looked surprised, but then, after a slight pause, a deep breath, and a soft sigh, she said, "Thank you for trusting me." Then she grew quiet. The left side of her mouth pulled down, and her eyes narrowed as she looked at Hamelin. It was obvious she was thinking. She said nothing for what seemed like a very long time.

Finally, she said, "What I think is this: I trust your word, and I believe what you are telling me, even though it is very unusual. Also, I think these things involving the cave and the eagle are very important for you, Hamelin." She paused again. Then almost in a rush—as if she didn't want to say it—she added, "Wanting desperately to go back through is part of the answer, and I think you'll never be satisfied with yourself either now, or even years from now, unless you try to go back."

Hamelin sat silently. He really hadn't expected this answer from a grown-up, even though it was Mrs. Eastland.

"However," she continued, "wanting to go back is not enough. I think it's very important for you to go at the *right time*."

Hamelin's forehead tightened. "That's sorta what the eagle said."

"Well, it's true. There are times when things should be done and times when they shouldn't. Maybe the first time was the right time, but the last two times weren't. Maybe you missed the right time, and it will never come back. Or maybe you'll get another chance."

"But how will I know?"

"I can't tell you that. There are lots of ways. Maybe even this conversation is part of it. But I can tell you that there is a right time, and if that time comes, you'll know."

Hamelin nodded and smiled. He thought he understood.

"Now," she said, "it's getting late, and the bus left long ago. Shall I give you a ride home?"

Hamelin agreed, and they closed up her classroom and left. He was relieved that Mrs. Eastland had been so understanding. It felt good to have an adult listen to him so closely. And he was especially glad to get her advice.

When they arrived at the children's home, he thanked her for the ride and for what she had told him. Just as he opened the car door, however, she put her hand on his shoulder.

"Hamelin," she said, "thank you for confiding in me. I know it wasn't easy. Just remember, wait for the right time. You'll know."

"Yes, ma'am."

She gave him a friendly wink and added, "And be sure to tell me what happens." Hamelin smiled and nodded. He trusted her, which made him think hard about what she said. He would have to be ready for the right time, but he was now more willing to wait if he had to—and somehow it made him even more sure that he would be going back into the cave.

Chapter 37

How Hamelin
Knew When

THAT AFTERNOON HAMELIN WROTE A LONG LETTER TO
Layla and Bryan and told them everything that
Mrs. Eastland had said. He wanted to write the letter
while her words were still fresh in his mind.

Later, when he joined the others for supper, he had the
strong feeling that change was in the air. He couldn't say
why, but he could feel it. Even the light in the room seemed
different. And before supper was over, the Kaleys had news.

Mrs. Kaley's father, who was eighty-one years old, had
rather suddenly fallen ill. Mr. and Mrs. Kaley explained that
she would have to travel back north to take care of him for
a while. The children were immediately quiet. Losing parents was something they all knew well. And the fact that they
would be losing Mrs. Kaley, even if only for several weeks,
saddened them all. But there was nothing else to be done
about it, and Mr. Kaley would still be there.

That night Hamelin went to the Kaleys' apartment and
offered to help in any way he could. Though she was in a

hurry to pack, Mrs. Kaley sat down with him for a few minutes on the edge of her bed and explained again why she needed to leave.

"But," she said, "I promise you I won't be gone any longer than I have to, and I'll try very hard to be back for Christmas." She looked closely at Hamelin's face and then quickly looked away.

He took a deep breath. He was relieved.

"You know, Hamelin, maybe I will take you up on your offer to help. Would you go up into the attic, find my large brown suitcase, and bring it to me? I really don't remember exactly where I put it—maybe somewhere toward the back."

"Sure," he yelled as he hurried out the apartment door, eager to help.

The children's home had an attic above the second floor, but there wasn't a proper set of stairs to get to it. It was used simply as storage space, and it ran the full width of the house and most of its length. It was an unfinished space, so Hamelin had to use a stepladder in the hall on the second floor even to get to the opening.

He climbed the ladder and removed the wooden cover that lay over the square opening in the ceiling. Then he pulled himself up into the attic, turned on the flashlight he had brought along, and found the suitcase just about where Mrs. Kaley guessed it would be. He glanced around and could see that the attic was full of all kinds of other stuff: boxes marked "Christmas decorations," others marked "clothes," dusty unused furniture, and various other things he had seen in use at the home in previous years.

He got the suitcase down for Mrs. Kaley and tried to find other ways to help her, but there wasn't much else he could do.

"Maybe someday you'll get to meet my father," she said as she told him good-night.

———✧———

A few days after Mrs. Kaley left, Hamelin received a letter from Layla and Bryan. They thought Mrs. Eastland had given him good advice, and they trusted that he would know when the time was right. They reminded him that he would let them know before he returned to the cave, but they would see him soon anyway.

Hamelin wrote them back, agreeing with their request and also telling them about Mrs. Kaley's father and her trip north. For the time being at least, the burden lifted a little from his mind. He was confident he would go back; now it was just a question of when.

But the days began to drag for him. He missed Mrs. Kaley. Of course, Mrs. Parker was her usual cheery self. And Mr. Kaley, though a little quieter without his wife, was mostly the same as he always was.

As the days went by, Mr. Kaley regularly gave everyone a report at mealtime. It started to sound like Mrs. Kaley's father was doing better. Hamelin hoped she would be home soon.

———✧———

That year Christmas was on a Tuesday, so that meant the last day of school before the holidays would be Friday, December 14. It was going to be a nice long break, a little more than two weeks, with school starting back on Wednesday, January 2.

While everyone was looking forward to the end of school on Friday, it was the preceding afternoon that made the holidays start early. About five o'clock that Thursday, Mr. Kaley surprised everyone when he walked through the front door with Mrs. Kaley. She came back early—and in time for the Christmas holidays!

"My father is doing much better now, and I think I'm home for good!" she said as the children crowded around her. Everyone laughed and hugged her.

With Mrs. Kaley back, the whole house looked and felt lighter. Around the dinner table, the kids laughed, Mr. Kaley had more jokes than usual, and everyone enjoyed hearing again Mrs. Kaley's singsong voice and her favorite saying— "Oh, John!"

After the meal, Mr. and Mrs. Kaley visited with the children a long time but finally went to their apartment. Hamelin took his homework downstairs near the living room and foyer area, hoping to see Mrs. Kaley again.

And he did. A little later that evening, she came out of their apartment and, after spying him, said quickly, "Oh, Hamelin, I was hoping to find you. Would you mind taking my suitcase back to the attic?"

"Sure!"

Once again he got the stepladder and the flashlight. He pushed away the wooden cover, boosted the suitcase up through the opening, and pulled himself up. But as he made his way across the attic, looking down to watch where he stepped, he unexpectedly bumped his head hard against a low-hanging rafter. He lost his balance and fell back onto some plywood flooring.

Hamelin wasn't knocked out, but he didn't get up immediately. His head was pounding, so he just sat there for a minute, dazed. The flashlight had fallen out of his hand, but it hadn't broken. It lay near his feet still on, and its beam shot across the attic into the corner opposite from where

Mrs. Kaley's suitcase was stored, shining on something that looked familiar to him. He pressed his fingers to the bridge of his nose and waited another minute to let the throbbing in his head ease up a little more. Then, bending from the waist to make sure he didn't bump his head again, he got up and slowly made his way across the wood flooring toward what the light had struck.

When he reached the other side of the attic, he realized that the flashlight beam had indeed fallen on something he recognized. It was his old backpack.

He hadn't seen it in more than three years. He thought back and reconstructed what must have happened. When he had slipped back into the children's home early that morning after running away, the backpack was so muddy and scratched up that he had just shoved it under his bed. He really hadn't known what to do with it, because he didn't want anyone to see it and ask how it got so beat up. So it had stayed there, and then he had forgotten about it, until some time later he had realized it was gone. But no one had asked him about it, so he had figured that maybe someone had found it under his bed and thrown it away—probably during the flurry of housecleaning when the Kaleys first arrived. But instead, here it was, up in the attic.

Hamelin picked it up and felt a bulge in the back of it. He pulled on the half-closed zipper—at first it stuck—to see what it was. Something definitely was in there. He stuffed his fingers into the pouch and pulled out a crumpled ball of stiff cloth. It was gloves. A pair of gloves. And then he felt a rush of surprise fill his chest. It was the pair of gloves the eagle had given him!

Hamelin's heart began to race. He returned the backpack to the corner where he had found it and made his way back to the other side of the attic. He put Mrs. Kaley's suitcase where it belonged, climbed out of the attic, and returned the stepladder. He hurried to his area in the boys' bedroom and looked at the gloves, his mind flooding with memories of that night.

He pushed his fingers into the stiff cloth. And though the gloves were still a touch too big, they were a much better fit now. He stared at them for a moment and then placed them in the trunk at the foot of his bed. His mind was whirling.

He went back to see Mr. and Mrs. Kaley. They visited for a while, but all Hamelin could think about was the gloves. He thought about telling the Kaleys everything, and at one point he almost started a sentence. But he just couldn't. He finally told them good-night and went back to the boys' long room. As he lay there in his bed, he took a deep breath. He knew the right time was near.

Chapter 38

Showdown with Patton McBoggerson

THE NEXT MORNING, AS HAMELIN DRESSED FOR SCHOOL on the last day before the Christmas break, he grabbed the gloves at the last second. The weather had turned cold during the night, so he figured he had a good excuse to wear them. Usually he wouldn't have bothered, even when it was very cold. But he sensed that he had found those gloves for a reason.

The day passed quickly, and the atmosphere in class was relaxed. Mrs. Eastland had a small gift for each child, and some of the children were able to bring a gift for her. The class had a party that afternoon with cupcakes, cookies, and a special apple punch.

At the end of the day, when Mrs. Eastland dismissed the class, Hamelin told her good-bye and thanked her again for what she had told him. He then gathered up his books to take home for the holidays and, because it was cold outside, put on his coat. He remembered again the gloves he had found the previous night, so he put them on too.

He went outside to get on the bus and, as he usually did, took a quick glance around for Paul so they could ride home together. That's when he saw Patton McBoggerson. From the looks of things, there was a crowd of kids gathering around him—he must have been picking on some poor kid. Then, to Hamelin's shock, he realized that the one Patton was standing in front of, blocking, pushing, and slapping on the head, was *Paul!*

Hamelin ran as hard as he could to the crowd and pushed his way to the center.

"Hey, what're you doing?" he hollered, even before he got to Paul. "Pick on somebody your own size!"

"Well, look who's here," Patton said with a wicked grin on his face. Hamelin realized that he was almost the same height as Patton, but the bully still outweighed him by a good forty pounds. At this point, however, size didn't matter. He had to protect Paul.

"So what are you going to *do* about it, Hamelin Stoop? I'll push your little buddy around anytime I *want* to."

With that, Patton turned his attention again to Paul, but Hamelin instinctively stepped between the two, shielding Paul from the bully.

"Oh, aren't you brave!" said Patton sarcastically.

"At least I don't pick on first graders," Hamelin shot back.

Patton's face turned red, and he suddenly lunged toward Hamelin and pushed him hard. Hamelin stumbled backward but didn't fall. He kept his eyes on Patton and quickly moved Paul to the side. "Just get away from here," he said.

Paul glared at Patton but did move away slowly.

"Yeah, that's right," said the bully. "You'd better run away, you little shrimp. I'll get you another time." He turned to Hamelin. "Right now, though, I'm gonna take care of Mr. Stoopid!"

Patton rushed at Hamelin and this time pushed him in the chest with both hands before he could get his arms up to defend himself. He lost his balance and fell backward. Patton laughed and then, before Hamelin could get up, jumped on top of him, straddling him at the waist.

"How brave do you feel now, Hambone?" he sneered.

"I feel fine, except for your *lard* all over me!" Some of the kids nearby laughed.

"I oughta smash your stupid *face!*" snarled Patton.

"I don't care what you do to me," Hamelin yelled back. "You're *still* a bully!"

Furious, Patton closed his right hand into a fist and threw a punch. As Hamelin instinctively lifted his hands and forearms to block the oncoming blow, the fist came down violently against the palm of Hamelin's right hand—but stopped as suddenly as if it had hit a brick wall.

"Owwwww!" Patton screamed. "What the . . . ?" Then, furious and embarrassed that he had cried out, he coiled his left hand into a fist and again tried to slug Hamelin in the face. But Hamelin instinctively moved his hands a little to his right to protect himself, as if he were going to catch a baseball two-handed. Again he blocked Patton's oncoming fist. This time, however, the fist didn't just hit the palm of Hamelin's hand. Instead, Hamelin caught it in both hands in midair, and when he squeezed his gloves around it, Patton's face twisted in agony.

"Yaow!" he yelled. "My hand! You broke my hand!"

Patton held both of his forearms up to about his own shoulder height, but his hands hung limp from the wrists, and he wailed.

Hamelin really didn't understand what had happened, but with a screaming Patton McBoggerson still on top of him, and the bully's chest exposed, he didn't hesitate. He pulled back his gloved hands and smashed Patton in the middle of the chest with the sides of both his fists.

The result was stunning—to Patton and everyone else. The children who had crowded around and were watching what was going on were, later on, not exactly sure how to describe what they saw. Hamelin's two-fisted blow to Patton's chest didn't just knock him off balance; it knocked him completely off of Hamelin and sent him flying backward. Now it was the bully lying on his back, wailing, both hands still held in the air and a wild-eyed look of shock and pain on his face.

Between his cries, he blubbered, "What did you *do* to me?"

Hamelin quickly got up, took a look at Patton, still sprawled on the ground, and walked away. The children who were standing by made a path for him, and he could hear several of them whispering in astonishment.

Hamelin himself was amazed at what had happened, but he also felt very self-conscious and even embarrassed. He kept walking away from the crowd while at the same time looking for Paul. He felt like he was walking in slow motion. He could still hear Patton wailing and crying behind him, and he thought he saw Mr. Litchie at the edge of the crowd, but he didn't look long enough to be sure.

Paul wasn't far away, because he had wanted to stay and help. Hamelin saw him, nodded, and the two of them headed straight for the bus. It all happened so fast that no one knew what to think, though there was lots of talking and whispering going on. And the buzz was all about Hamelin.

On the bus, the other children, even the older boys, stared at him. No one could believe what they had seen, and those who hadn't seen it heard in quick whispers the wildly spreading story of how Hamelin had knocked the big ninth-grade bully for a loop.

Hamelin sat on the bus in silence, trying to put together what had just happened—and wondering where all that strength had come from. And then it hit him. He looked down at his hands. The *gloves.*

His mind started whirling back to when he had first worn the gloves more than three years ago—when he held the swinging footbridge and then forcibly pushed away from it and when he dug his fingers into the ground to avoid falling over the cliff. He remembered that his grip had felt really strong. It must have been these gloves . . . the gloves from the Great Eagle . . . that had given him such extraordinary strength against Patton.

Nervous at the thought, Hamelin quickly took the gloves off and put them in his coat pocket. If they were somehow magic, then he wanted to make sure nothing else happened, at least not until he figured things out.

Within minutes after the bus arrived at the home, word of the fight quickly reached Mr. and Mrs. Kaley.

When Hamelin and Paul entered the house, Mr. Kaley was waiting. He eyed Hamelin and then asked to speak to Paul.

The two walked away, and Hamelin worried that he was in trouble.

———

"I didn't squeal on you, Hamelin, I promise!" Paul said as they walked together to supper that night. "I told him you were just protecting me."

Later at the dinner tables, all the children were still whispering about it, how Hamelin "pounded Patton on the chest and sent him flying" and how Patton "maybe even broke his wrists when he tried to hit Hamelin."

Hamelin never heard anyone mention his gloves, probably because there was nothing unusual about them. And since he had taken them off on the bus, maybe no one even noticed them. Maybe everyone thought it was just a surge of adrenaline that had given him a bit more strength.

Near the end of supper, Mr. Kaley got up from his place and walked toward Hamelin. He had something in his hand. The room got quieter as everyone, especially the children, saw Mr. Kaley approach Hamelin. Hamelin saw him coming too and figured now was the time he was going to get scolded, maybe even punished. But Mr. Kaley just stood next to him at the table and said in a calm voice, "I hear you had a pretty interesting day."

Hamelin looked up at him and nodded. "Yes, sir," he said.

"Glad you took care of Paul, and glad you know how to take care of yourself. By the way, here's a letter from Layla."

He winked at Hamelin, who took the letter and said, "Thanks." The whole room was still quiet, but most had heard what Mr. Kaley said, and they smiled and looked at Hamelin as Mr. Kaley walked away. Hamelin let out a quiet sigh of relief.

Hamelin didn't want to draw attention to the letter, so he kept it on the table until supper was over. Then he casually took it in one hand, put his dishes up, and went upstairs. He was by himself in his space in the boys' bedroom. As he opened the envelope, he felt a combination of excitement and dread. *Will it be about the note from my mother?*

Inside the envelope, he found two sheets of paper. He unfolded them and saw that the one on top was a letter from Layla. The other sheet was also something that looked like Layla's handwriting, but he started with the top one, which read,

```
Dear Hamelin,

When we got back to Abilene, Bryan immediately
contacted his friend in the police department.
He asked him if he could help us with the
note that was on the porch when you were left
at the children's home. It took several days,
and Bryan's friend didn't know how to do it
himself, but he got another person in the
department who knew something about this kind
of thing. It took a while, but the results
came back.

    I didn't want to send you the original note
in the mail, because I didn't want to take
any chance of it being lost. It's something
you'll want to save.

    So I copied it word for word. The next page
is my handwriting, of course, but it's exactly
what the note on the screened porch said.

    Bryan and I look forward to talking to
you about it. It says some very scary and
strange things. We know it might make you
want to go back to the cave immediately, but
please don't do anything without talking to
us. There are some other things that we need
to tell you.
```

```
So I better close. I know you want to read
the note that got left. We love you, and we
look forward to seeing you.

Love,
Layla
```

Hamelin felt his hands almost trembling as he reached for the other note. *Could this really be from my mother?* The note said,

```
Mrs. Frendle,

Please take care of my baby boy. I should've
talked to you more when I was there, but I
was so afraid. I'm very sorry now. Maybe you
could have helped.
     My story is strange, but I'm from Hamelin.
We were taken by Ren'dal from our families
long years ago. Please don't let them take
our son. Ren'dal's trackers are coming, and
they will either kill me or take me back to
Ventr
```

That was it. The note was short and unfinished, but Hamelin was overwhelmed with feelings. His mind was whirling. He read the letter again slowly and thought about every word. He wanted to make sure he picked up on everything. It was a lot for him to think about, and his emotions were so full at seeing the letter that he wasn't sure if he was thinking clearly. But several things seemed obvious—the letter was from one of his parents. Probably his mother, since

Mrs. Frendle thought it was written by a woman. And Layla apparently did too.

And his mother was from some place called Hamelin, wherever that was. Hamelin had heard of a town that had the same name as he did. Wasn't that the town Bryan said Mrs. Frendle mentioned?

Another thing that seemed obvious was that both parents were still alive when the note was written. She originally wrote "my baby boy" but later in the letter said "*our* son." If she were on her own or if his father were dead, Hamelin didn't think she would put it like that.

And obviously they were in danger. Someone was chasing them, and she didn't want Hamelin to be caught.

But the biggest and strangest thing was the odd name that appeared toward the bottom. The name Ren'dal. Hamelin couldn't remember it before when he was talking to Bryan and Layla, but he did now. That was one of the two strange names that the eagle had mentioned three and a half years ago when he had failed to cross the footbridge. "She is waiting," he had said, and then he said something about Ren'dal and somebody else.

And that's also when he said "and your own"—before he stopped. If his parents had been captured by Ren'dal, then it was obvious they were somewhere on the other side of the footbridge, and it now seemed even more likely to Hamelin that the eagle had been referring to them when he said "your own."

Hamelin stared at the letter, and even though it wasn't his mother's handwriting, it was his mother's words. He felt tears welling up in his eyes, and he pulled it up to the side of his face, though he wanted to be careful not to get any tears on it. He couldn't help it. He sat on the edge of his bed and glanced around quickly, glad that no one else was in the room. And he sobbed. Not out loud, but for a long minute or two, huge tears ran down his face.

But she hadn't put her name. Oh, he wished she had, but she was being chased, probably afraid, and got interrupted. The last word in the letter looked to be another odd name or maybe even only part of a word—*Ventr*. No period. No nothing. But the *V* was capitalized, and it clearly looked like a place that she didn't want to go back to.

Hamelin continued to sit on the bed for a long time, but now he knew for sure: it was the right time. And it was no accident he had found the gloves and used them today, the same day he had gotten his mother's letter from Layla.

Chapter 39

The Journey Begins

HAMELIN KNEW THAT THE TIME HAD COME TO RETURN TO the cave. He couldn't delay, but he also knew that he couldn't leave without telling Bryan and Layla—and maybe the Kaleys—what he was planning.

So, very early on Saturday morning, he asked Mr. Kaley if he could use the phone in the Kaleys' apartment. "I'll pay the charges, Mr. Kaley, but I really have to make an important call to Bryan and Layla." Mr. Kaley could tell by his voice that something unusual was going on, so he let him use the phone. He stepped outside while Hamelin placed the call. Bryan answered.

"Hello?"

"Bryan?"

"Yeah."

"This is Hamelin."

"Hey, Hamelin! What's going on?" Bryan called for Layla, and Hamelin could hear her voice in the background. "Everything okay?" Bryan asked.

"Yeah," Hamelin said, "but a lot's going on." There was a brief silence on the phone.

"You got the note, I'm sure. Hope it hasn't upset you. Maybe we shouldn't have sent it. Should have been there with you. I'm sorry. But Layla said, and I agreed, that you deserved to know as soon as possible. But we'll be there for the holidays in about a week—"

"I think it's time for me to go back to the cave."

"Hamelin—no, not yet! Look, we'll be there soon," said Bryan.

"It's not just the note. I found the gloves. The gloves the eagle gave me."

Hamelin then quickly told him about the gloves and the fight. Bryan explained the situation to Layla, and she immediately took the phone from her brother.

"Hamelin, listen, we understand why you want to go now. We really do," she said. "But we don't like this. Can't you wait 'til we get there?"

"I know . . . I mean . . . I wish I could wait," said Hamelin. "But I *know* the time is right. I just . . . I missed it before, so I have to at least *try*." He heard Layla take a deep breath. She handed the phone back to Bryan.

"Hamelin? Are you sure about this? What about the Kaleys?"

"I'll leave a note for them. But I can't tell them now. They'll just . . . try to stop me. But if they call you, you can tell them however much of the story you want."

"How long will you be gone?" Bryan asked.

"I don't know," he said. And then Hamelin's voice got stronger. "But I *know* that the time has come for me to try again to get into the cave and find the eagle."

Bryan said, "I . . . we . . . understand."

Hamelin quickly said good-bye, because he wasn't sure what else to say, but just before he put the phone down, he could hear Layla call out, "We love you, Hamelin!" He wished he had said it back, but he was already hanging up the phone. He left the Kaleys' apartment and didn't see either of them immediately, so he was glad to escape any further conversations right then.

Hamelin went back to his area in the boys' room and gathered up a few things. He wrote the Kaleys a note saying that he would be gone for several days and asking them not to worry about him. He told them that Bryan and Layla could explain things and that they knew where he had to go. He asked the Kaleys not to look for him and told them that he would contact them as soon as possible, that this was something he had to do.

Of course the Kaleys were going to worry, Hamelin knew, but he hoped they would understand. After breakfast that same Saturday morning, he left the note just inside their bedroom door, in a place where he was sure they would find it. He put on his sweater and jacket, placed the gloves carefully inside his coat pocket, and then casually walked through the dining hall to the kitchen, where he stuffed a few things to eat into his blue jean pockets. It was the first day of the Christmas holidays, so no one paid any attention when Hamelin walked out of the same screened porch where he had been left in a tomato box eleven and a half years earlier.

So that he wouldn't be seen walking up the road, he decided to go through the wooded area on that side of the house. Within fifty minutes, he had gone the two and a half miles north through the woods. He quickly slipped across the road and within another fifteen minutes, with the morning sun at his back, had made his way up the hill to the ledge.

The boulder that he, Bryan, and Layla had scraped the mud from looked just the same as they left it. The opening at the floor of the ledge was still there, but he obviously wasn't going to get into the cave unless it was bigger, so he set about digging and scraping around the boulder. The floor of the ledge was rock hard, so he couldn't widen the opening at its bottom, but he succeeded in pulling away more of the mud from the inner side of the rock. However, the opening still wasn't big enough to crawl through.

As he stood there pondering what to do next, he heard a strong, rushing wind. It had the sound of wings, but it was nothing at all like the fluttering of many small wings they had heard before. This sounded like powerful strokes, loud swishes of wind that seemed to come from just the other side of the boulder.

At first Hamelin was motionless, even afraid. He realized his heart was pounding. He slowly moved a step backward, away from the opening, and now leaned on his left shoulder against the rock wall of the hill. He hoped it was the eagle, but he also feared the strange, unpredictable bird, not to mention the other creatures that were obviously lurking in the cave.

He stood completely still, almost afraid to breathe. He glanced to his right at the drop-off, looking to see if he could make a sudden dash for it, jump off the ledge, and scramble down the hill. But as he looked to his right, the morning sun shone directly in his eyes, and the woods in the eastern horizon beyond him seemed to merge with the shrubs just below the ledge. He squinted his eyes as things were turning dark on him with the sun so bright in his face. He took a deep breath to calm himself. And just as he was telling himself that he couldn't back out and run away again, he heard a strange sound, almost like two planks of wood being rubbed together in short bursts. Hamelin looked back toward the opening and could tell that something was happening on the other side of the boulder. What was that? Did his eyes detect a movement of light just inside the opening? He leaned toward it.

Then a piercing voice startled him. It was breathy but strong and direct, and though he jerked back a step at the sound, it was still unmistakable: "Why don't you use the gloves?"

The gloves? The *gloves*! Hamelin had completely forgotten about them! He quickly reached inside his jacket, pulled on the gloves, and then, with his back up against the inner wall and his two hands gripping the rock, pushed. Almost immediately, he felt the boulder move. It didn't move easily, but it did move steadily. He was amazed at the strength that flowed from his hands. In fact, the more effort he exerted, the more the strength from his hands grew.

The boulder moved first six inches, then a foot, then two feet as Hamelin's arms extended. His hands had begun at his chest and were now pushed straight out in front of him. He then leaned forward and pushed with his full weight, and he felt the great boulder roll another foot over a small mound and into a low spot, a kind of resting place created by a small natural rut on the other side of the mound. The opening was still narrow but definitely wide enough to get through. But what attracted Hamelin's attention even more immediately was the stunning creature, the magnificent eagle who stood on the other side of the opening, waiting for him to begin again whatever it was he was summoned to do.

Now, in the morning light, Hamelin could see that the great bird was even bigger than he remembered, his head at shoulder height to Hamelin, despite the fact that he too had grown. Beyond the beauty and size of the creature, however, was his way of standing there, the look of majesty that he carried as the light radiated from him. But there was something else. The eagle looked stronger but also older. The times since Hamelin had seen him in the light had changed him. His eyes were a brownish gold. His chest was larger, but the gold of his feathers was darker, and the layers of black held tinges of gray. The Great Eagle looked wiser, and the radiance that came from him seemed thicker, almost heavier.

"You've come none too soon," he said. "Follow me. We have no time to waste."

With that, the great bird turned and strode off. Hamelin surprised himself by hesitating, but the eagle never looked back. Hamelin took a short breath and followed. He wanted to yell, "Where are we going?" but he figured he knew, and he didn't want the eagle to know how afraid he was.

Chapter 40

The Footbridge: Another Chance

HAMELIN HAD TO MOVE QUICKLY TO FOLLOW THE GREAT Eagle, but he stepped ahead with more confidence than he did as an eight-year-old. His mind was busy even as he walked the treacherous path. For the last three and a half years, he had often hoped he would get back to this very path, but now all he could think about was the past: all the books he had read and especially the friends he had made, like Marceya, Paul, Bryan and Layla, the Kaleys, and Mrs. Eastland. Walking in the darkness, he thought about growing up in the children's home, about not knowing his parents, and about Mrs. Regehr and Mrs. Frendle. For some reason, he even thought about Mrs. Kelliman and Patton McBoggerson.

And when he remembered Patton, he thought of the fight and the gloves, and then, again, he remembered the path in front of him. He needed to be careful. This second journey was only just beginning, and he knew he still had the footbridge to cross—but now he had hope that his parents would be somewhere on the other side.

For a second, the eagle was gone from sight, and the darkness of the cave reasserted itself immediately. The path on which they walked, as before, moved downward and grew narrower. Hamelin leaned left and strengthened his balance by touching his hand to the wall of the cavern. Now he could see the eagle's light again, so he picked up his pace. He had to stay as close as possible to the great bird.

Though Hamelin didn't remember every turn in the cave, he did recall that the path had grown more dangerous the farther they went. He remembered especially the last, cramped, wide curve and knew that before long they would reach the footbridge. He steeled himself to face it, the spot where he had failed before.

Perhaps it was his determination to stay closer to the eagle this time, or his dread of the walking bridge over the chasm, or maybe both, but the trip through the cavern seemed shorter than he expected. Now came that last narrow curve. He bent over, crawled, and then stood. Here he was again. The space still had a hot, musty smell to it. The eagle stopped and turned, and just beyond the great bird and with the light that flowed from him, Hamelin could see it—the silhouette of the upper ropes of the footbridge.

The eagle looked steadily at the boy, then turned and darted swiftly across the bridge. From the other side, he turned back to Hamelin and said, "Cross over."

Hamelin took one look at the footbridge, and his legs immediately felt weak. He took a deep breath and made himself walk toward it. This time, however, he stood straight, took a step onto the bridge, and then very lightly placed his gloved hands just above the upper ropes. He paused, and when he did, he felt his body go light. He could feel his knees starting to bend, and the sensation of falling moved across his upper body.

"Hamelin," called out the eagle, "stand up . . . and *breathe!*" Hamelin filled his chest with air and straightened up. He took a step, then another.

Don't pause or look down, he told himself fiercely. He strode forward for several quick paces and for a second thought the rest was going to be easy.

But he heard howling below him, and he instinctively looked down. The bridge began to sway left and right. The winds of the cavern had suddenly stirred.

And then a hot smell from below hit his face. Although he had not heard or felt any breeze before now, Hamelin found himself in the middle of whirling, whipping gusts, and the bridge began to rock and sway hard back and forth. He firmed up his grip on the upper ropes, then lifted his head and raised his line of vision, determined not to look down again. For one brief second, he shut his eyes. He told himself there was no way he would let himself turn back. Then he opened his eyes and looked forward again, and even though the winds were loud and the bridge was twisting violently, he saw the shining bird looking at him. Their eyes met. And Hamelin decided to keep his eyes on the eagle.

The bridge was swinging ever wider left and right. Hamelin clutched even more tightly to the upper rope rails and kept looking at the bird. The violent pitching of the footbridge was now swinging his legs to an almost ninety-degree angle—left and right—from their normal vertical position. And the noisy winds were adding to his increasing sense of imbalance. His fears once again made him glance down, and he felt waves of panic flood his head and stomach. His eyes were swinging with the bridge. He knew he couldn't just stand there. He had to act. He thought he heard the great bird yelling his name, so, fixing his eyes on the Great Eagle and timing his move—just as the arc of the footbridge approached its lowest point coming down from his left—he bent his knees and quickly took several more steps, and then waited while the bridge swung on high to his right.

Then as soon as the bridge came back to the bottom of the twisting arc—Hamelin ran. He got to within five feet of the other side when disaster struck. Even the eagle looked surprised. The lower rope on Hamelin's left came untied from its post across the bridge, and the eagle had not noticed that it was coming loose just at his right foot. He had been so intent on extending his right wing toward Hamelin that he didn't see the knot gradually slipping. The eagle screeched loudly above the howling winds, but it was too late.

The bridge was still connected at its other points, the four points, upper and lower, behind Hamelin and three of the points in front of him. But the sudden loss of support from the planks on his left immediately caused Hamelin to drop. Fortunately, he was gripping the two ropes that served as handrails, and as he fell through the collapsed left side of the footbridge, his grip held firm. His footing, however, was completely gone, and he was suspended in midair over the chasm below.

The strength in the gloves enabled him to pull himself up, so that for a moment he looked like a gymnast doing the iron cross, though of course his feet were not even or stable. Even though he could hold on, he knew that he would be better off with both hands on the same rope. He quickly let go with his left hand and reached over to the right-hand rope and then pulled himself up so that his feet were on the one lower rope that still stretched across the chasm on his right. Now, however, with both feet on the same lower rope and his hands holding the upper rope just below his waist level, his balance was more precarious than ever. Instead of facing the eagle, who was now to his left, Hamelin was facing the blackness below. The bridge was still swinging and twisting left to right, but the loss of the lower left supporting rope, with all of Hamelin's weight now on one side, made it even worse.

He looked quickly at the eagle and shouted, "What should I do?"

The eagle screeched back, "Keep coming this way. There is no going back."

"But the rope is still tied back there," Hamelin yelled.

"You can't go back!" said the eagle again.

"But I can't hang on forever—I'm going to fall."

"You could fall either way."

Hamelin was close to panicking. He continued to hold the rope with his hands but was afraid to keep standing tall. For balance, he crouched on his right knee as he still faced sideways over the abyss. He wrapped his right arm as much as he could around the rope so that it ran from his wrist through his elbow and under his armpit. Then he slowly lowered himself to his knees on the right-hand rope. Being lower helped his balance, but now he was frozen in place.

"Did you just bring me out here to fall?" he yelled in frustration.

"No! I did bring you out here—but I brought you out here to succeed. Either way, it is a test."

The wind now whipped the rope bridge more violently than ever. The sound of the howling winds below and the heat coming up from the abyss swamped Hamelin's senses. But he wouldn't let go. He also knew he couldn't stay there and that going back was something he couldn't do again. So he took a deep breath—even if it was a breath that filled his nostrils and mouth with the smell and taste of burning rubber. He continued to grip with both hands, but he looped his right leg and then his left over the top rope so that his legs were wrapped around it. These movements spun him around so that his face, chest, and lower body were now horizontal and facing up and the rope was running through his clenched hands—which were just above his head—across his chest, and against his legs just under the knees. Gripping the rope with hands and knees, he couldn't see the eagle anymore, but he could hear the great bird.

"You can do it, Hamelin. I know you can. Keep coming this way. Even if it's slow, it's the right direction."

Hamelin began to pull himself in a horizontal shinny toward the side of the bridge where the eagle stood. He was moving head first, but he was making progress. Hand over hand, he pulled himself with the rope burning between his thighs and knees.

The wind continued to howl, but above it all, Hamelin could hear the eagle in that strange voice that had shrieks and screeches in it. "You're almost here," the bird yelled. "Just a little more. Your hand is close to the post on this side."

"Just grab me and pull me in!" yelled Hamelin.

The eagle continued to stand there.

"You can do it," he yelled. His voice was now closer, and though Hamelin couldn't see him, he could almost feel his presence. His eyes were closed, but he had the feeling that the eagle's wings were above him, sheltering him. And he could hear the eagle's voice, closer and closer.

He felt his head touch the post on the other side of the bridge, though his hands and legs were still clinging to the upper rope and his full body was still suspended over the abyss.

He could figure out only one way to get himself to safety. He would have to let go with one hand. He took another deep breath, and as the bridge swung now to his right, he released the rope with his left hand and grabbed the post near its base, sunk deep into the rock on the other side. He still held the rope with his legs and one hand, but now he could pull with his left hand on the post and also scoot closer with his right hand. Getting his full body up to ground level on the other side was still the problem, but he was for the moment slowly gaining valuable inches.

The only way to do it now was to let go with the other hand and try to grab the post before his left arm gave way—and quickly enough not to fall below the level of the post. He waited until the howling wind and the twisting bridge put him in just the position he wanted, with his left arm slightly above the level of the land, and he let go with his legs and then, a split second later, with his right hand. His body swung down and banged hard against the rock just below the post as his right hand grabbed it and the lower rope, which was still attached on that side. He got his right hand around the post, but as he hugged it with both hands and arms, his body now dangled vertically over the abyss.

Now he would find out just exactly how strong the gloves were. Amazingly, he seemed to grow stronger the more he used the strength that he had. He pulled and was able to raise himself partway up the post, and at just the right moment, he swung his left leg up and then managed to get his knee on the ground. Then, pulling in and regripping higher on the post simultaneously, he finally lifted his right knee up. He was then able, with a powerful pull followed by a two-handed push against the post, to swing and at the same time rotate his upper body so that he landed on his back at the eagle's feet. He rolled over a couple of times to make sure he was away from the drop-off, and then, panting and still lying on his back, he looked up into the face of the eagle.

They stared at each other, and Hamelin finally gasped, "Why didn't you help me?"

"I did. By staying here. It wasn't easy."

For a split second, Hamelin actually thought the eagle was kidding, but then he realized that the bird probably meant it. He rolled over one more time and then sat up. The eagle glanced at him for an instant—Hamelin was pretty sure he saw a momentary look of approval in the great bird's eyes— and without warning launched himself down into the abyss.

Hamelin immediately feared that the strange bird was leaving him in one of his sudden and unannounced departures. Soon, however, the light from the Great Eagle was visible enough for Hamelin to see the bird spread his wings and fly halfway to the other side of the chasm. In one swooping move, the glorious bird grabbed the dangling lower rope in his beak and flew it back to Hamelin before dropping it and then quickly stepping on it to hold it on the ground.

"Tie it back," the great bird said. "Someone else might need this bridge."

Hamelin looked puzzled for a moment and then remembered that he did know how to tie things. Mr. Moore had taught him several knots for ropes and chains, as they had often had to use the old tractor to pull some trailer or pickup out of a muddy spot in the pasture.

Hamelin quickly wrapped the loose end of the rope around the post where it belonged. It was a good thing the rope had only come untied and not broken—there was still plenty of slack for tying another knot. He used the best knot he could remember and, with the strength in his hands, pulled it tight. It would hold. He then turned and stood, looking at the eagle. "I made it," he said. "I finally made it."

The eagle nodded, turned his back, and began to run. The light radiating from him projected forward and—as far as Hamelin could tell—revealed what looked like a smaller, horizontal shaft just in front of them. The eagle was moving quickly toward it.

Chapter 41

The Tunnel of Times, the Atrium of the Worlds, and Beyond

"**W**AIT," SAID HAMELIN, MORE SHARPLY THAN HE intended. The eagle turned and looked at him.

"I made it. I passed the test—which is what you called it, right?"

"Yes, young man, you have indeed passed the test. Well done."

"So I've got some questions." The eagle looked at him and blinked in a way that gave Hamelin the courage to go on. "What about the girl who was waiting? You mentioned her the first time I tried to cross the bridge and failed."

"She's gone. Lost to the other side."

Hamelin wasn't sure what that meant, but he went on to his next question. "What about Ren'dal? Isn't that the name you used along with some other name that I can't remember?"

"Yes, I mentioned Ren'dal and Chimera. They *are* the other side."

"Are they waiting?"

"Not for you, nor are they expecting you. But they'll learn about you soon enough."

Hamelin then hesitated before asking his last question. It was really the main one he was aiming at, but he was building up to it. "You also started to say something else. You said something about 'your own,' but then you stopped. You were going to say 'your own *parents*,' weren't you?"

The eagle stared at him. And then he said simply, "Yes."

"Are they waiting on me?"

The eagle seemed to think for a minute but then replied, "No, but they are waiting. They're hoping to be set free, but I can't say they're waiting on you."

"Where are they?"

"I can't say," replied the eagle.

"What do you mean? You mean you don't know, or you don't want to say?"

The eagle took what appeared to be a deep breath, filling his chest and about the same time giving his wings half a flutter. He looked impatient with Hamelin but, on the other hand, almost seemed like he had to answer the question, even if he didn't want to.

"There are some things I know and can answer. There are other things that only the Ancient One knows."

Before the eagle could continue, Hamelin said, "So which one is this?"

"Neither. This is one of those things that I know, that I'm not permitted to say."

"But that's why I came," said Hamelin, his voice a little louder than before. "To find them."

"Perhaps, but never forget that you were summoned here. Finding your parents might be one thing, but you were summoned for many other reasons as well."

"You mean there's something more important than finding my parents?" Hamelin vaguely remembered something similar about Diamond and the back of the North Wind and life's deep mysteries, but none of that mattered as much to him now.

"Many things. We can never know all the Ancient One's reasons for what he does, but, I assure you, he often has bigger reasons and purposes than simply making us happy."

Hamelin glared at the eagle. Even while he was doing it, he knew it wasn't wise. "So I'm just supposed to give up my reasons?"

The eagle's eyes softened a bit, as did his voice. He leaned toward Hamelin and said, "No, it's just that the Ancient One often has unusual and surprising things in mind. I suspect he wants to include your reasons within his. It's possible that your reasons were the only way he had to connect with you. But this is a fight for kingdoms, for exiles, and ultimately to determine the rightful ruler of the Land of Gloaming."

"But I just . . . I just—"

"Your own reasons to come have been good, but they're not enough. There are other things to consider."

Hamelin looked down and began to feel angry. All the reasons he had to come back over here—to prove himself, to overcome his fears, to find his parents and learn his name—now seemed unimportant to the eagle and whoever this Ancient One was that the eagle served.

He stood still. Staring at the eagle. The eagle was silent, looking back but now waiting.

Hamelin looked away from the great bird. *I just wanted to prove myself, and I did!* But then he also remembered that he wanted to prove himself because he had failed, and his failure had cost other people, especially the girl who was waiting for him, and his anger shifted to regret.

"I'm sorry about her—the girl who was waiting."

"Yes, much suffering and pain have come about because of your failure three and a half years ago, yet now it appears that the Ancient One has given us another opportunity—but we must go soon if we're to seize it!"

"Where to?"

The eagle nodded his head toward the large dark space behind him, the one that looked like a shaft. "We must go through the Tunnel of Times."

"What's that?"

"It's where the times change. Time still moves at the same rate across this tunnel as it does over here, but the times will change. You will end up in a different time, one where people speak and dress as they would have many hundreds of years ago, according to your history books."

"What am I going to do?"

"I'll tell you more as we go. For now, time is short. There's not a moment to lose. But first, through the Tunnel of Times, and then on to the Atrium of the Worlds."

Hamelin wanted to ask what that was, but he knew he would find out from the eagle soon enough.

Johnnie bolted upright in bed with a gasp. "Oh!" she said out loud.

Simon sat up in bed next to her. "What is it, honey? Are you okay?"

"I had the dream again."

"Which one?"

"The terrible one. The one where I'm pulled up by the ropes . . ."

"You mean the one with the animals and the thrones?"

"Yes, and all the other things I've mentioned before too. Lots of people, and I'm being lashed while everyone laughs and counts—"

"But, honey, remember what I told you when the lightning struck? I saw that room too, and most of those things you mentioned weren't there. Remember, there was no young teenage boy and no animals—"

"Yes, but . . ."

"But what?"

"There's something different about this dream. It isn't about the past. I keep having it, and I think it's got to be something that's still going to happen."

"How can you be sure it's not just the same dream over and over?"

"Because," Johnnie said, "there are different things I see each time. It's becoming clearer."

"Like what?"

"The boy. I've recognized the boy."

"The boy? The young teenage boy?"

"Yes."

"So," said Simon slowly, "who is he?"

And now Johnnie turned more toward Simon. It was dark, but there was enough light in the room for her to see his face. She leaned in toward him. She whispered, "He looks like you."

"Me?" Simon whispered back. "So it was me?"

"No . . . it was . . ." And then Johnnie leaned over and whispered in Simon's ear.

As he listened, his eyes got wider. He was still. Finally, he whispered, "Oh, my God."

Acknowledgments

I WANT TO BEGIN BY THANKING OUR CHILDREN, THEIR spouses, and a few other family members for allowing me to borrow their names for this series. The characters are completely fictional, but it has been a lot of fun to use these names. I hope it might be amusing for our grandchildren in the future. In addition, I should note that several of our children and their spouses have read different drafts of this volume, and I have received many helpful suggestions from them.

I continue by especially acknowledging a huge debt of gratitude to Judy Ferguson, my senior administrative assistant. To say she has transcribed and word processed this manuscript through many versions would be true, but it would not be nearly enough. For some years, she's been a combination of proofreader, copyeditor, plot advisor, and thoughtful, constructive critic. I will truly never be able to acknowledge fully her amazing help. She knows the characters and plot as well as I do and has therefore not only saved me from many grammatical and syntactical errors but also rescued the text from numerous substantive scene and plot inconsistencies. This volume—whose remaining faults are the author's alone—has been immeasurably strengthened by Judy's wide-ranging expertise. She is truly a great friend and colleague.

I also want to acknowledge my indebtedness to the father and son duo of Jerry and Jeremiah Johnston. Their persistent encouragement and their great and complementary insights into the world of book production, marketing, promotion, and distribution, among other things, have been and remain invaluable.

I must also thank Sharon Saunders, Karen Francies, and Margaret Patterson for their support and encouragement to complete this project.

And then there are our partners at Scribe—a great company from which I've learned and benefited so much. David Rech, the principal, and his coworkers Danny Constantino, Tim Durning, Jeff DeBlasio, and more recently Jamie Harrison have become our friends. David has been a patient instructor and mentor regarding all things touching book production. Danny, an expert copyeditor, has done far more than look for comma blunders and content redundancies. He has kept an eye out for substantive plot issues and strengthened the final product significantly. Tim, Jeff, and Jamie are true artists in book design and cover creation.

I also want to thank the Trustees of Houston Baptist University, who have allowed me opportunities to work on this project from time to time.

Most of all, I thank my wife, Sue, whose support, encouragement, and disciplined business expertise have made possible the beginning, the continuation, and the completion of this project. It would not have happened without her. Again and again—and with great kindness—she has encouraged me to continue the project, especially during times when I thought it would never be finished. At one point, the draft lay untouched for more than a year. She wouldn't let me stop. I'm grateful.

It's a pleasure to dedicate this first volume of the Hamelin Stoop series to my wife Sue and to our seven children and their spouses. Whether they know it or not, they have been instrumental in all the factors that have motivated me to begin and finish this work.

Look for the second volume of the Hamelin Stoop series, *Hamelin Stoop: The Lost Princess and the Jewel of Periluna.*

I N THE NEXT EXCITING VOLUME, HAMELIN DISCOVERS THAT CROSS-ing the footbridge is not enough. He has passed the test set by the Ancient One, but now his mission to find his parents has only begun. Guided still by the Great Eagle, he must enter and pass through the mysterious Atrium of the Worlds, where he faces enchantment from a pond whose waters can bring both death and life. Hamelin then meets new friends who seek a captured princess and a stolen jewel of light and life. Though he longs to fulfill his quest to find his parents, he must first help his friends accomplish theirs. With a scarf that gives sight, shoes of speed, and a strange sword—not to mention Hamelin's gloves of strength—he and his friends do battle against Tumultor, a son of Chimera. Travel with Hamelin and his friends to a world of adventure and strange creatures, where courage and loyalty are the difference between life and death.

———◆———

If you enjoyed *Hamelin Stoop: The Eagle, the Cave, and the Footbridge*, share its message with others:

Mention Hamelin Stoop in a Facebook post, Twitter update, or blog post using the hashtag #HamelinStoop.

Recommend *Hamelin Stoop: The Eagle, the Cave, and the Footbridge* to your friends, small group, or book club.

Be sure to "Like Us" at www.hamelinstoop.com and join our e-mail list for more information and updates on the next books in the series.

About the Author

Robert B. Sloan is married to his college sweetheart, Sue. With seven married children and twenty young grandchildren, they especially enjoy large family gatherings with good food and lively conversation around the table. Favorite family activities include table and parlor games, writing and reading stories, coloring, and, of course, storytelling.